JOEY FLY
PRIVATE EYE

IN CREEPY CRAWLY CRIME

written by
AARON REYNOLDS

illustrated by
NEIL NUMBERMAN

HENRY HOLT AND COMPANY

NEW YORK

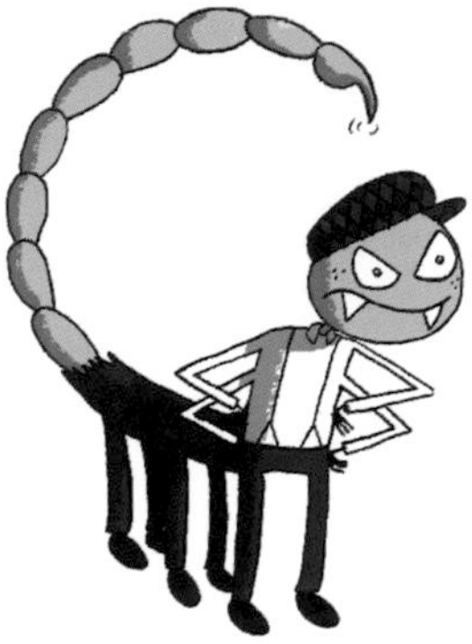

Henry Holt and Company, LLC
Publishers since 1866
175 Fifth Avenue
New York, New York 10010
www.HenryHoltKids.com

Distributed in Canada by H. B. Fenn and Company Ltd.

Library of Congress Cataloging-in-Publication Data
Reynolds, Aaron.
Joey Fly, private eye, in Creepy crawly crime / by Aaron Reynolds;
illustrations by Neil Numberman.—1st ed.
p. cm. — (Joey Fly, private eye ; bk. 1)
ISBN 978-0-8050-8242-5 (hardcover)
3 5 7 9 10 8 6 4
ISBN 978-0-8050-8786-4 (paperback)
3 5 7 9 10 8 6 4 2
1. Graphic novels. I. Numberman, Neil. II. Title. III. Title: Creepy crawly crime.
PN6727.R45J64 2009 741.5'973—dc22 2007040041

First Edition—2009
Book designed by Laurent Linn and April Ward
Printed in November 2009 in China by South China Printing Company Ltd.,
Dongguan City, Guangdong Province, on acid-free paper. ∞

Answer key for page 46: A. 64; B. 52; C. 66; D. 66; E. 21; F. 30; G. 12; H. 56; I. 33; J. 30; K. 6; L. 7; M. 50; N. 7; O. 6; P. 13, 26, 34, 49, 55, 63, 68, 93.

To Ethan:

Though we sometimes bug each other,
it's no mystery why I love you.

—A. R.

To my parents,
for your love, encouragement, and money

—N. N.

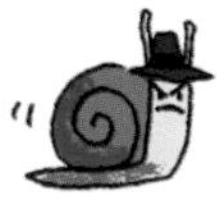

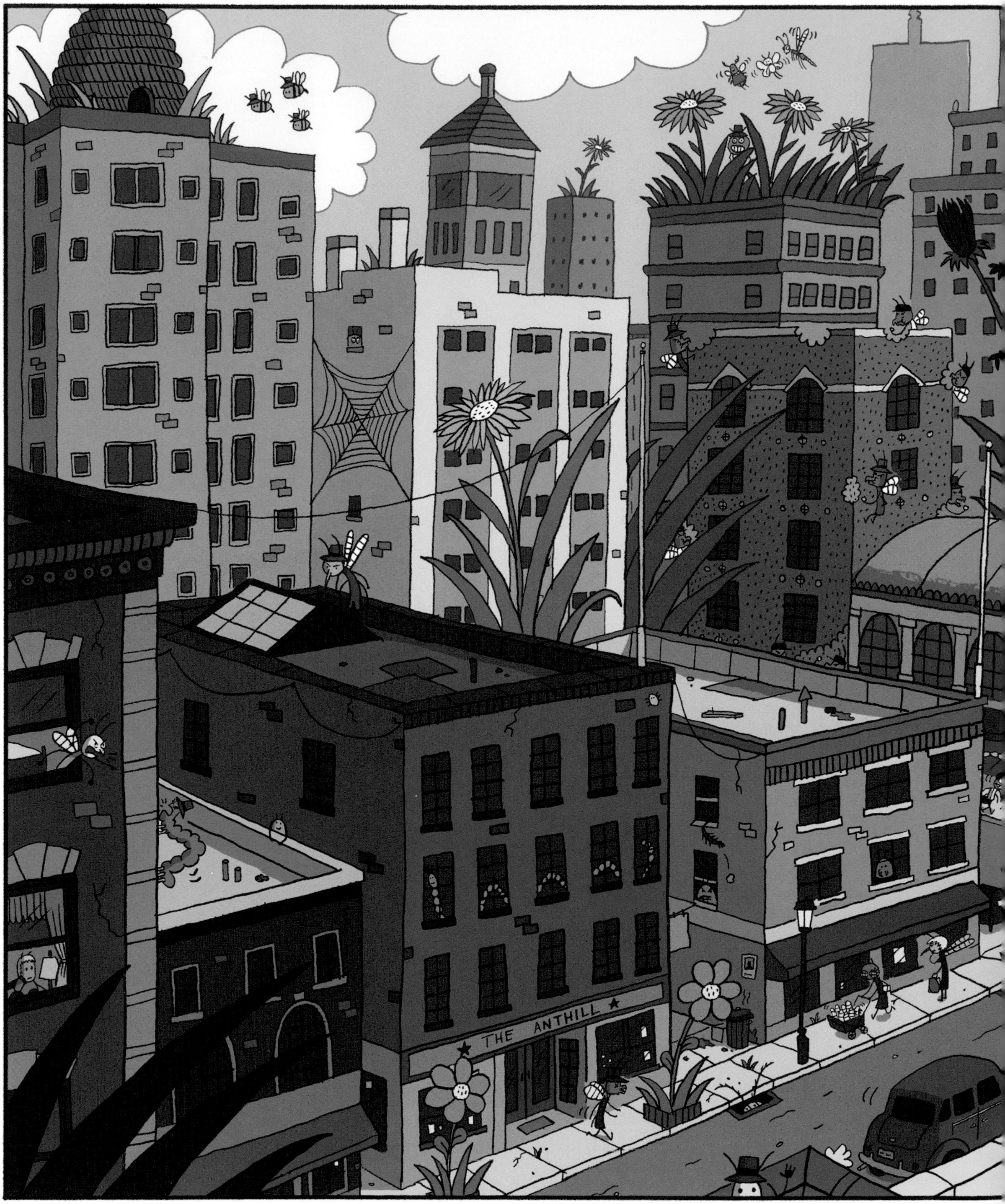
★ THE ANTHILL ★

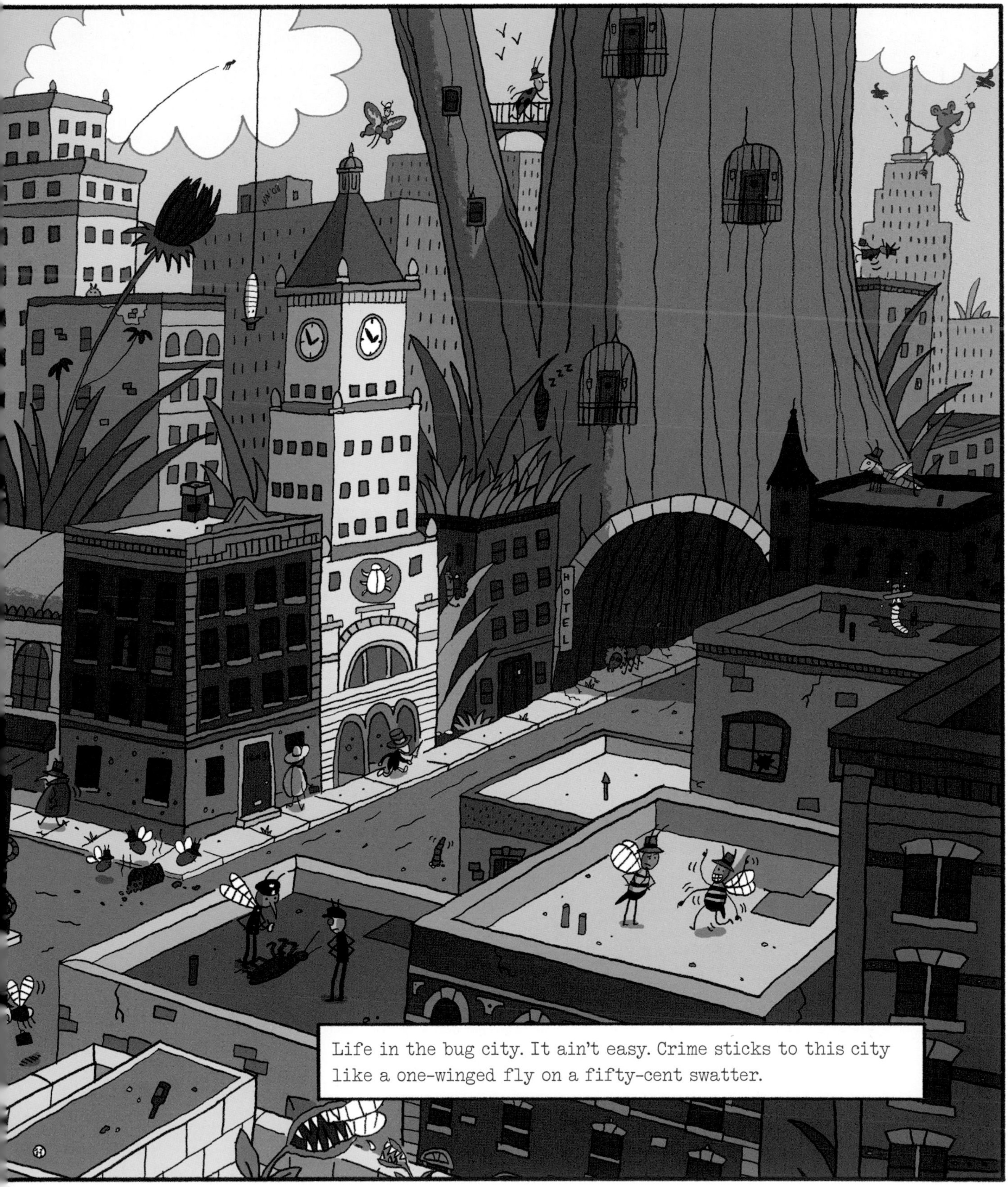
HOTEL
Life in the bug city. It ain't easy. Crime sticks to this city like a one-winged fly on a fifty-cent swatter.

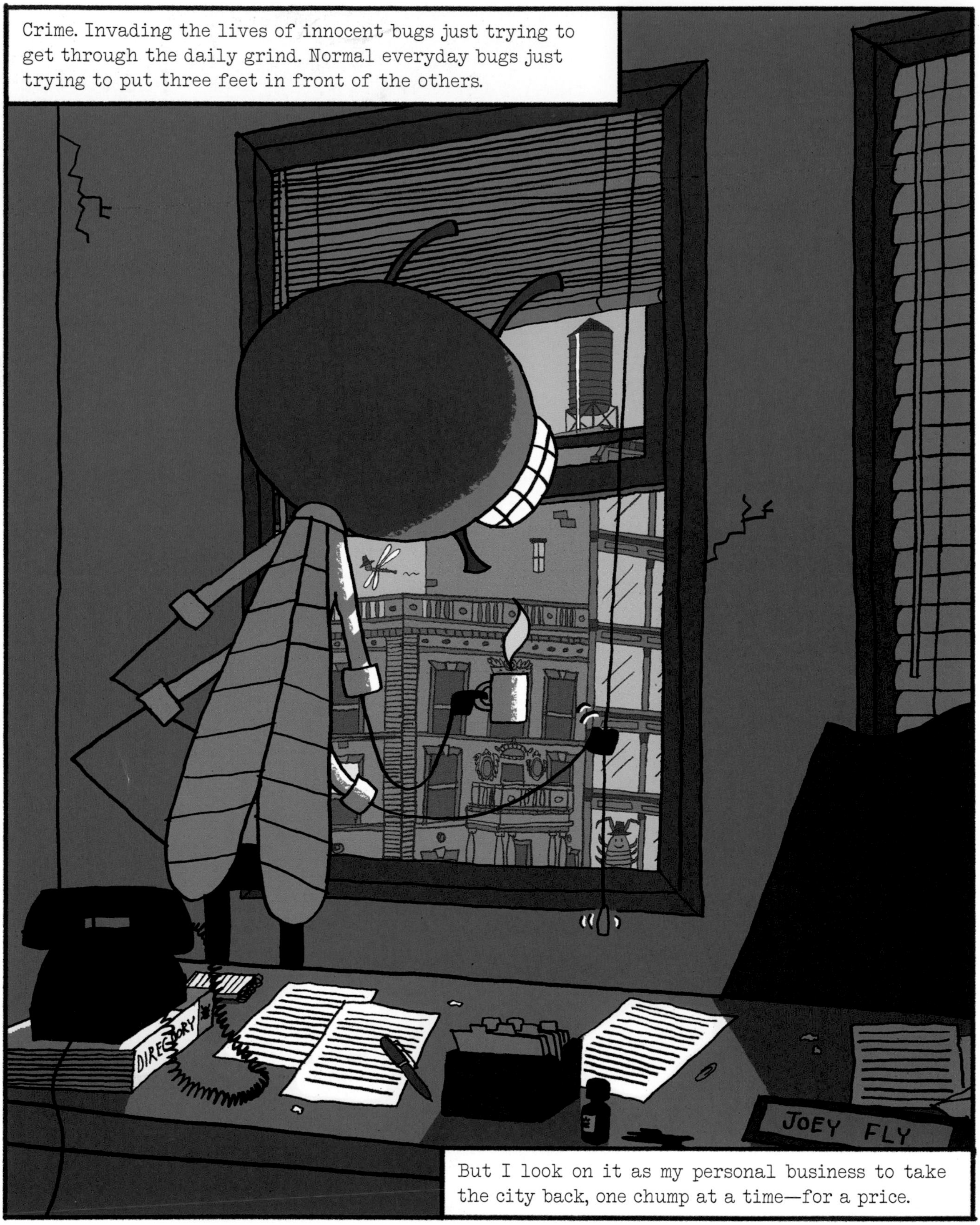
Crime. Invading the lives of innocent bugs just trying to get through the daily grind. Normal everyday bugs just trying to put three feet in front of the others.
DIRECTORY
JOEY FLY
But I look on it as my personal business to take the city back, one chump at a time—for a price.

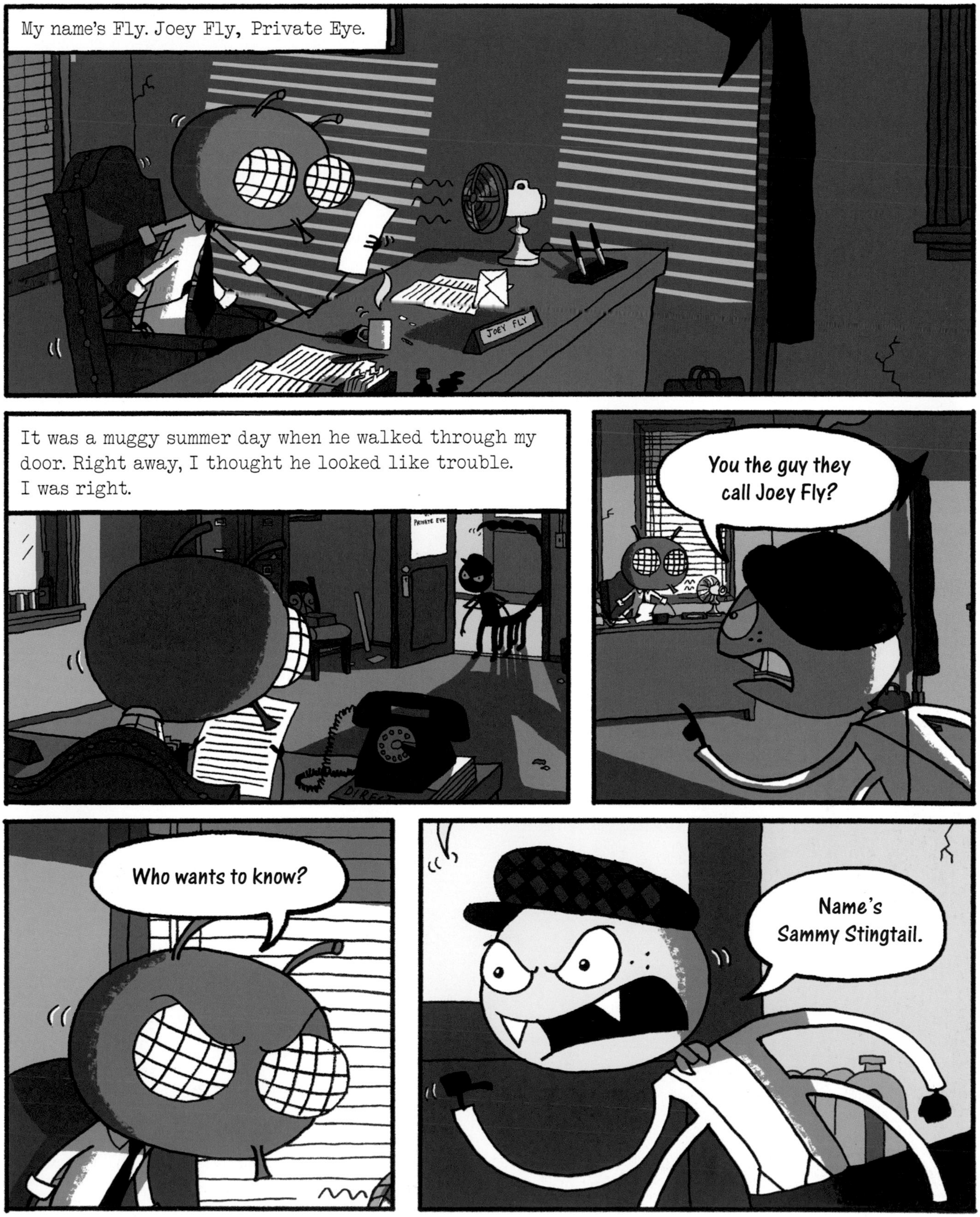
My name's Fly. Joey Fly, Private Eye.
JOEY FLY
It was a muggy summer day when he walked through my door. Right away, I thought he looked like trouble. I was right.
PRIVATE EYE
You the guy they call Joey Fly?
Who wants to know?
Name's Sammy Stingtail.

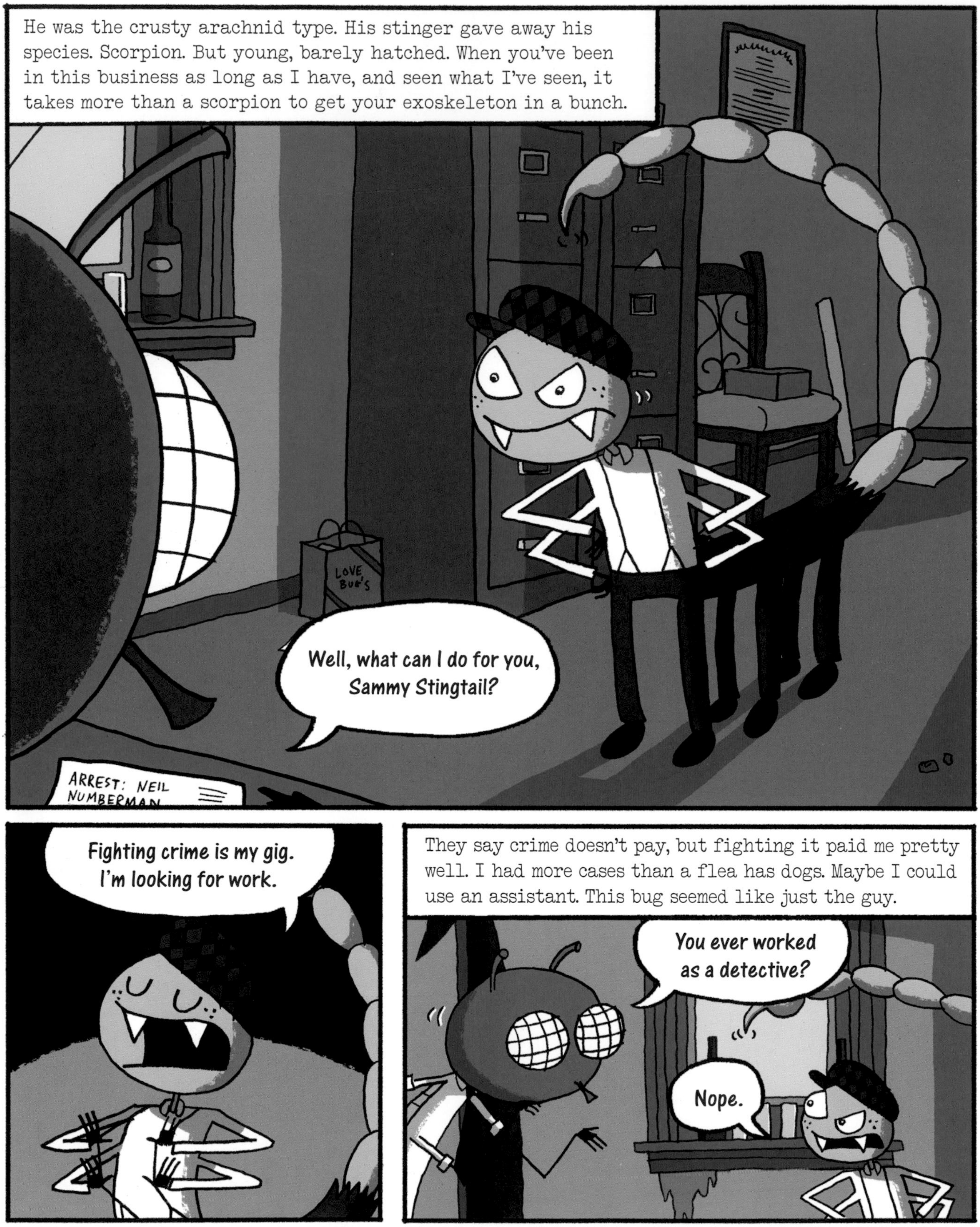

He was the crusty arachnid type. His stinger gave away his species. Scorpion. But young, barely hatched. When you've been in this business as long as I have, and seen what I've seen, it takes more than a scorpion to get your exoskeleton in a bunch.
LOVE BUG'S
Well, what can I do for you, Sammy Stingtail?
ARREST: NEIL NUMBERMAN
Fighting crime is my gig. I'm looking for work.
They say crime doesn't pay, but fighting it paid me pretty well. I had more cases than a flea has dogs. Maybe I could use an assistant. This bug seemed like just the guy.
You ever worked as a detective?
Nope.

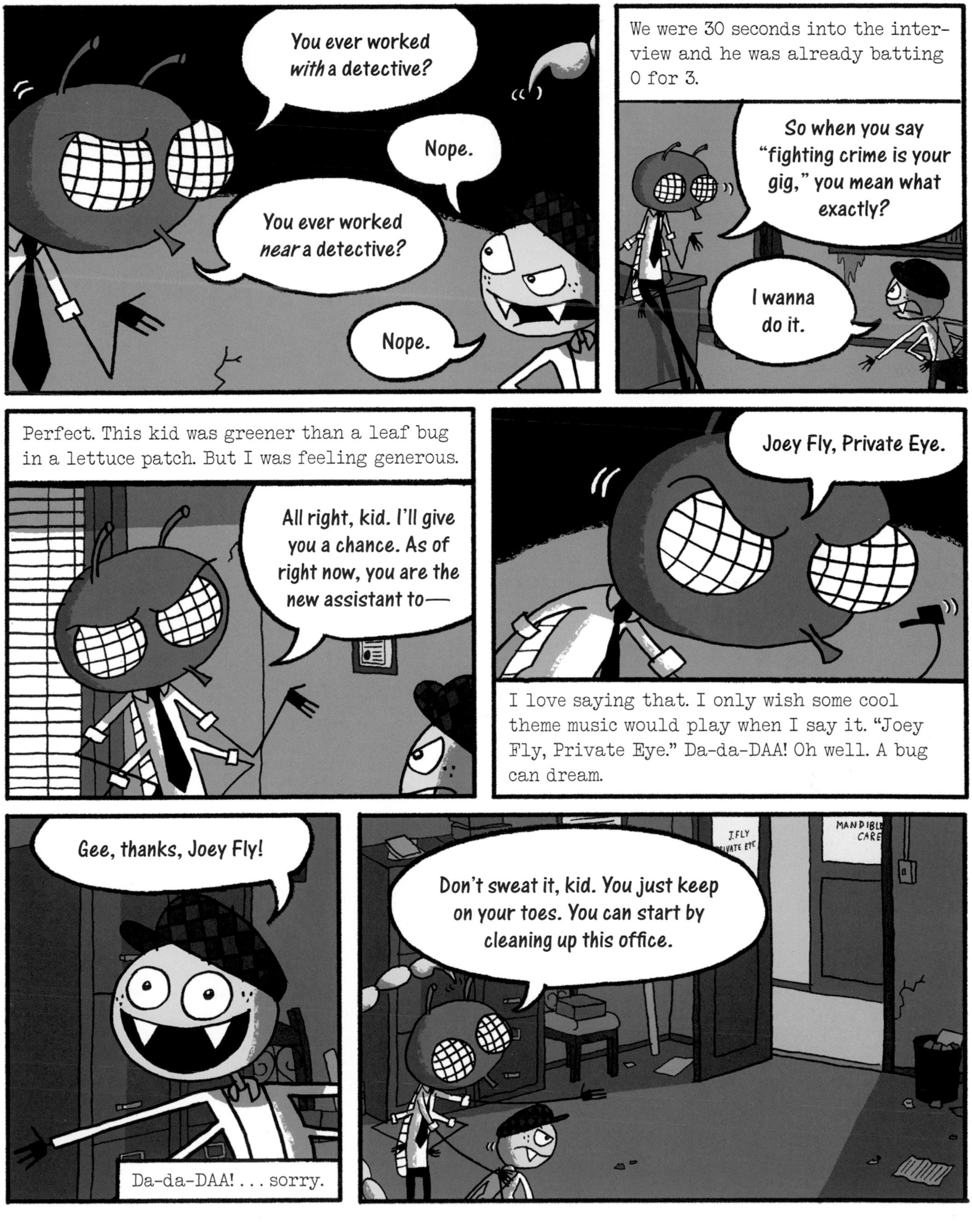
You ever worked *with* a detective?
Nope.
You ever worked *near* a detective?
Nope.
We were 30 seconds into the interview and he was already batting 0 for 3.
So when you say "fighting crime is your gig," you mean what exactly?
I wanna do it.
Perfect. This kid was greener than a leaf bug in a lettuce patch. But I was feeling generous.
All right, kid. I'll give you a chance. As of right now, you are the new assistant to—
Joey Fly, Private Eye.
I love saying that. I only wish some cool theme music would play when I say it. "Joey Fly, Private Eye." Da-da-DAA! Oh well. A bug can dream.
Gee, thanks, Joey Fly!
Da-da-DAA! . . . sorry.
Don't sweat it, kid. You just keep on your toes. You can start by cleaning up this office.
J.FLY PRIVATE EYE
MANDIBLE CARE

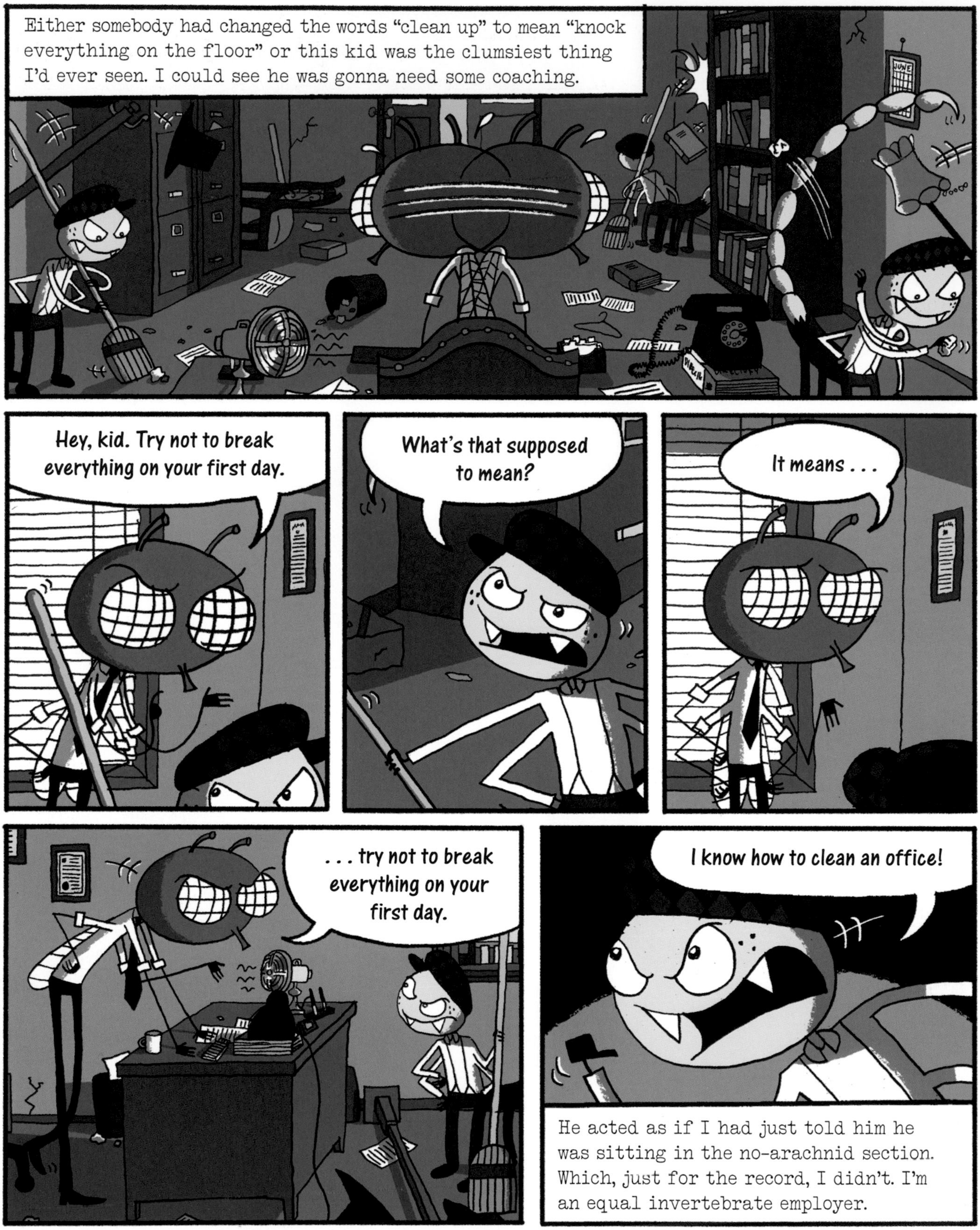
Either somebody had changed the words "clean up" to mean "knock everything on the floor" or this kid was the clumsiest thing I'd ever seen. I could see he was gonna need some coaching.
Hey, kid. Try not to break everything on your first day.
What's that supposed to mean?
It means . . .
. . . try not to break everything on your first day.
I know how to clean an office!
He acted as if I had just told him he was sitting in the no-arachnid section. Which, just for the record, I didn't. I'm an equal invertebrate employer.

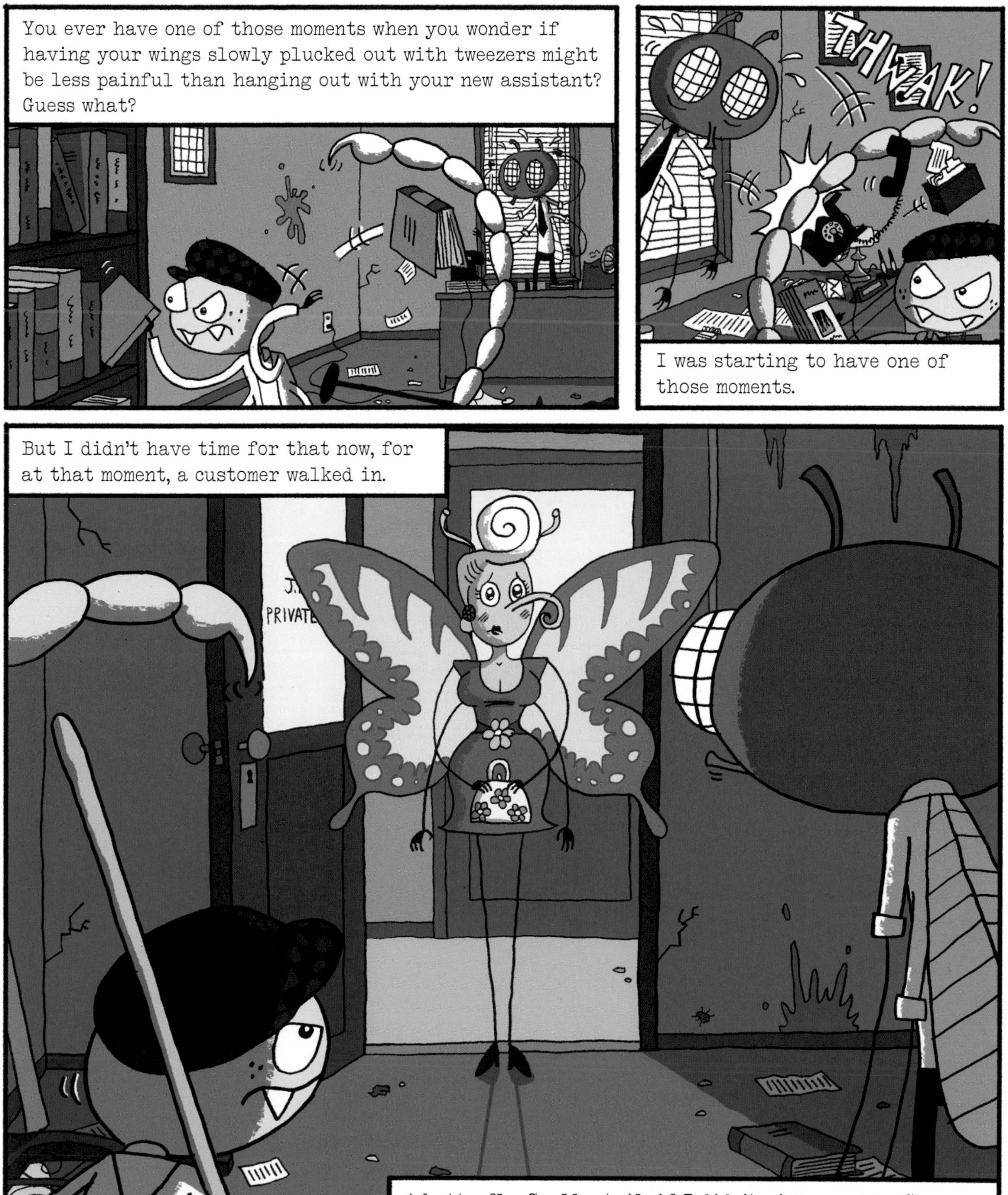
You ever have one of those moments when you wonder if having your wings slowly plucked out with tweezers might be less painful than hanging out with your new assistant? Guess what?
THWAK!
I was starting to have one of those moments.
But I didn't have time for that now, for at that moment, a customer walked in.
PRIVATE
A butterfly. Swallowtail, if I didn't miss my guess. She was a tall drip of water. And I was suddenly feeling parched.

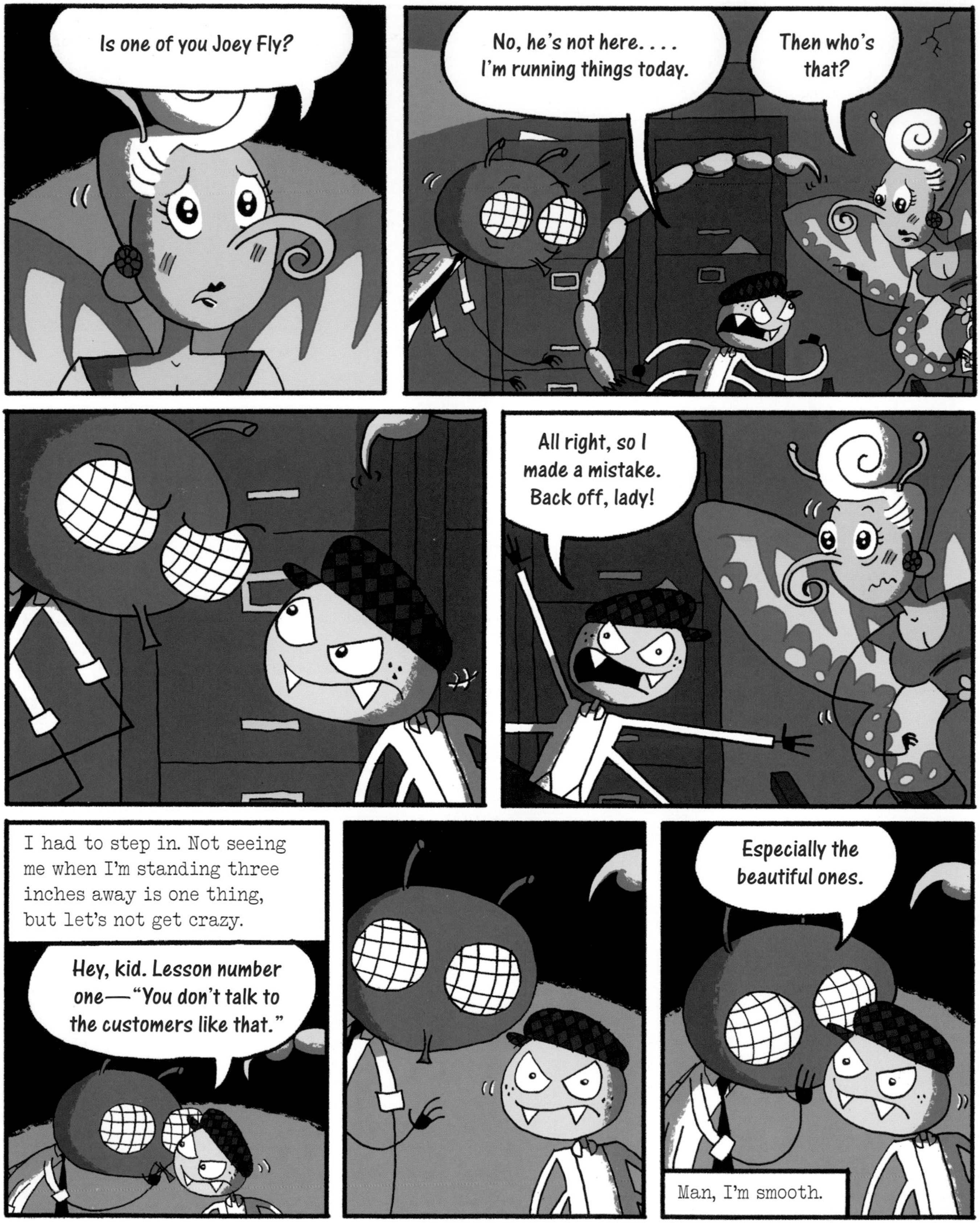
Is one of you Joey Fly?
No, he's not here. . . . I'm running things today.
Then who's that?
All right, so I made a mistake. Back off, lady!
I had to step in. Not seeing me when I'm standing three inches away is one thing, but let's not get crazy.
Hey, kid. Lesson number one—"You don't talk to the customers like that."
Especially the beautiful ones.
Man, I'm smooth.

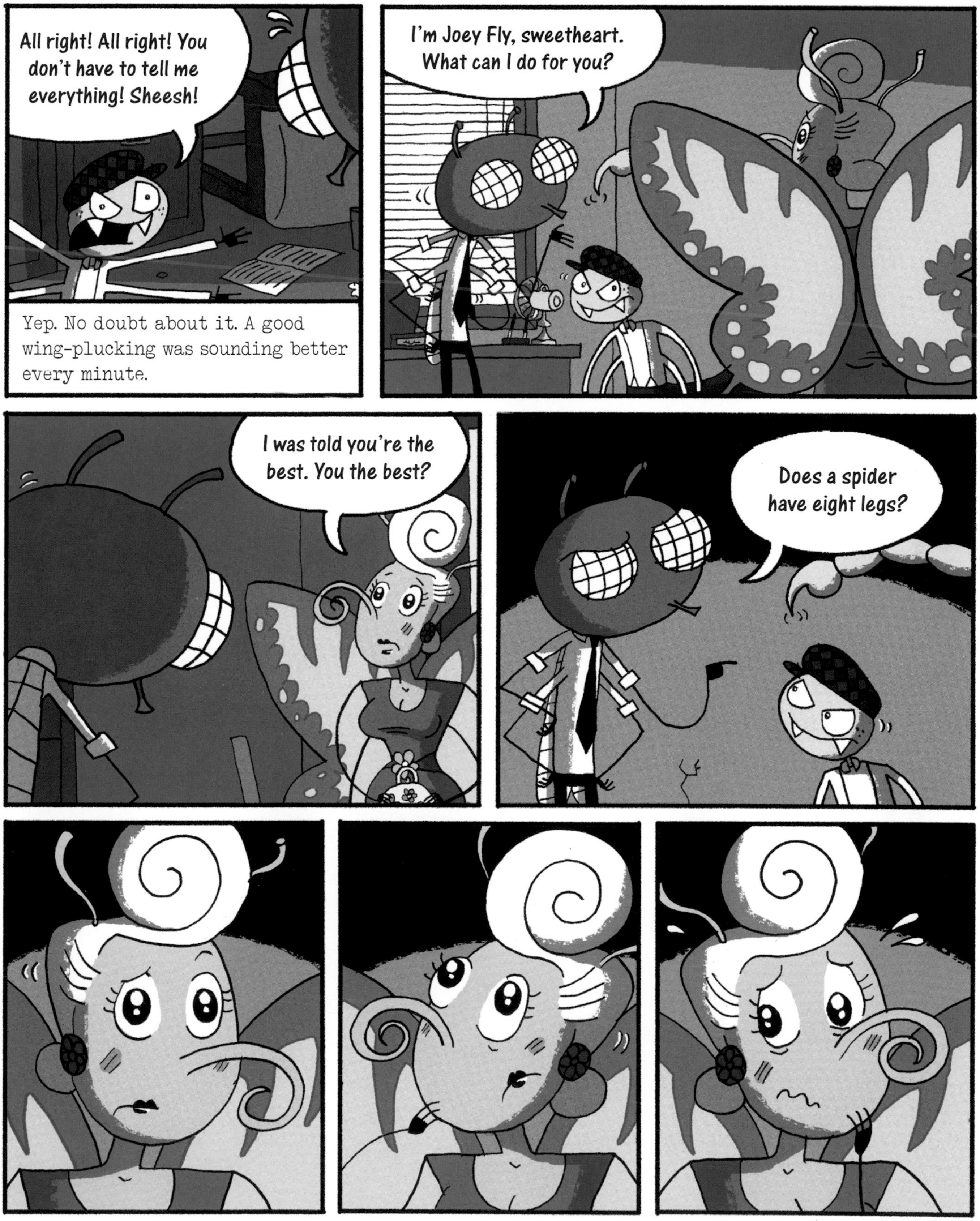

All right! All right! You don't have to tell me everything! Sheesh!
Yep. No doubt about it. A good wing-plucking was sounding better every minute.
I'm Joey Fly, sweetheart. What can I do for you?
I was told you're the best. You the best?
Does a spider have eight legs?

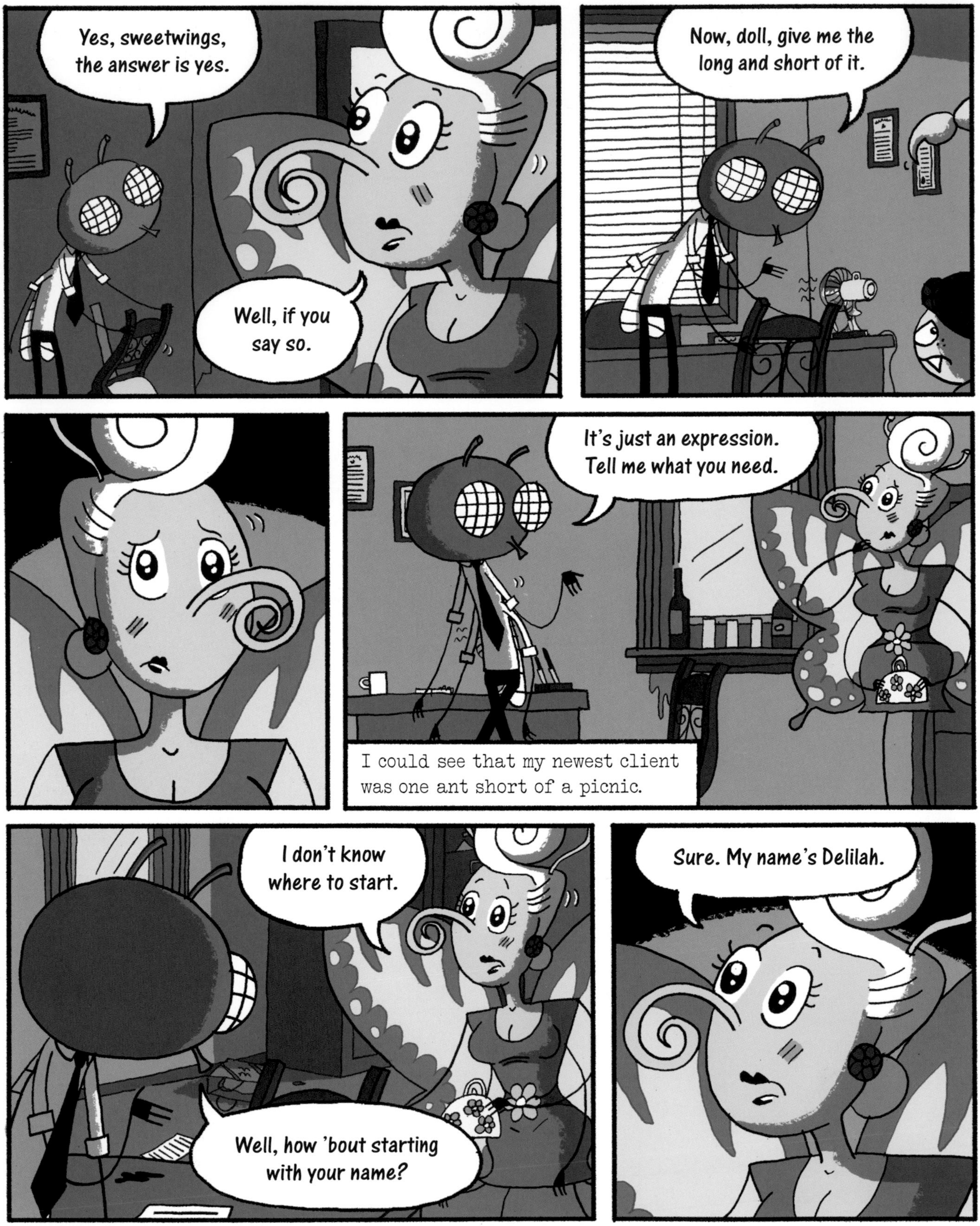
Yes, sweetwings, the answer is yes.
Well, if you say so.
Now, doll, give me the long and short of it.
It's just an expression. Tell me what you need.
I could see that my newest client was one ant short of a picnic.
I don't know where to start.
Well, how 'bout starting with your name?
Sure. My name's Delilah.

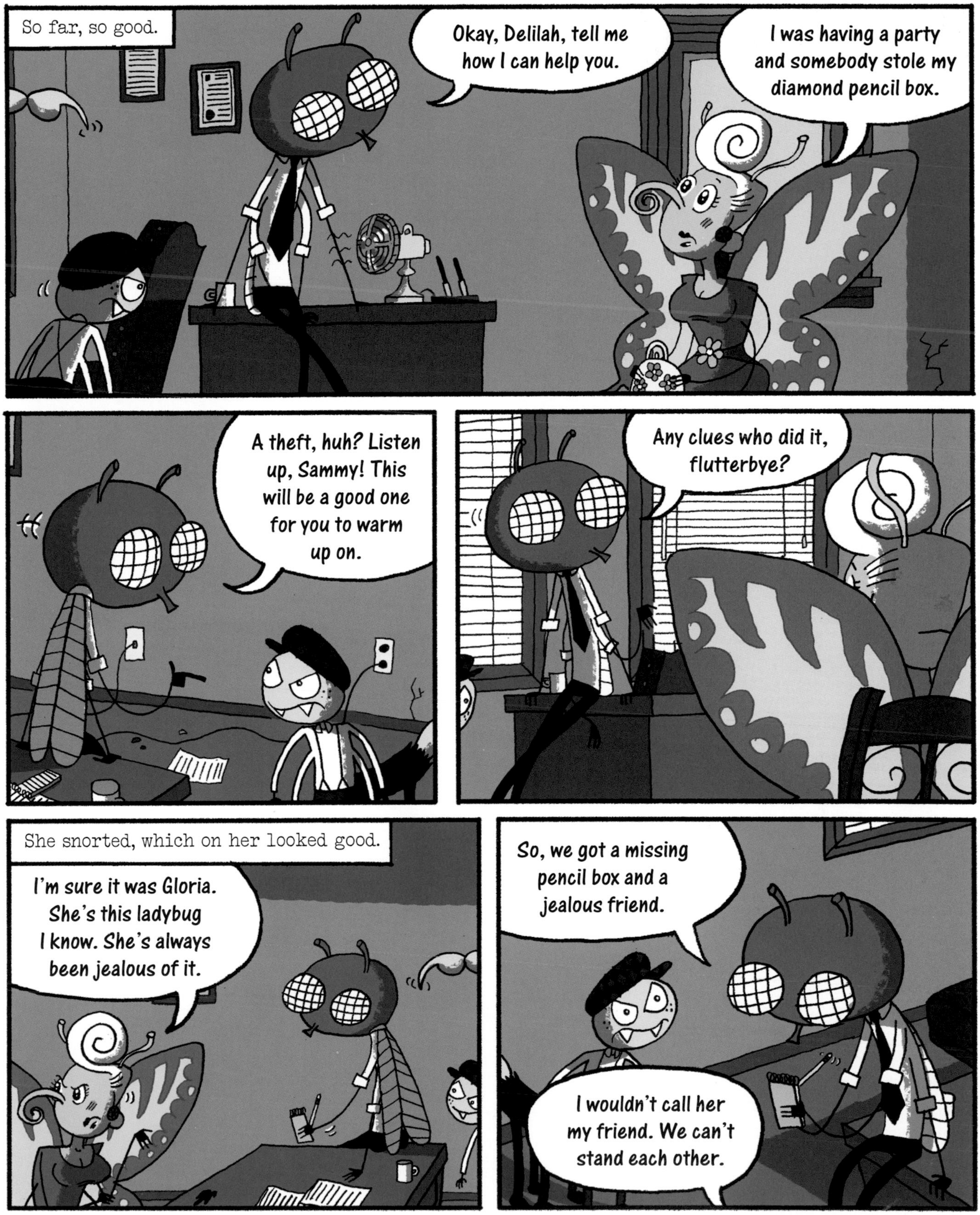
So far, so good.
Okay, Delilah, tell me how I can help you.
I was having a party and somebody stole my diamond pencil box.
A theft, huh? Listen up, Sammy! This will be a good one for you to warm up on.
Any clues who did it, flutterbye?
She snorted, which on her looked good.
I'm sure it was Gloria. She's this ladybug I know. She's always been jealous of it.
So, we got a missing pencil box and a jealous friend.
I wouldn't call her my friend. We can't stand each other.

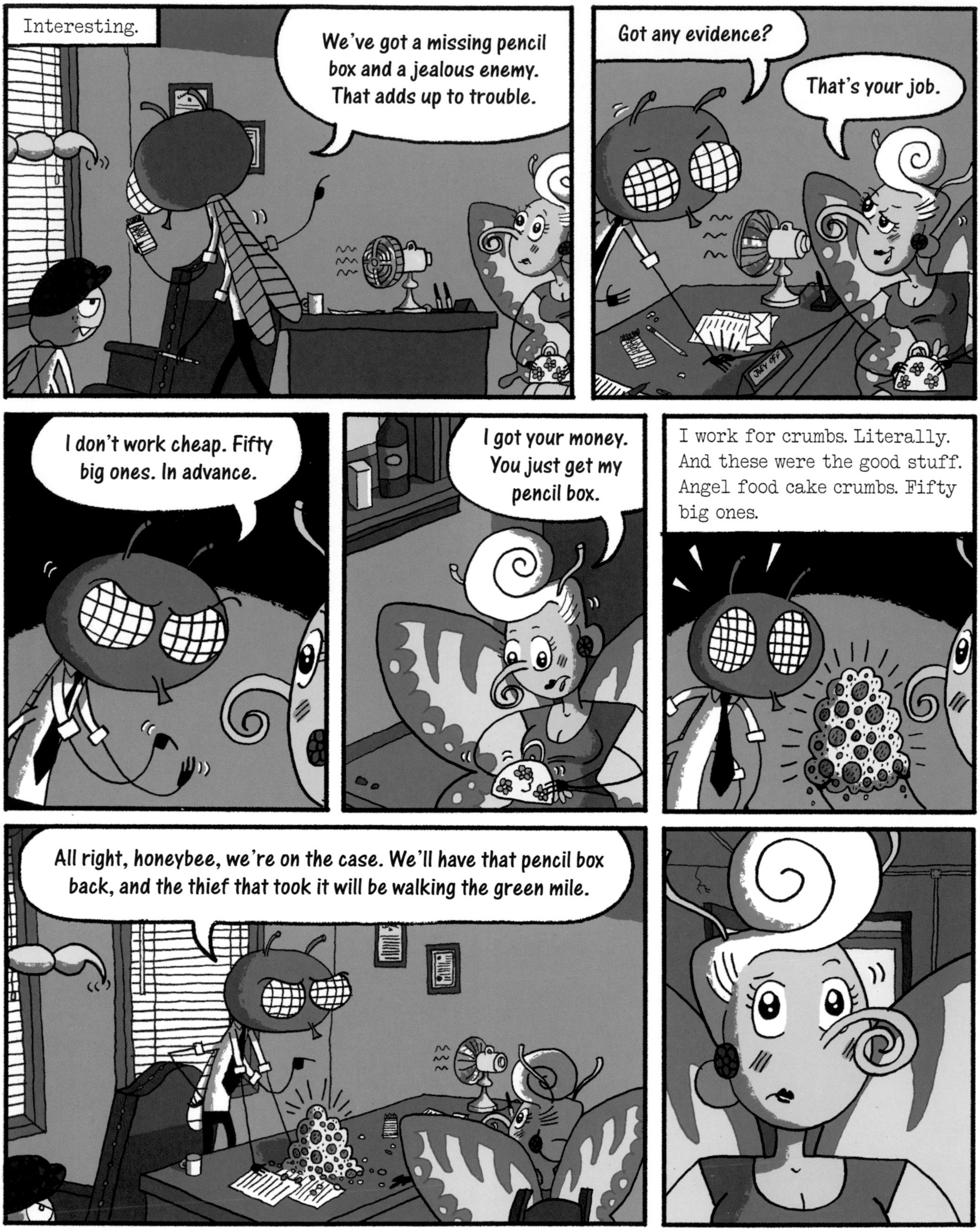

Interesting.
We've got a missing pencil box and a jealous enemy. That adds up to trouble.
Got any evidence?
That's your job.
I don't work cheap. Fifty big ones. In advance.
I got your money. You just get my pencil box.
I work for crumbs. Literally. And these were the good stuff. Angel food cake crumbs. Fifty big ones.
All right, honeybee, we're on the case. We'll have that pencil box back, and the thief that took it will be walking the green mile.

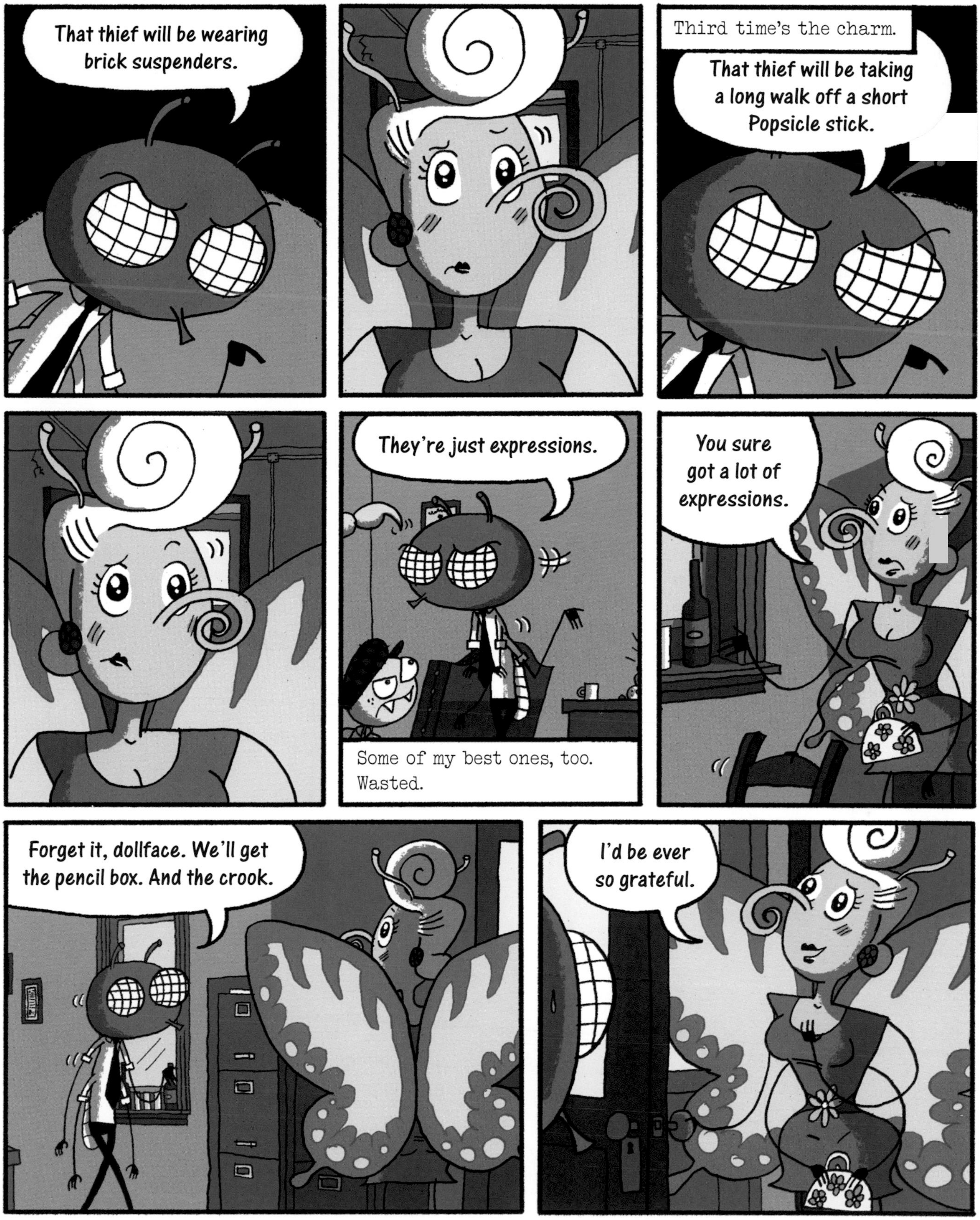

That thief will be wearing brick suspenders.
Third time's the charm.
That thief will be taking a long walk off a short Popsicle stick.
They're just expressions.
Some of my best ones, too. Wasted.
You sure got a lot of expressions.
Forget it, dollface. We'll get the pencil box. And the crook.
I'd be ever so grateful.

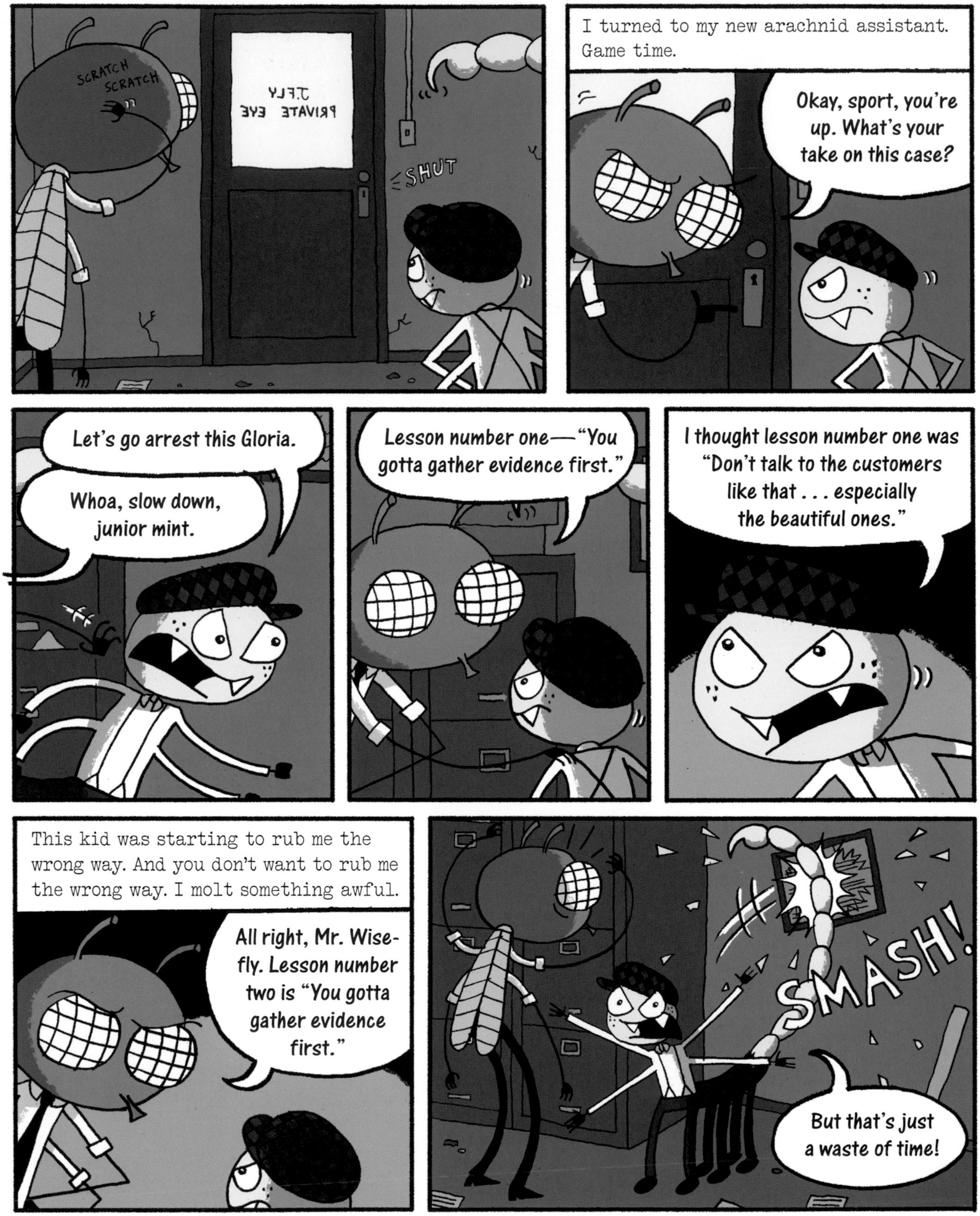

SCRATCH SCRATCH
J. FLY PRIVATE EYE
SHUT
I turned to my new arachnid assistant. Game time.
Okay, sport, you're up. What's your take on this case?
Let's go arrest this Gloria.
Whoa, slow down, junior mint.
Lesson number one—"You gotta gather evidence first."
I thought lesson number one was "Don't talk to the customers like that . . . especially the beautiful ones."
This kid was starting to rub me the wrong way. And you don't want to rub me the wrong way. I molt something awful.
All right, Mr. Wise-fly. Lesson number two is "You gotta gather evidence first."
SMASH!
But that's just a waste of time!

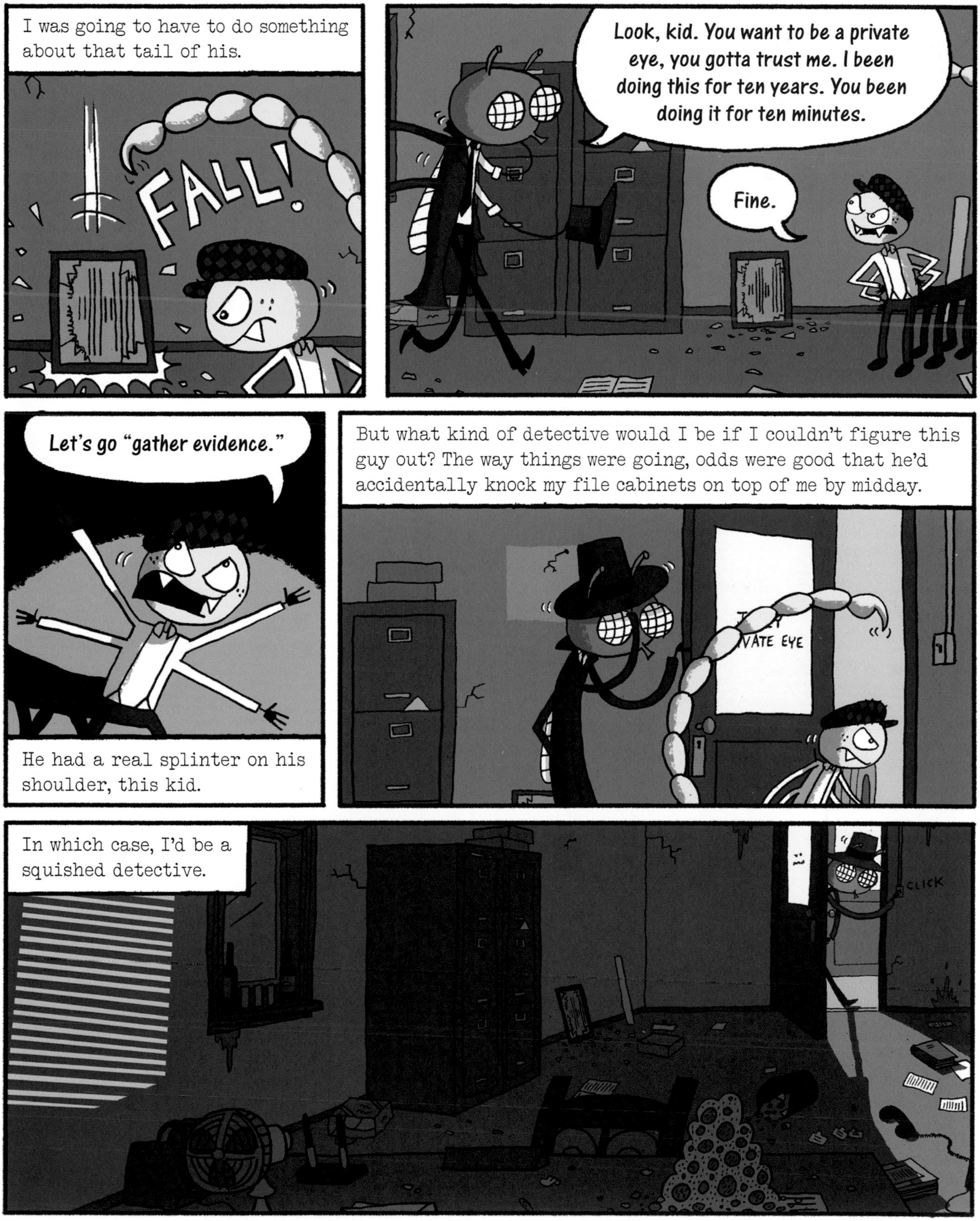

I was going to have to do something about that tail of his.
FALL!
Look, kid. You want to be a private eye, you gotta trust me. I been doing this for ten years. You been doing it for ten minutes.
Fine.
Let's go "gather evidence."
He had a real splinter on his shoulder, this kid.
But what kind of detective would I be if I couldn't figure this guy out? The way things were going, odds were good that he'd accidentally knock my file cabinets on top of me by midday.
In which case, I'd be a squished detective.
CLICK

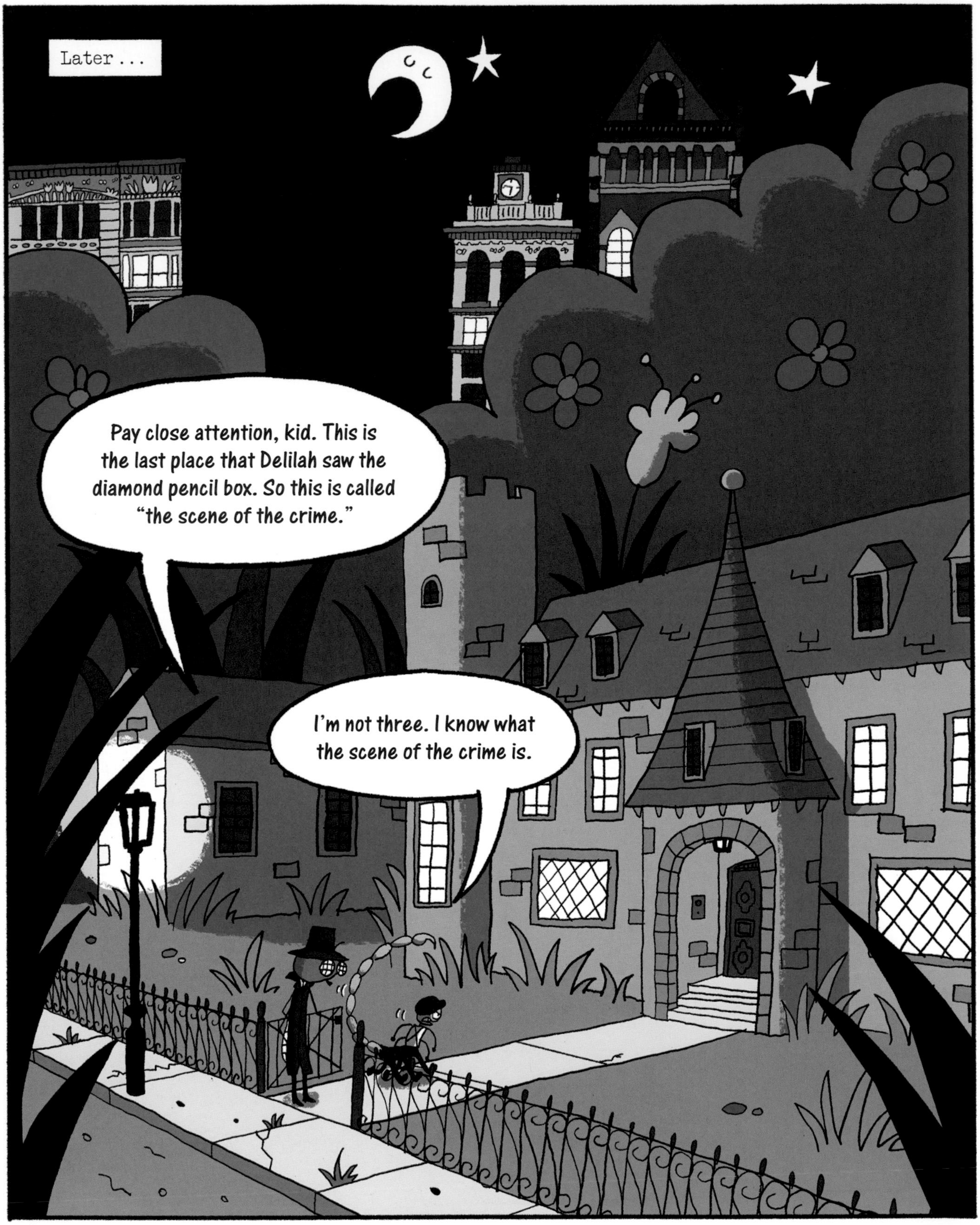
Later . . .
Pay close attention, kid. This is the last place that Delilah saw the diamond pencil box. So this is called "the scene of the crime."
I'm not three. I know what the scene of the crime is.

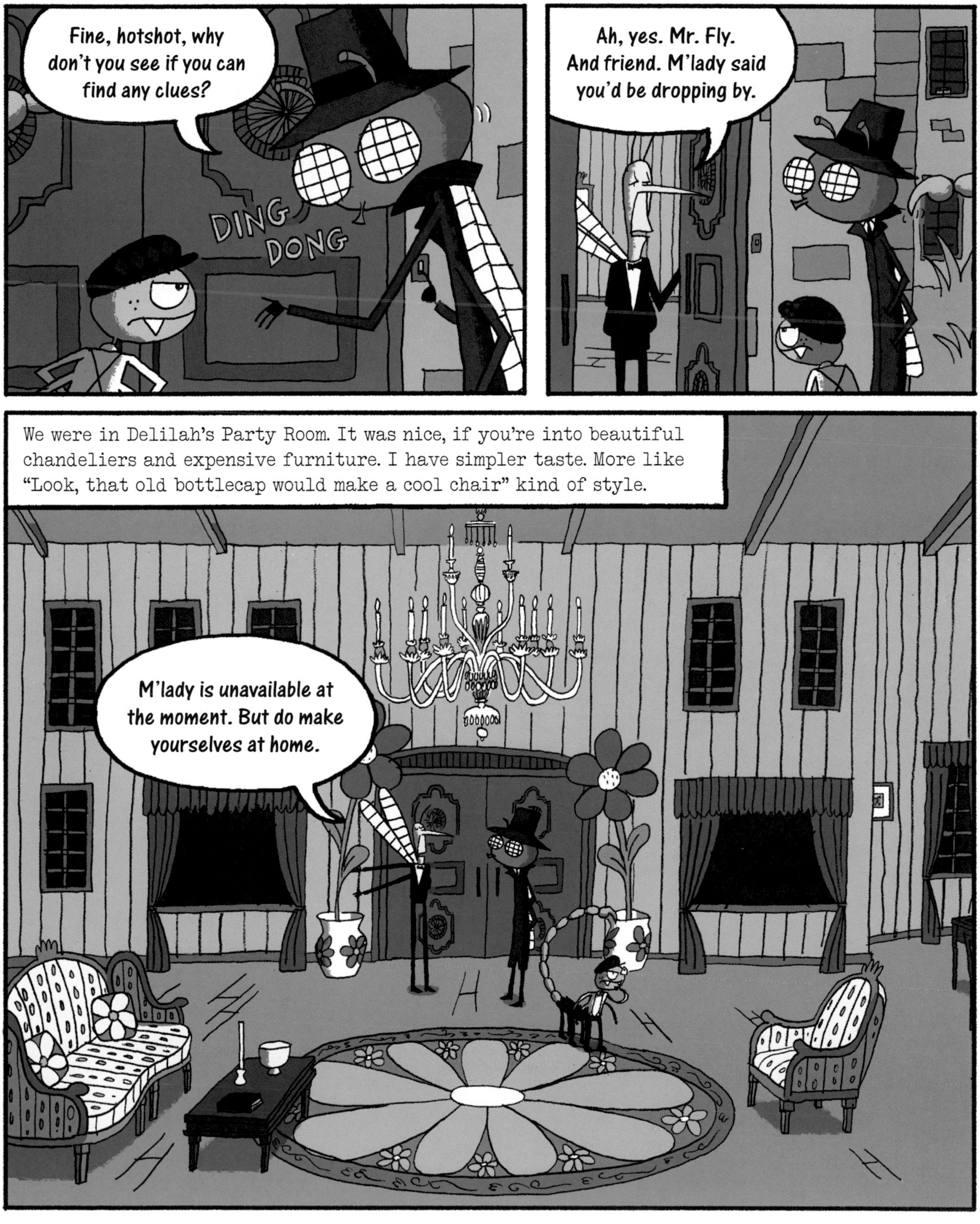
Fine, hotshot, why don't you see if you can find any clues?
DING DONG
Ah, yes. Mr. Fly. And friend. M'lady said you'd be dropping by.
We were in Delilah's Party Room. It was nice, if you're into beautiful chandeliers and expensive furniture. I have simpler taste. More like "Look, that old bottlecap would make a cool chair" kind of style.
M'lady is unavailable at the moment. But do make yourselves at home.

No matter how slick a crook thinks he is, he almost always leaves a little nugget of evidence. If you can snoop out that evidence, well, the case is usually wrapped up tighter than a fly in a web.

By the way, most private flies don't like that particular phrase. But I prefer to stare fear right in the face.

Hey, Joey, I found something.

Great work, kid! I knew you had it in you. What is it?

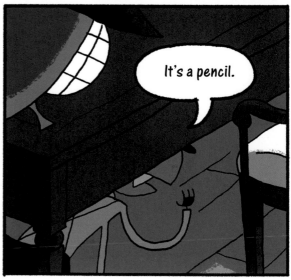

It's a pencil.

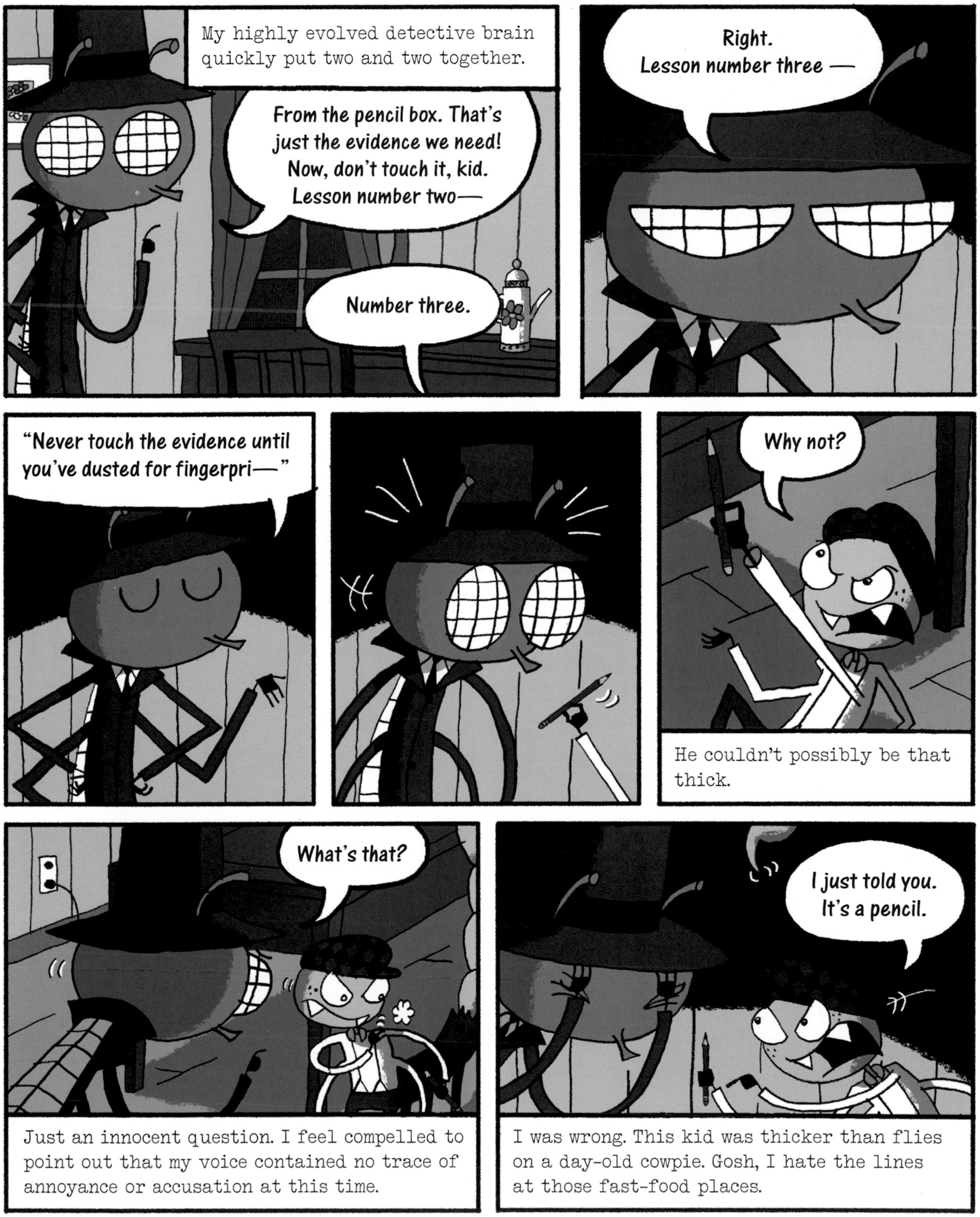
My highly evolved detective brain quickly put two and two together.
From the pencil box. That's just the evidence we need! Now, don't touch it, kid. Lesson number two—
Number three.
Right. Lesson number three —
"Never touch the evidence until you've dusted for fingerpri—"
Why not?
He couldn't possibly be that thick.
What's that?
Just an innocent question. I feel compelled to point out that my voice contained no trace of annoyance or accusation at this time.
I just told you. It's a pencil.
I was wrong. This kid was thicker than flies on a day-old cowpie. Gosh, I hate the lines at those fast-food places.

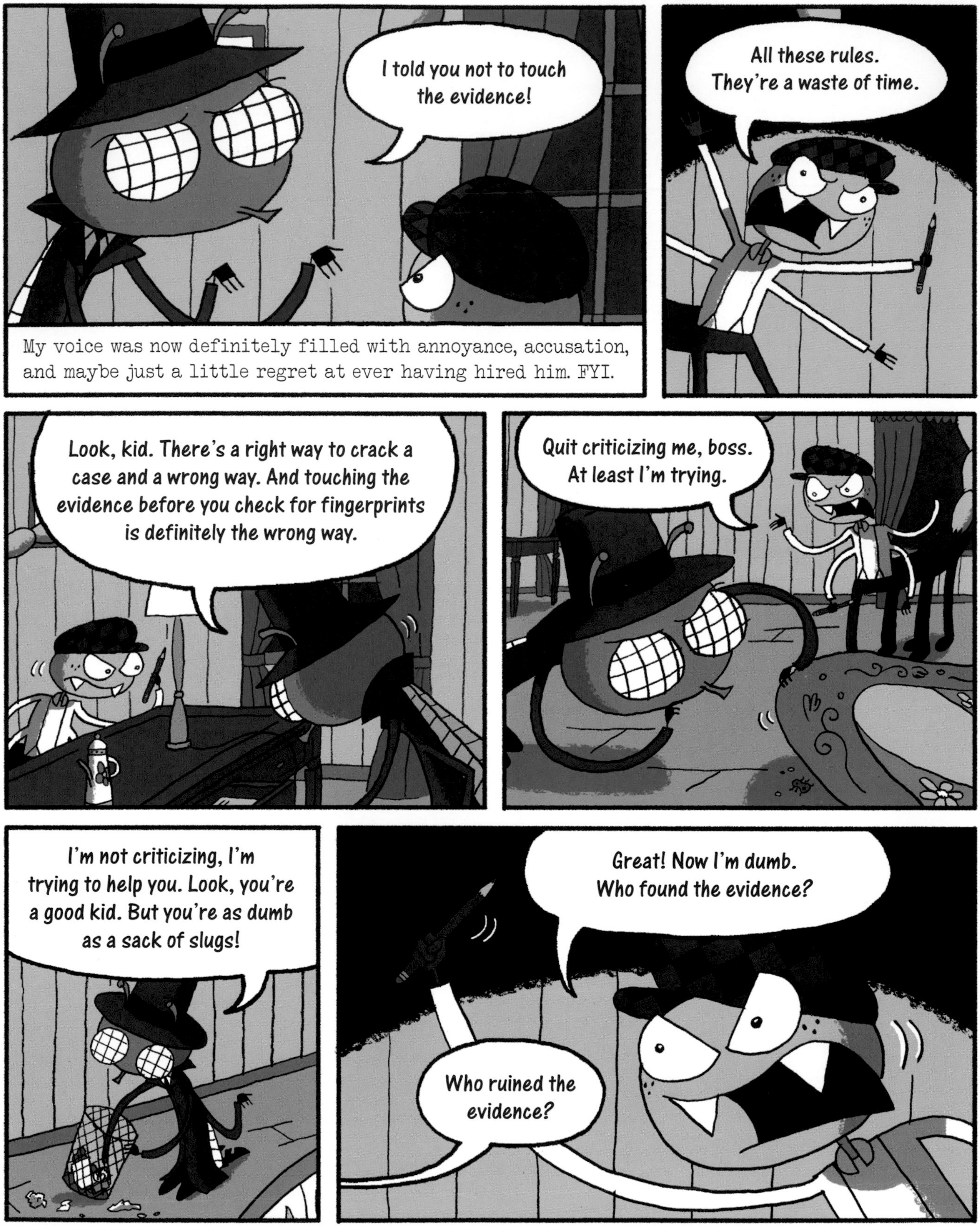
I told you not to touch the evidence!
My voice was now definitely filled with annoyance, accusation, and maybe just a little regret at ever having hired him. FYI.
All these rules. They're a waste of time.
Look, kid. There's a right way to crack a case and a wrong way. And touching the evidence before you check for fingerprints is definitely the wrong way.
Quit criticizing me, boss. At least I'm trying.
I'm not criticizing, I'm trying to help you. Look, you're a good kid. But you're as dumb as a sack of slugs!
Great! Now I'm dumb. Who found the evidence?
Who ruined the evidence?

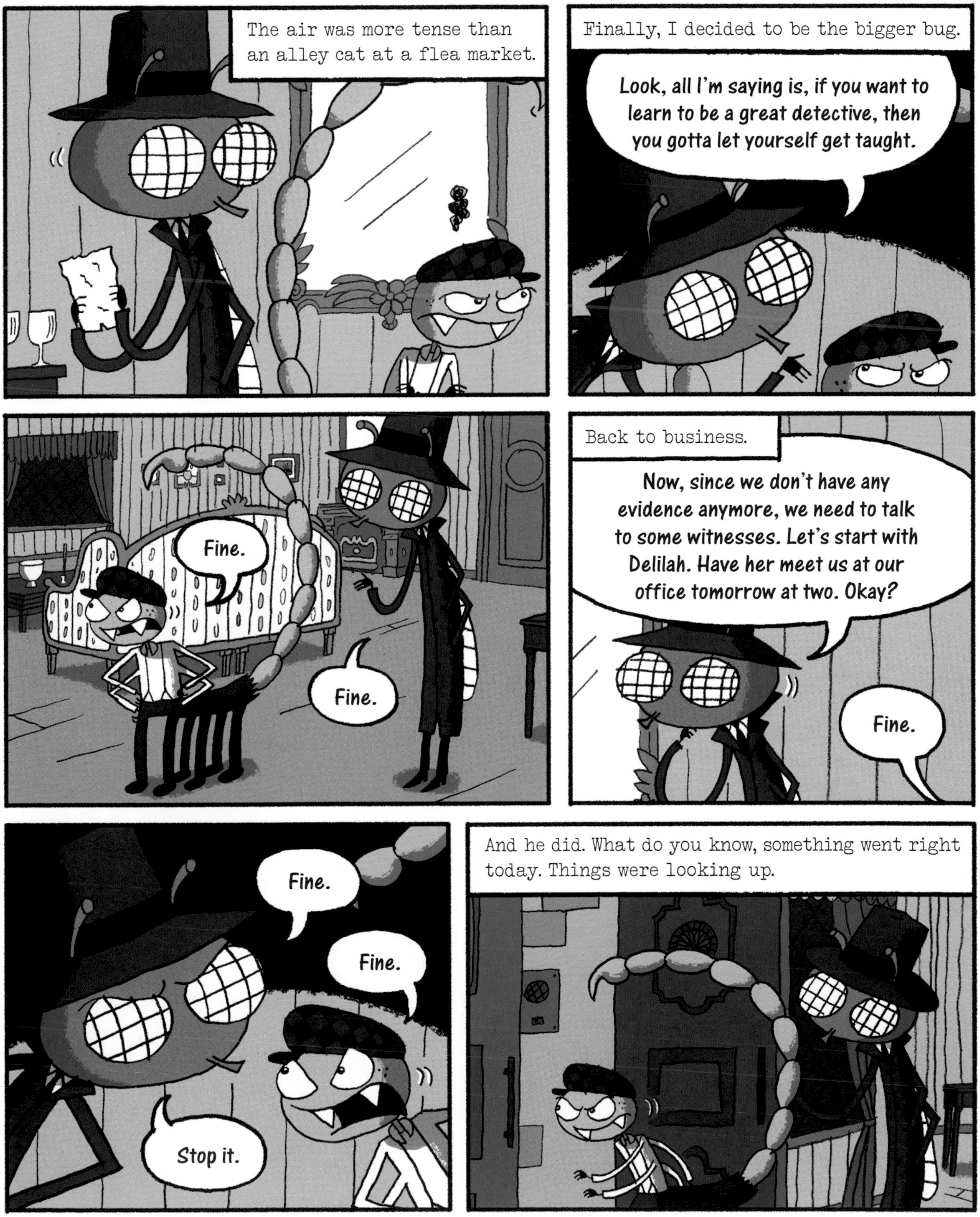
The air was more tense than an alley cat at a flea market.
Finally, I decided to be the bigger bug.
Look, all I'm saying is, if you want to learn to be a great detective, then you gotta let yourself get taught.
Fine.
Fine.
Back to business.
Now, since we don't have any evidence anymore, we need to talk to some witnesses. Let's start with Delilah. Have her meet us at our office tomorrow at two. Okay?
Fine.
Fine.
Fine.
Stop it.
And he did. What do you know, something went right today. Things were looking up.

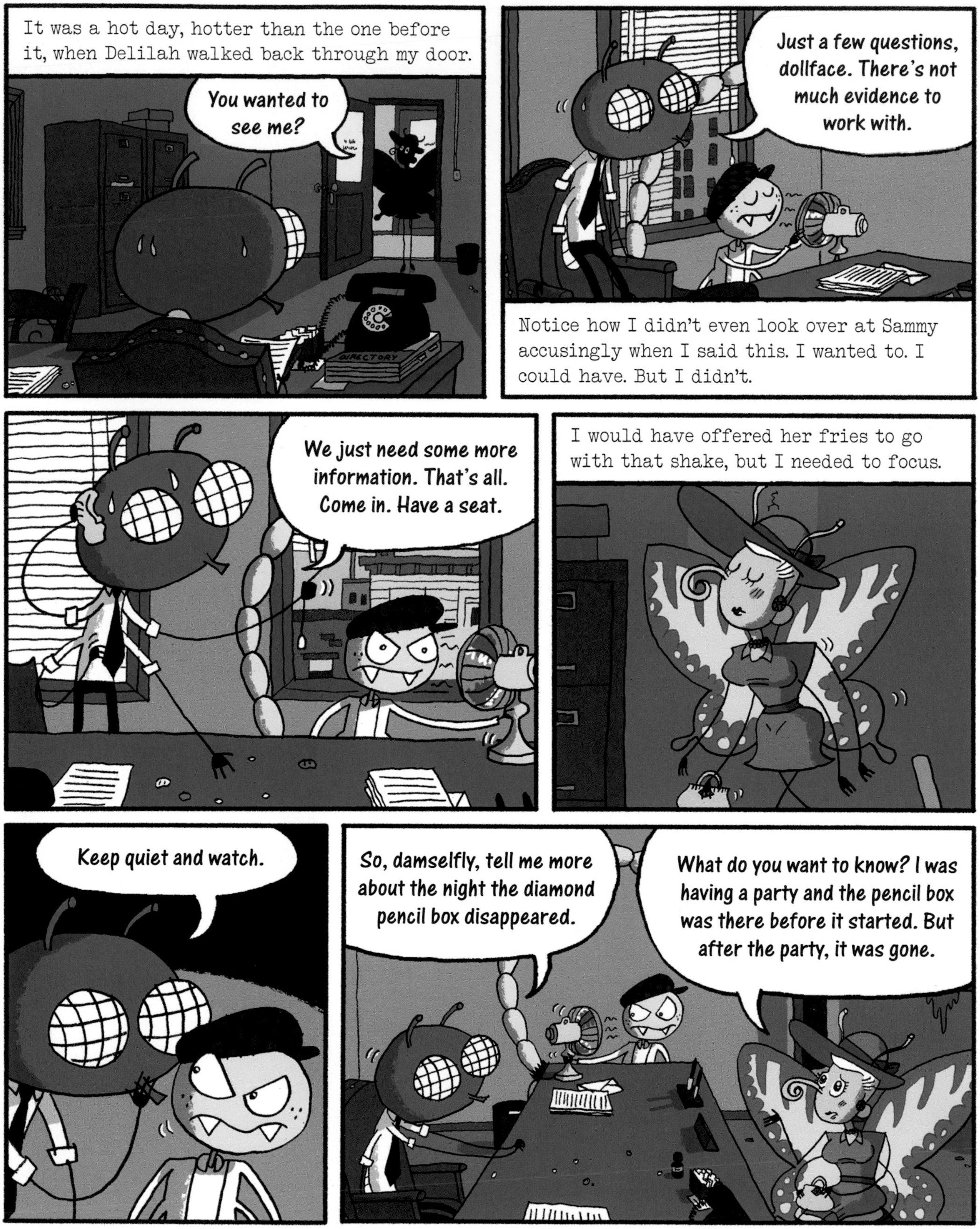

It was a hot day, hotter than the one before it, when Delilah walked back through my door.
You wanted to see me?
Just a few questions, dollface. There's not much evidence to work with.
Notice how I didn't even look over at Sammy accusingly when I said this. I wanted to. I could have. But I didn't.
DIRECTORY
We just need some more information. That's all. Come in. Have a seat.
I would have offered her fries to go with that shake, but I needed to focus.
Keep quiet and watch.
So, damselfly, tell me more about the night the diamond pencil box disappeared.
What do you want to know? I was having a party and the pencil box was there before it started. But after the party, it was gone.

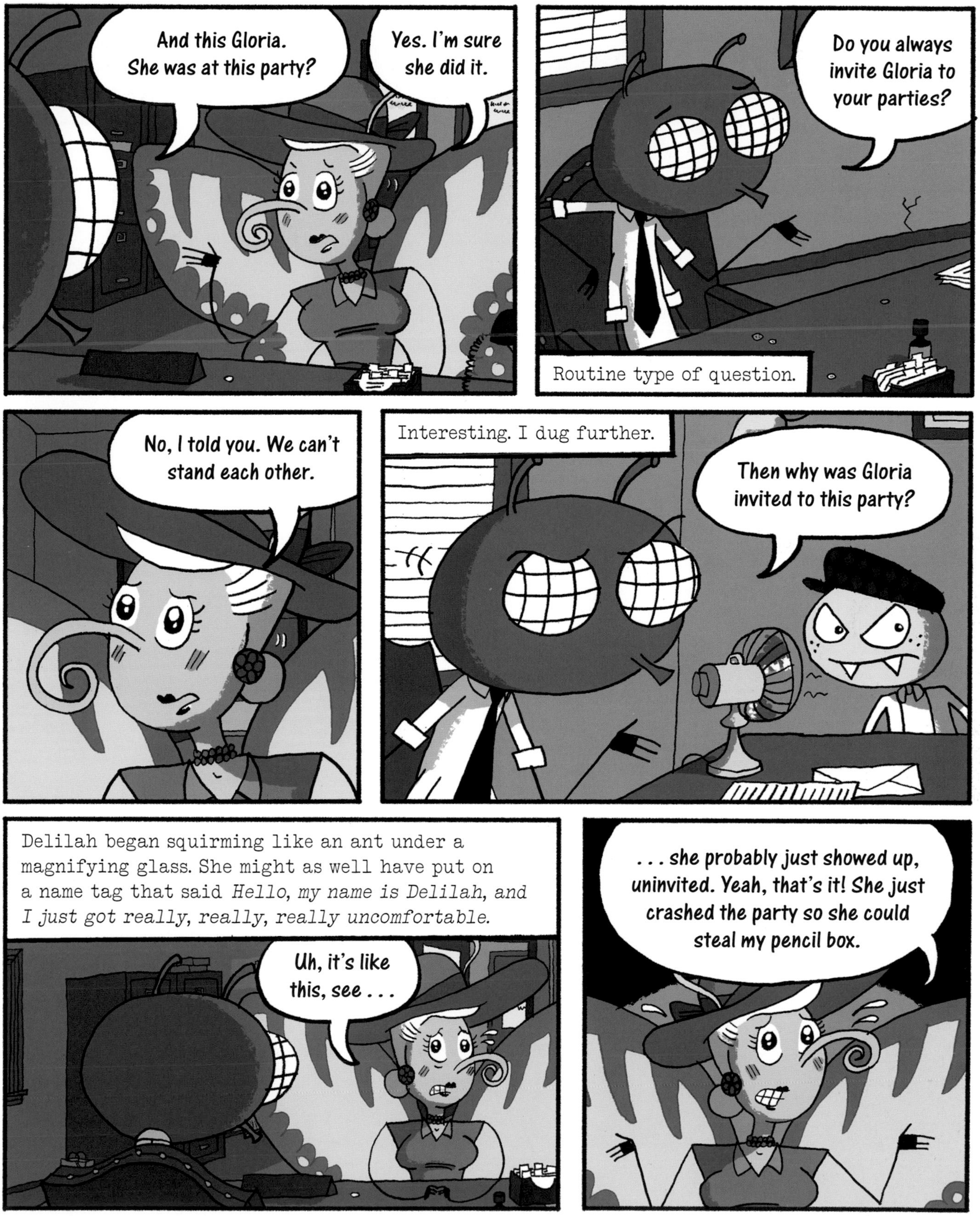

And this Gloria. She was at this party?
Yes. I'm sure she did it.
Do you always invite Gloria to your parties?
Routine type of question.
No, I told you. We can't stand each other.
Interesting. I dug further.
Then why was Gloria invited to this party?
Delilah began squirming like an ant under a magnifying glass. She might as well have put on a name tag that said *Hello, my name is Delilah, and I just got really, really, really uncomfortable.*
Uh, it's like this, see . . .
. . . she probably just showed up, uninvited. Yeah, that's it! She just crashed the party so she could steal my pencil box.

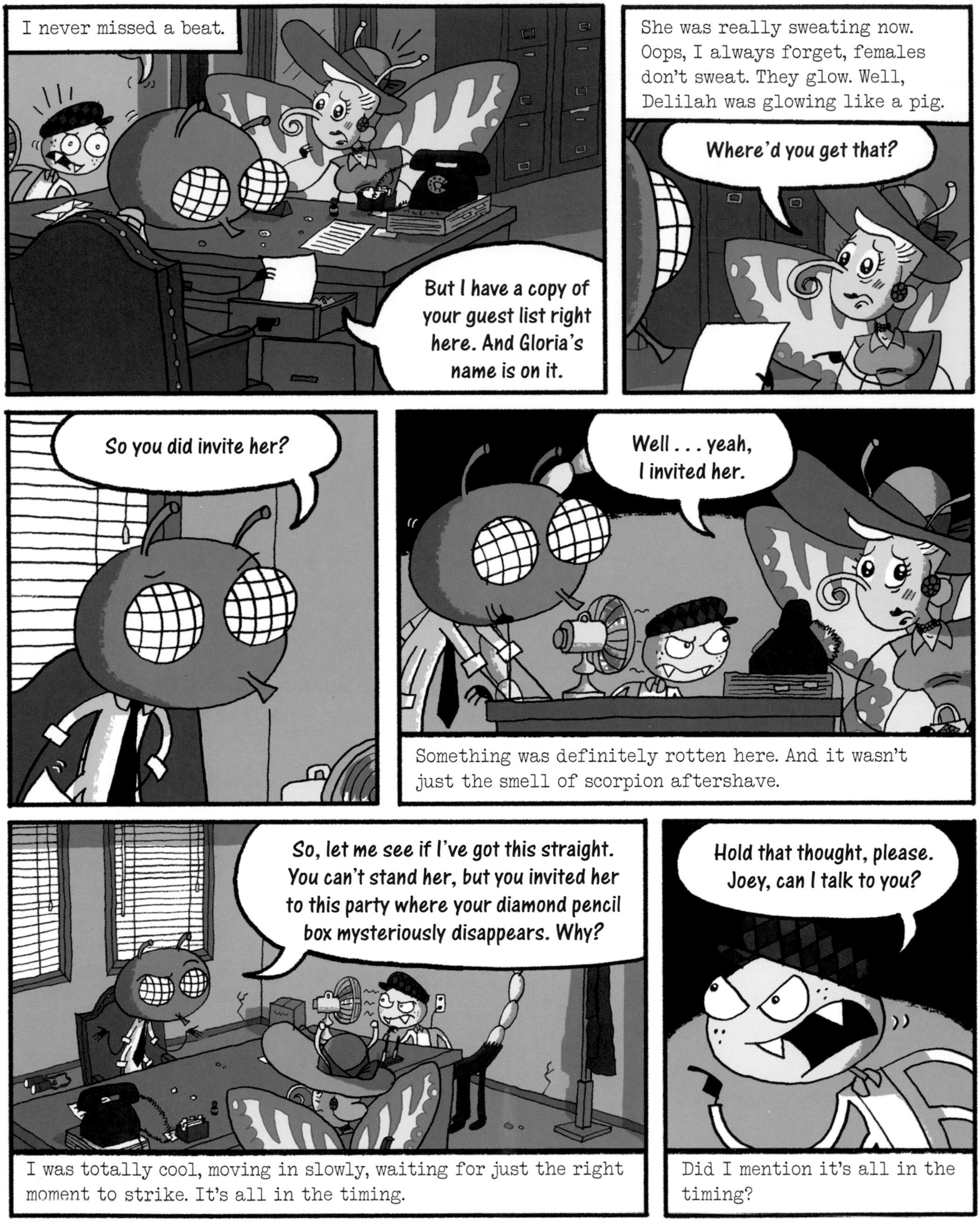
I never missed a beat.
But I have a copy of your guest list right here. And Gloria's name is on it.
She was really sweating now. Oops, I always forget, females don't sweat. They glow. Well, Delilah was glowing like a pig.
Where'd you get that?
So you did invite her?
Well . . . yeah, I invited her.
Something was definitely rotten here. And it wasn't just the smell of scorpion aftershave.
So, let me see if I've got this straight. You can't stand her, but you invited her to this party where your diamond pencil box mysteriously disappears. Why?
I was totally cool, moving in slowly, waiting for just the right moment to strike. It's all in the timing.
Hold that thought, please. Joey, can I talk to you?
Did I mention it's all in the timing?

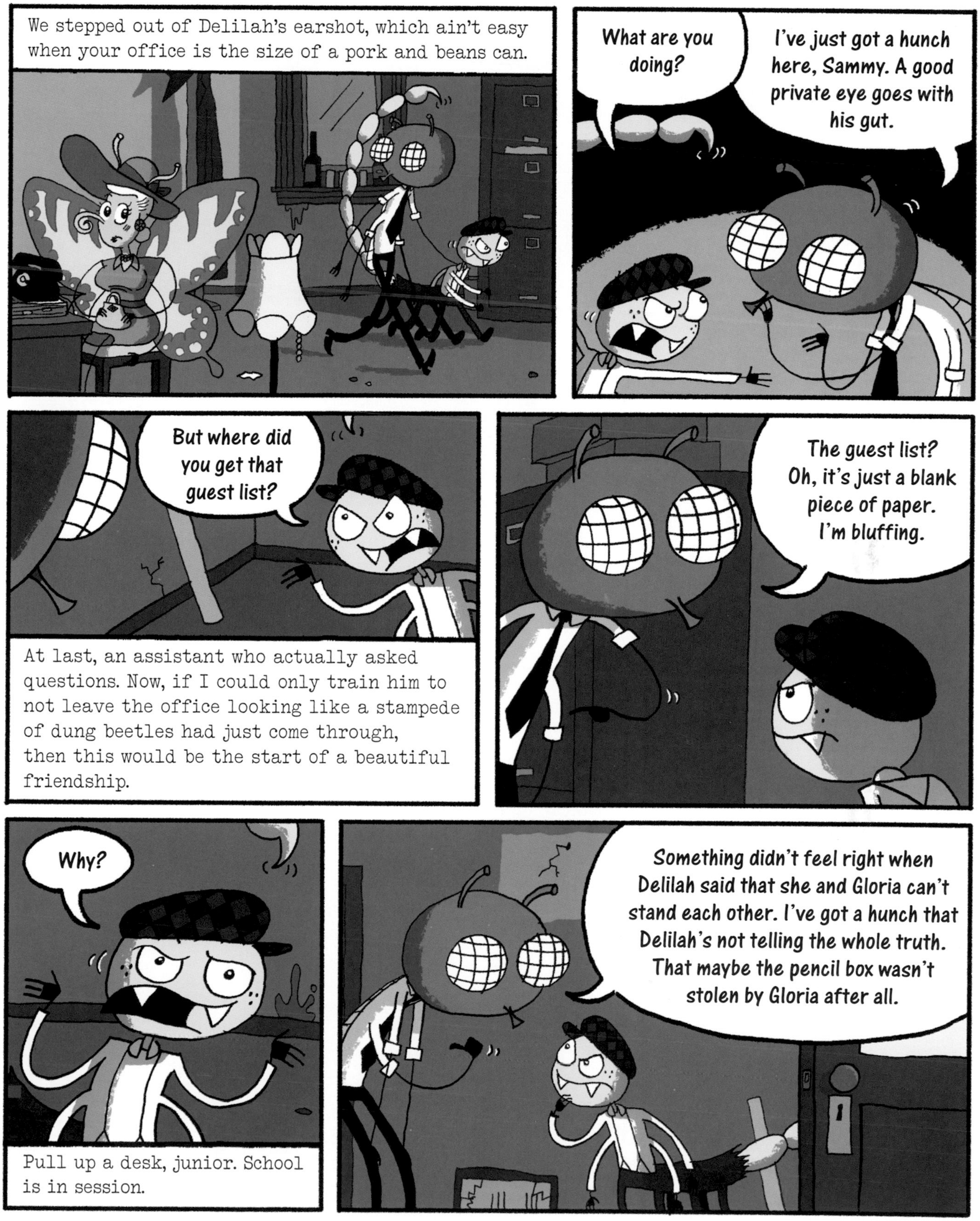
We stepped out of Delilah's earshot, which ain't easy when your office is the size of a pork and beans can.
What are you doing?
I've just got a hunch here, Sammy. A good private eye goes with his gut.
But where did you get that guest list?
At last, an assistant who actually asked questions. Now, if I could only train him to not leave the office looking like a stampede of dung beetles had just come through, then this would be the start of a beautiful friendship.
The guest list? Oh, it's just a blank piece of paper. I'm bluffing.
Why?
Pull up a desk, junior. School is in session.
Something didn't feel right when Delilah said that she and Gloria can't stand each other. I've got a hunch that Delilah's not telling the whole truth. That maybe the pencil box wasn't stolen by Gloria after all.

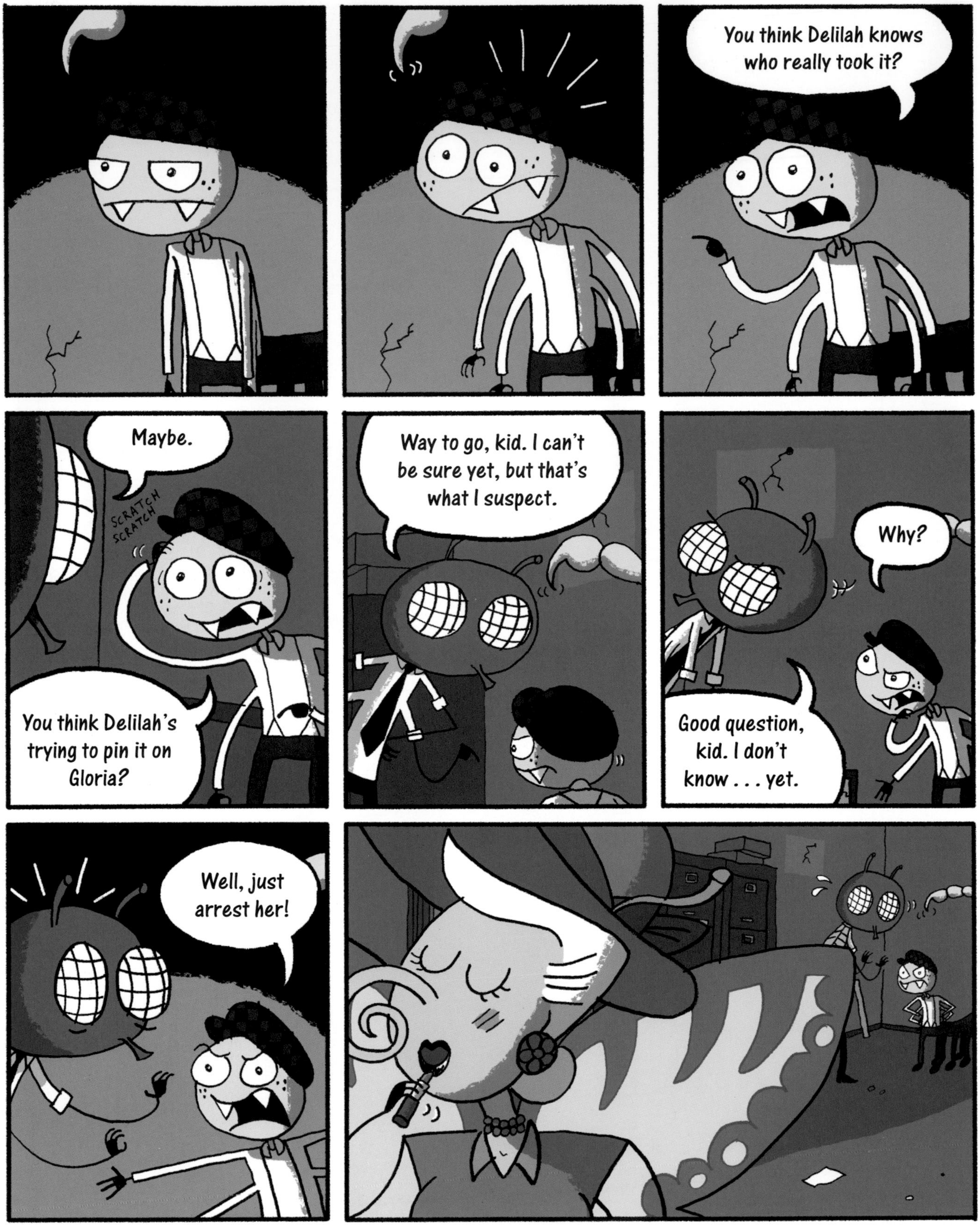
You think Delilah knows who really took it?
Maybe.
SCRATCH SCRATCH
You think Delilah's trying to pin it on Gloria?
Way to go, kid. I can't be sure yet, but that's what I suspect.
Why?
Good question, kid. I don't know . . . yet.
Well, just arrest her!

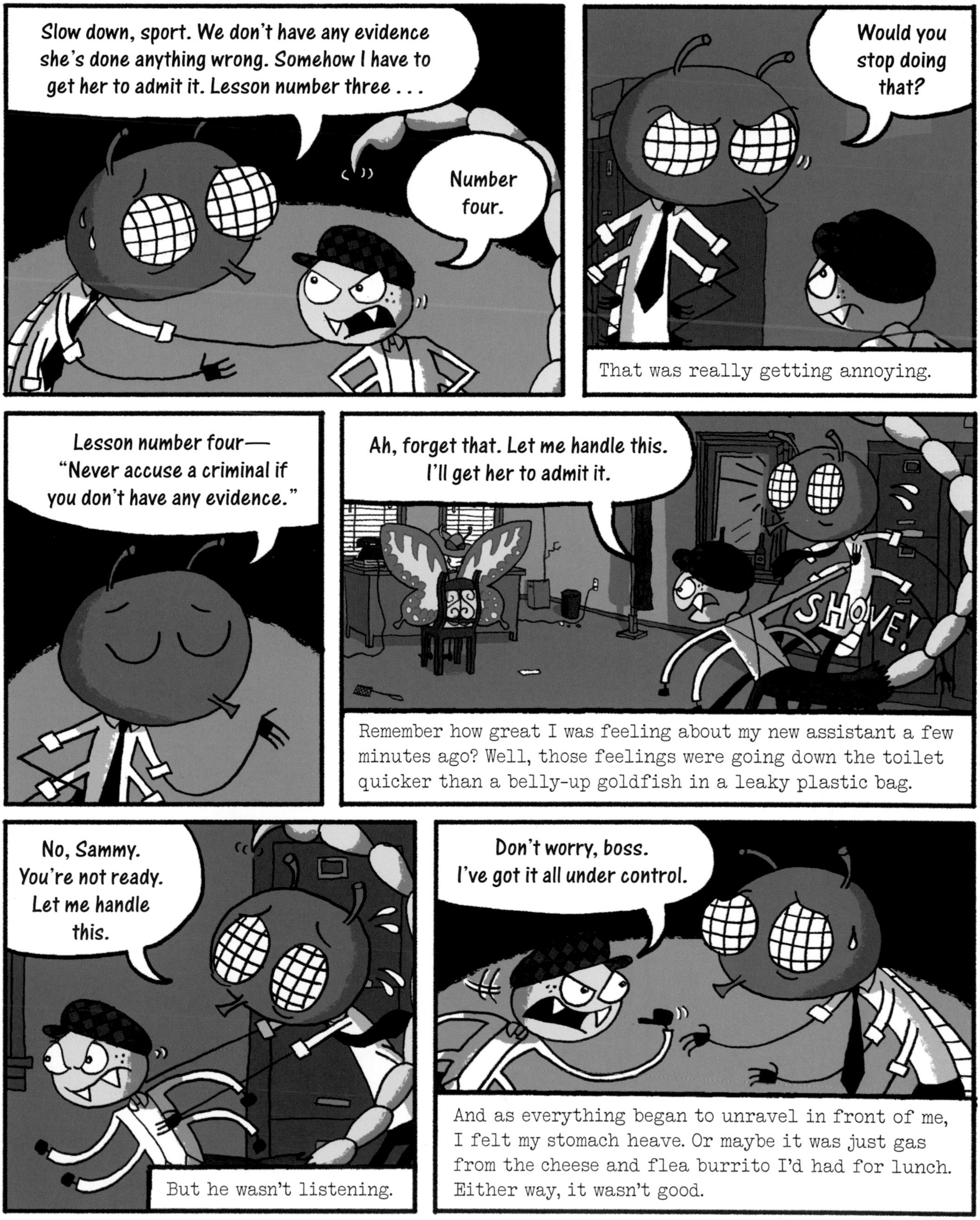
Slow down, sport. We don't have any evidence she's done anything wrong. Somehow I have to get her to admit it. Lesson number three . . .
Number four.
Would you stop doing that?
That was really getting annoying.
Lesson number four—"Never accuse a criminal if you don't have any evidence."
Ah, forget that. Let me handle this. I'll get her to admit it.
SHOVE!
Remember how great I was feeling about my new assistant a few minutes ago? Well, those feelings were going down the toilet quicker than a belly-up goldfish in a leaky plastic bag.
No, Sammy. You're not ready. Let me handle this.
But he wasn't listening.
Don't worry, boss. I've got it all under control.
And as everything began to unravel in front of me, I felt my stomach heave. Or maybe it was just gas from the cheese and flea burrito I'd had for lunch. Either way, it wasn't good.

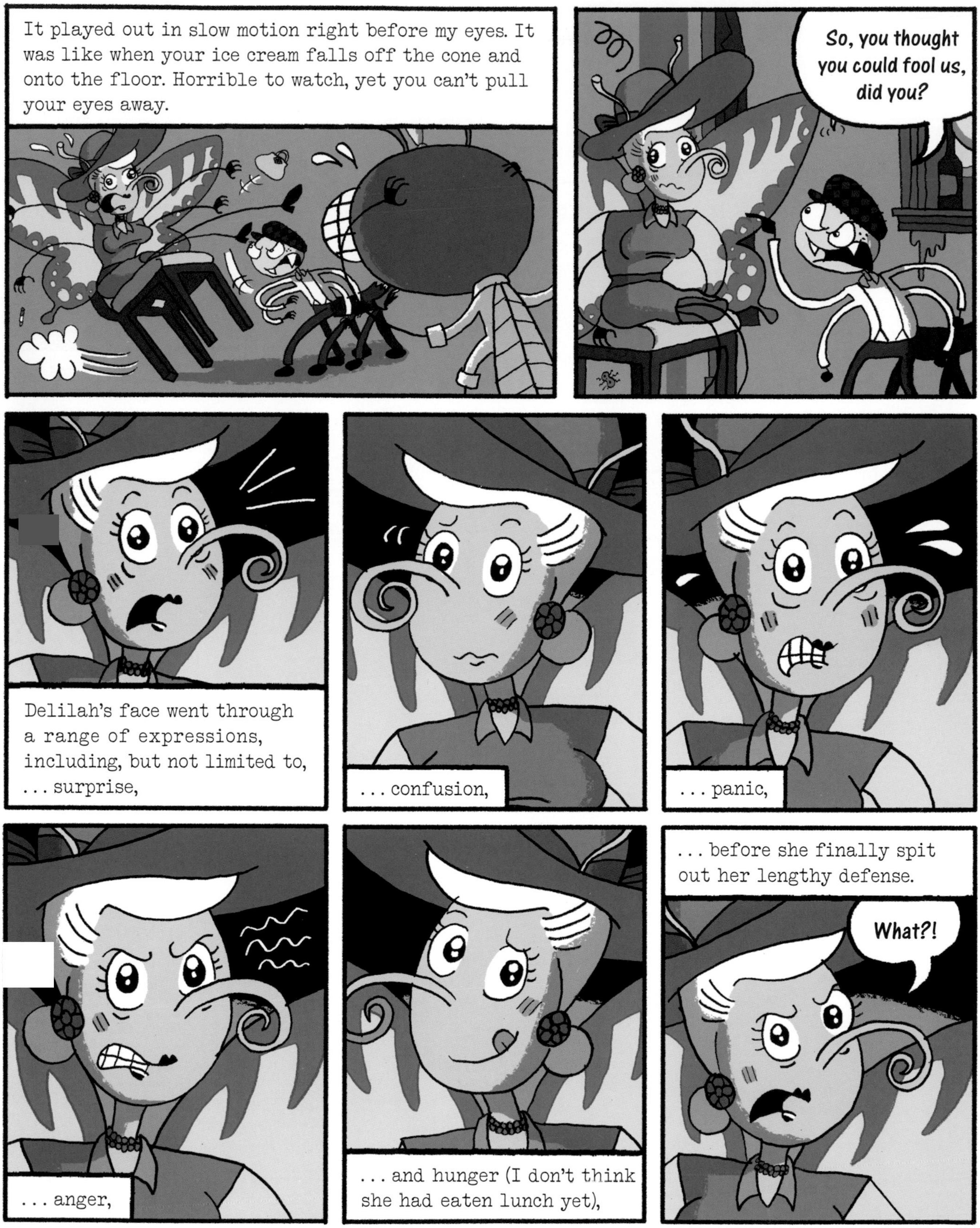
It played out in slow motion right before my eyes. It was like when your ice cream falls off the cone and onto the floor. Horrible to watch, yet you can't pull your eyes away.
So, you thought you could fool us, did you?
Delilah's face went through a range of expressions, including, but not limited to, . . . surprise,
. . . confusion,
. . . panic,
. . . anger,
. . . and hunger (I don't think she had eaten lunch yet),
. . . before she finally spit out her lengthy defense.
What?!

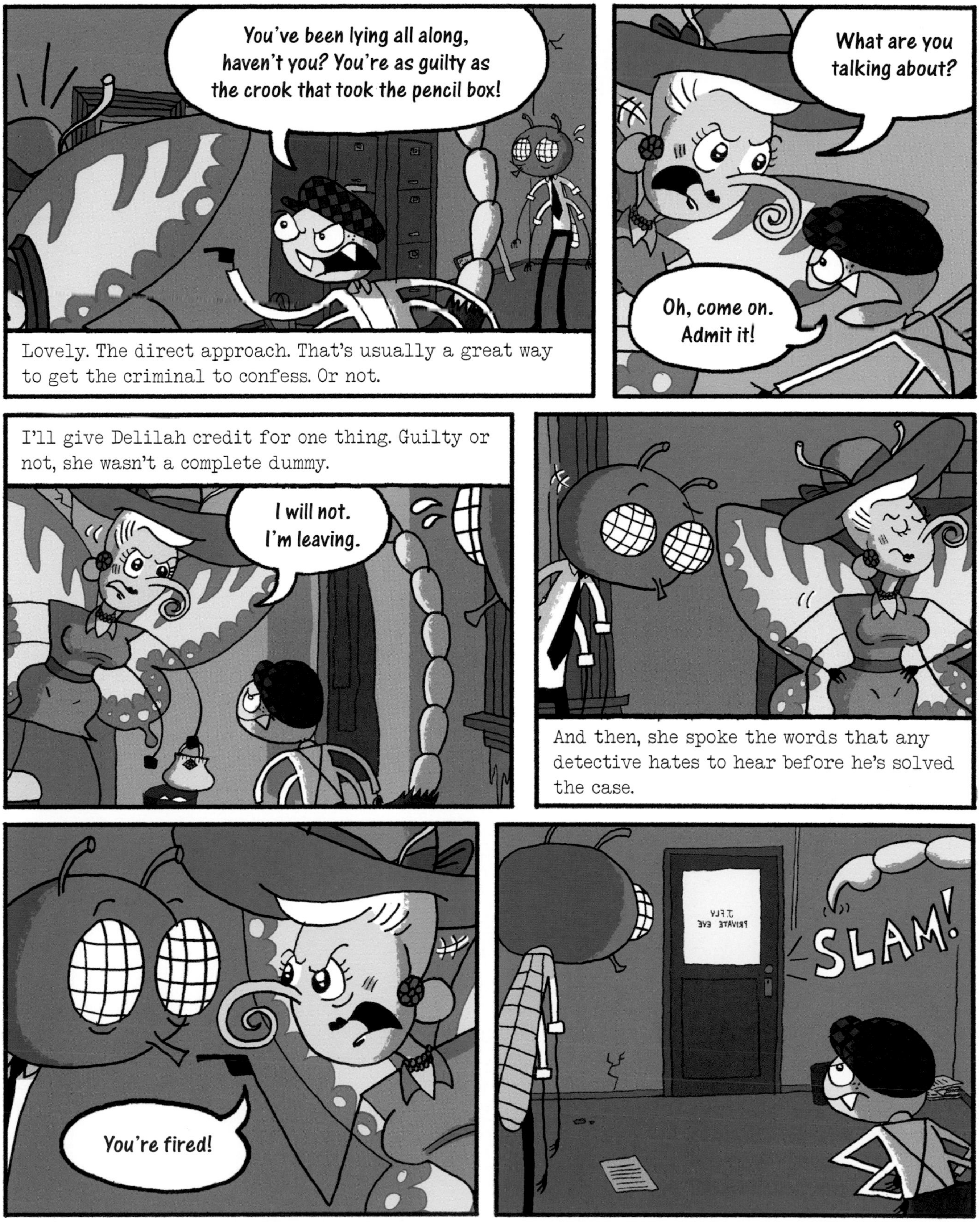
You've been lying all along, haven't you? You're as guilty as the crook that took the pencil box!
Lovely. The direct approach. That's usually a great way to get the criminal to confess. Or not.
What are you talking about?
Oh, come on. Admit it!
I'll give Delilah credit for one thing. Guilty or not, she wasn't a complete dummy.
I will not. I'm leaving.
And then, she spoke the words that any detective hates to hear before he's solved the case.
You're fired!
SLAM!

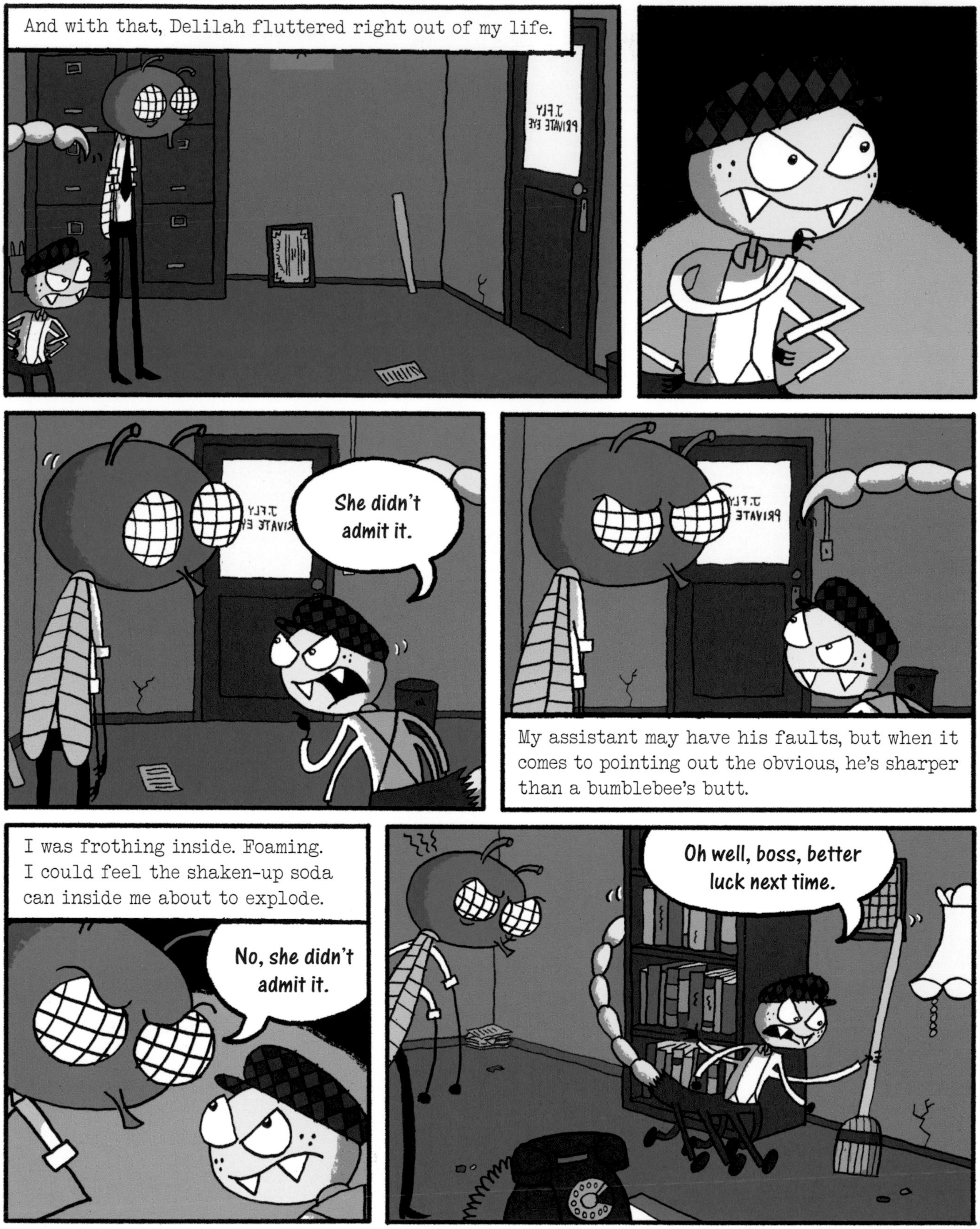

And with that, Delilah fluttered right out of my life.
J. FLY PRIVATE EYE
She didn't admit it.
My assistant may have his faults, but when it comes to pointing out the obvious, he's sharper than a bumblebee's butt.
I was frothing inside. Foaming. I could feel the shaken-up soda can inside me about to explode.
No, she didn't admit it.
Oh well, boss, better luck next time.

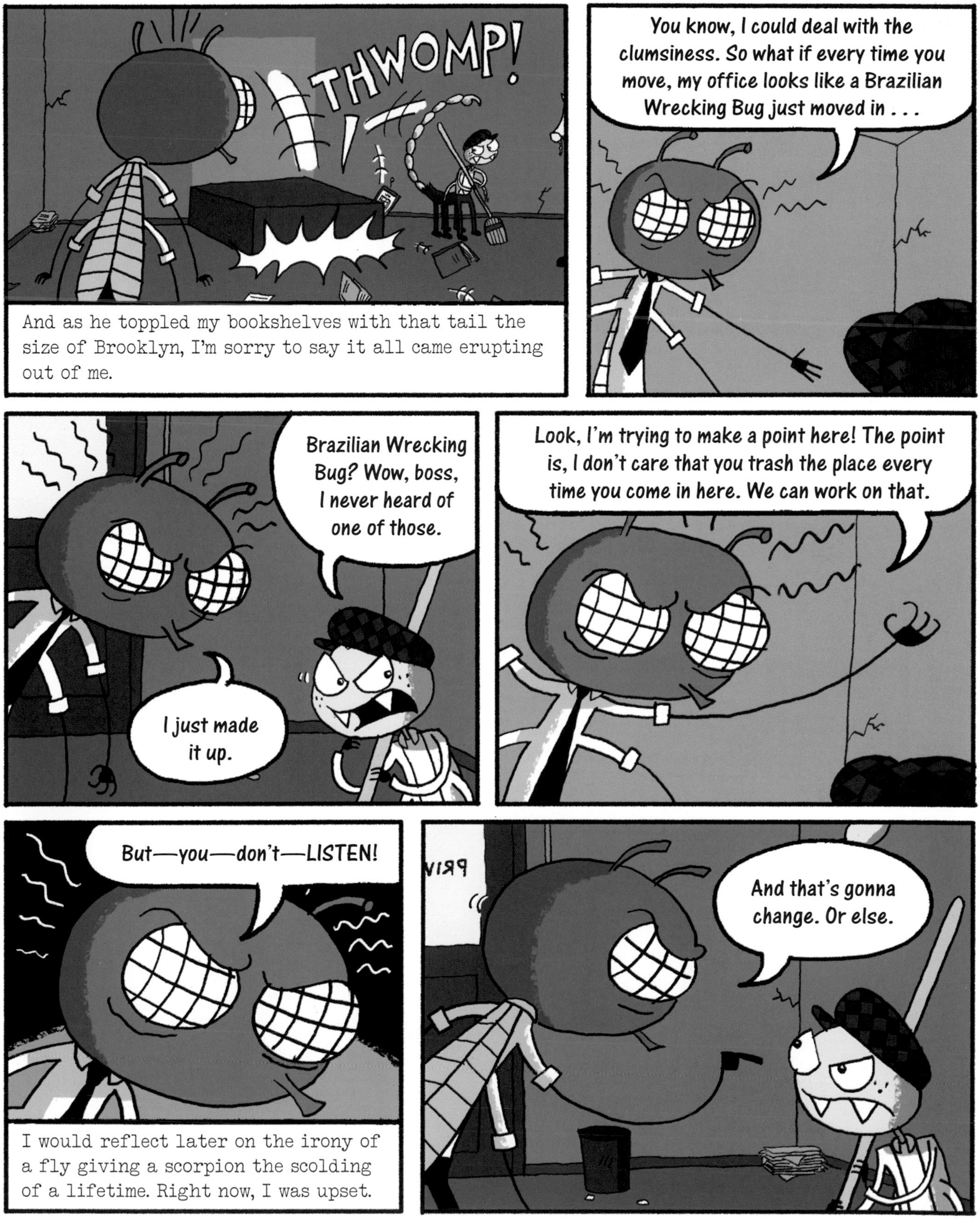
THWOMP!
And as he toppled my bookshelves with that tail the size of Brooklyn, I'm sorry to say it all came erupting out of me.
You know, I could deal with the clumsiness. So what if every time you move, my office looks like a Brazilian Wrecking Bug just moved in . . .
Brazilian Wrecking Bug? Wow, boss, I never heard of one of those.
I just made it up.
Look, I'm trying to make a point here! The point is, I don't care that you trash the place every time you come in here. We can work on that.
But—you—don't—LISTEN!
I would reflect later on the irony of a fly giving a scorpion the scolding of a lifetime. Right now, I was upset.
PRIV
And that's gonna change. Or else.

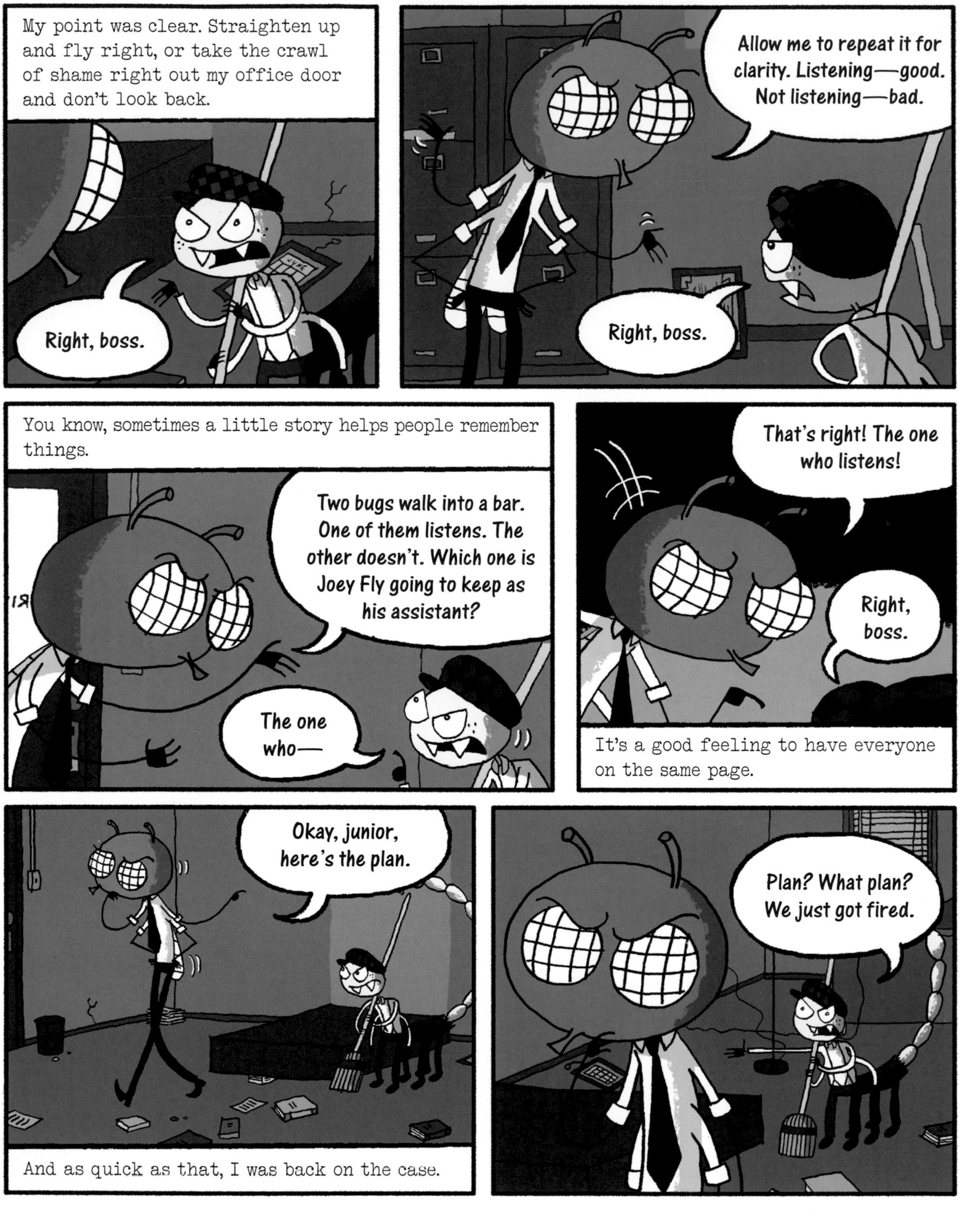
My point was clear. Straighten up and fly right, or take the crawl of shame right out my office door and don't look back.
Right, boss.
Allow me to repeat it for clarity. Listening—good. Not listening—bad.
Right, boss.
You know, sometimes a little story helps people remember things.
Two bugs walk into a bar. One of them listens. The other doesn't. Which one is Joey Fly going to keep as his assistant?
The one who—
That's right! The one who listens!
Right, boss.
It's a good feeling to have everyone on the same page.
Okay, junior, here's the plan.
And as quick as that, I was back on the case.
Plan? What plan? We just got fired.

Lesson number . . .

. . . well, whatever number we're on . . .

. . . "A good detective never lets a little thing like getting fired stop him from solving his case."

Something stinks worse than skunk cabbage about this whole thing.

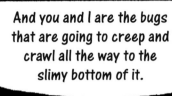

And you and I are the bugs that are going to creep and crawl all the way to the slimy bottom of it.

Right, boss.

And with that, Sammy knew that things had been forgiven. Maybe not completely forgotten. I had meant what I said to him. But definitely forgiven.

But what can we do? I mean, we've got no evidence, and we're fired.

We're playing the last card we've got. And it had better be an ace.

It's time to talk to Gloria.

We were hiding in the high grass a short hop from Delilah's place. And with that gargantuan tail of his, I use the word hiding here loosely. We were gonna have to figure out a way to disguise that thing.

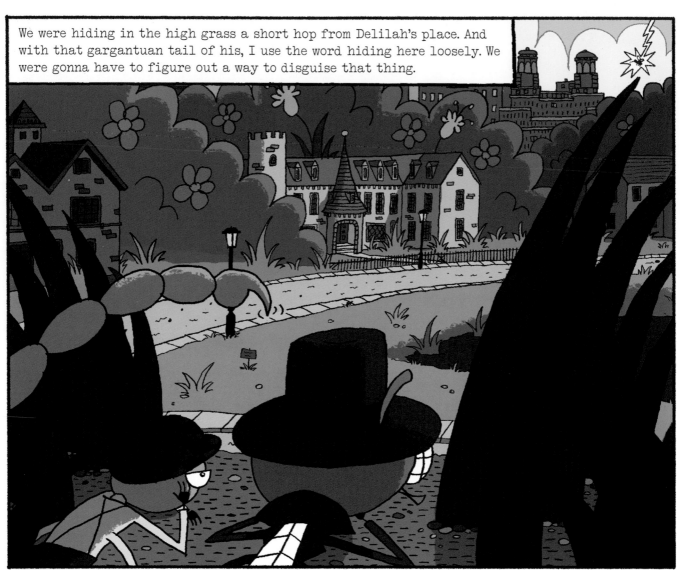

How are we going to find Gloria?

These hot days were going to kill me. The humidity was fogging up my exoskeleton from the inside out. Sammy's constant whining was starting to get on my nerves. And the gnats were eating me alive.

Trust me.

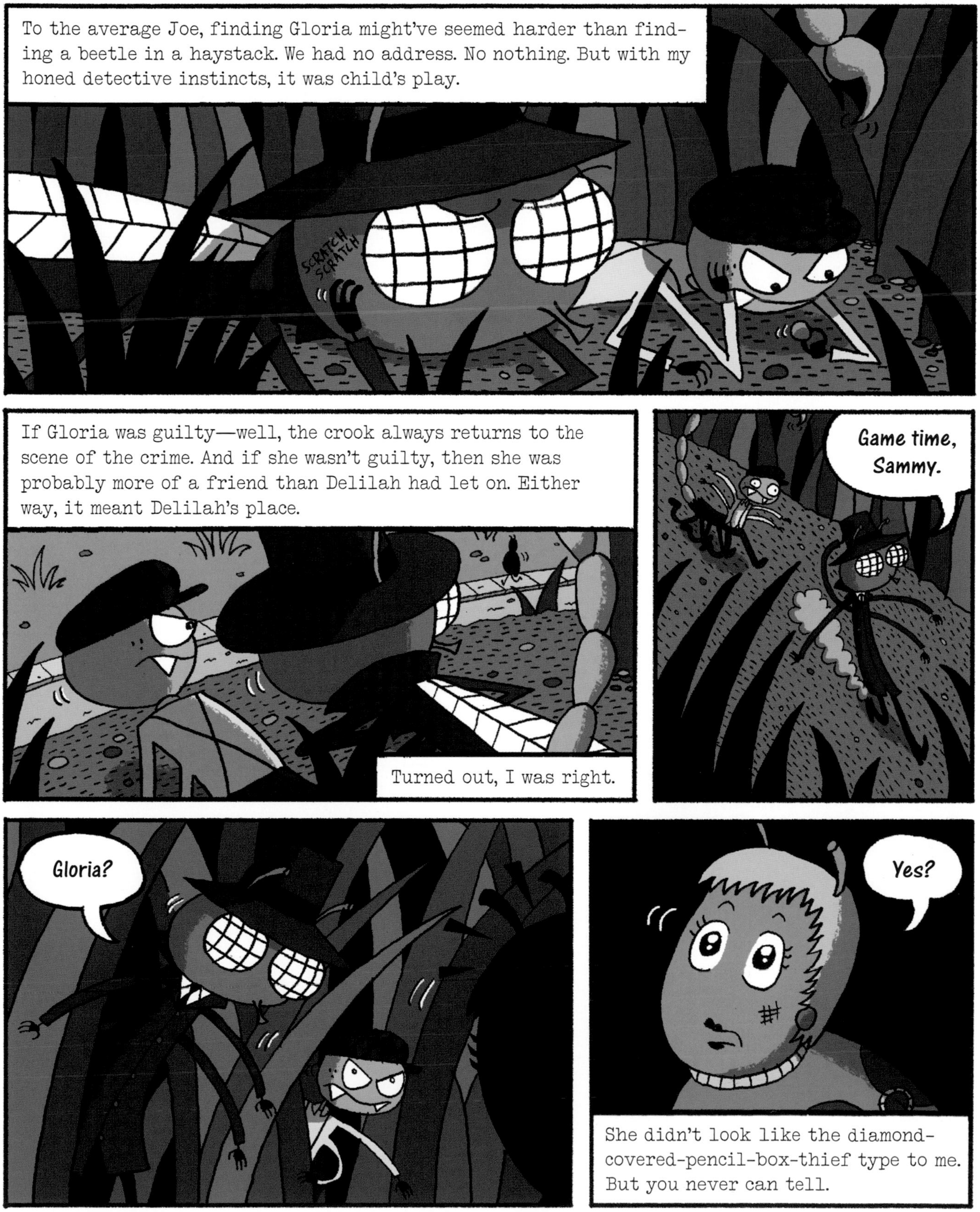

To the average Joe, finding Gloria might've seemed harder than finding a beetle in a haystack. We had no address. No nothing. But with my honed detective instincts, it was child's play.
SCRATCH SCRATCH
If Gloria was guilty—well, the crook always returns to the scene of the crime. And if she wasn't guilty, then she was probably more of a friend than Delilah had let on. Either way, it meant Delilah's place.
Turned out, I was right.
Game time, Sammy.
Gloria?
Yes?
She didn't look like the diamond-covered-pencil-box-thief type to me. But you never can tell.

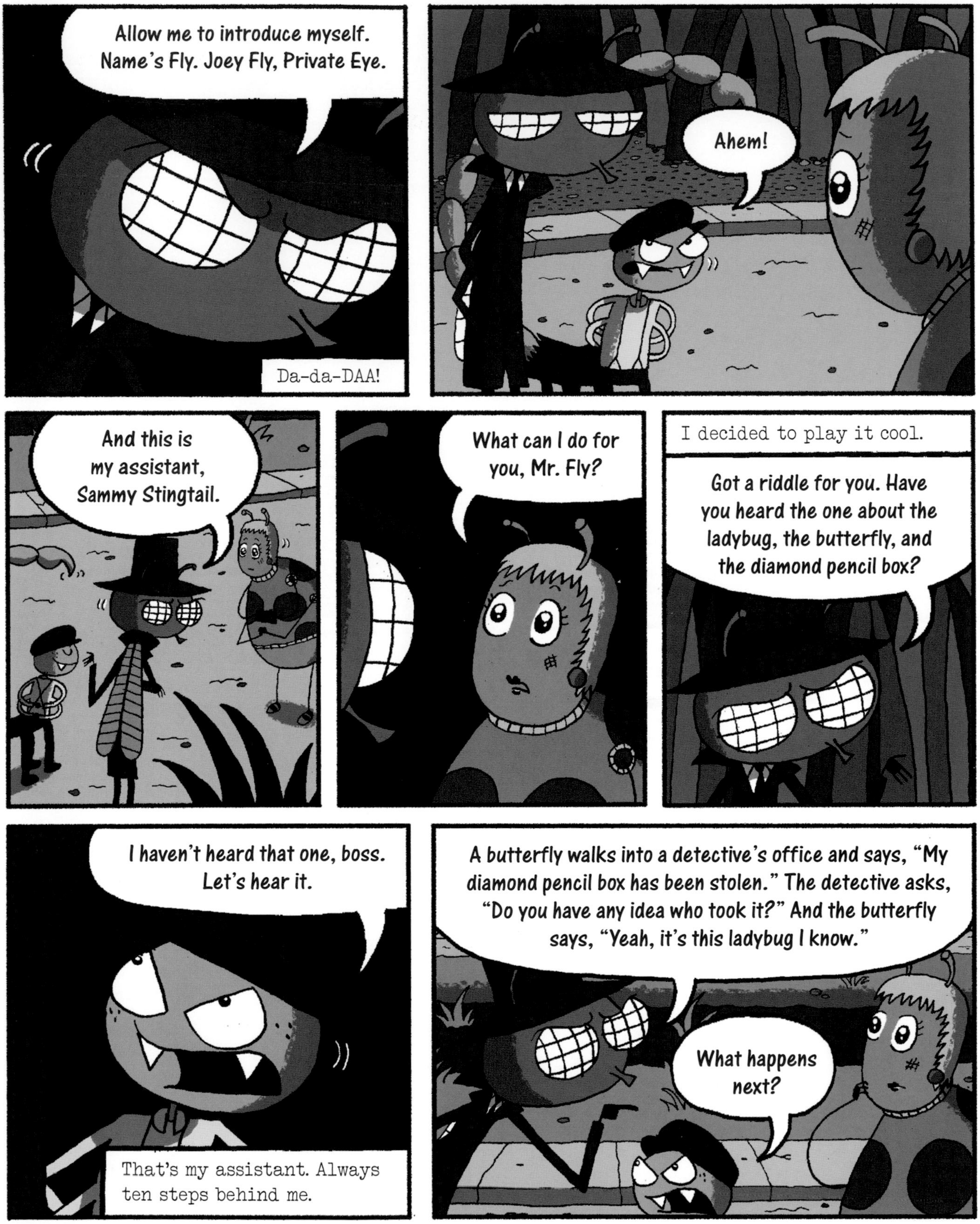
Allow me to introduce myself. Name's Fly. Joey Fly, Private Eye.
Da-da-DAA!
Ahem!
And this is my assistant, Sammy Stingtail.
What can I do for you, Mr. Fly?
I decided to play it cool.
Got a riddle for you. Have you heard the one about the ladybug, the butterfly, and the diamond pencil box?
I haven't heard that one, boss. Let's hear it.
That's my assistant. Always ten steps behind me.
A butterfly walks into a detective's office and says, "My diamond pencil box has been stolen." The detective asks, "Do you have any idea who took it?" And the butterfly says, "Yeah, it's this ladybug I know."
What happens next?

That's as much as I know.

Is that a joke? Because it's not a very funny one.

She was more right than she knew. Crime is no joke. And if she was the criminal, it was a lesson she was about to learn the hard way.

Wow, boss, you know what? That sounds just like that thing that happened with us and Delilah! Weird.

Life had been so much simpler in the days before I had an assistant. Like last week.

It is that thing that happened with us and Delilah. It's a little thing called style, which is clearly being wasted on this crowd.

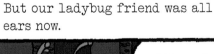

But our ladybug friend was all ears now.

Did you just say Delilah?

Now we were getting somewhere. I decided to get right to the point.

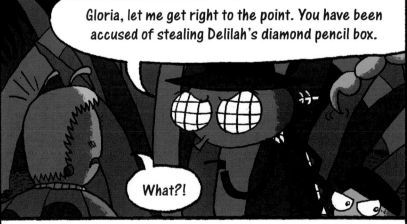

Gloria, let me get right to the point. You have been accused of stealing Delilah's diamond pencil box.

What?!

Clearly, this was news to Gloria. Or she wanted us to think it was news to her.

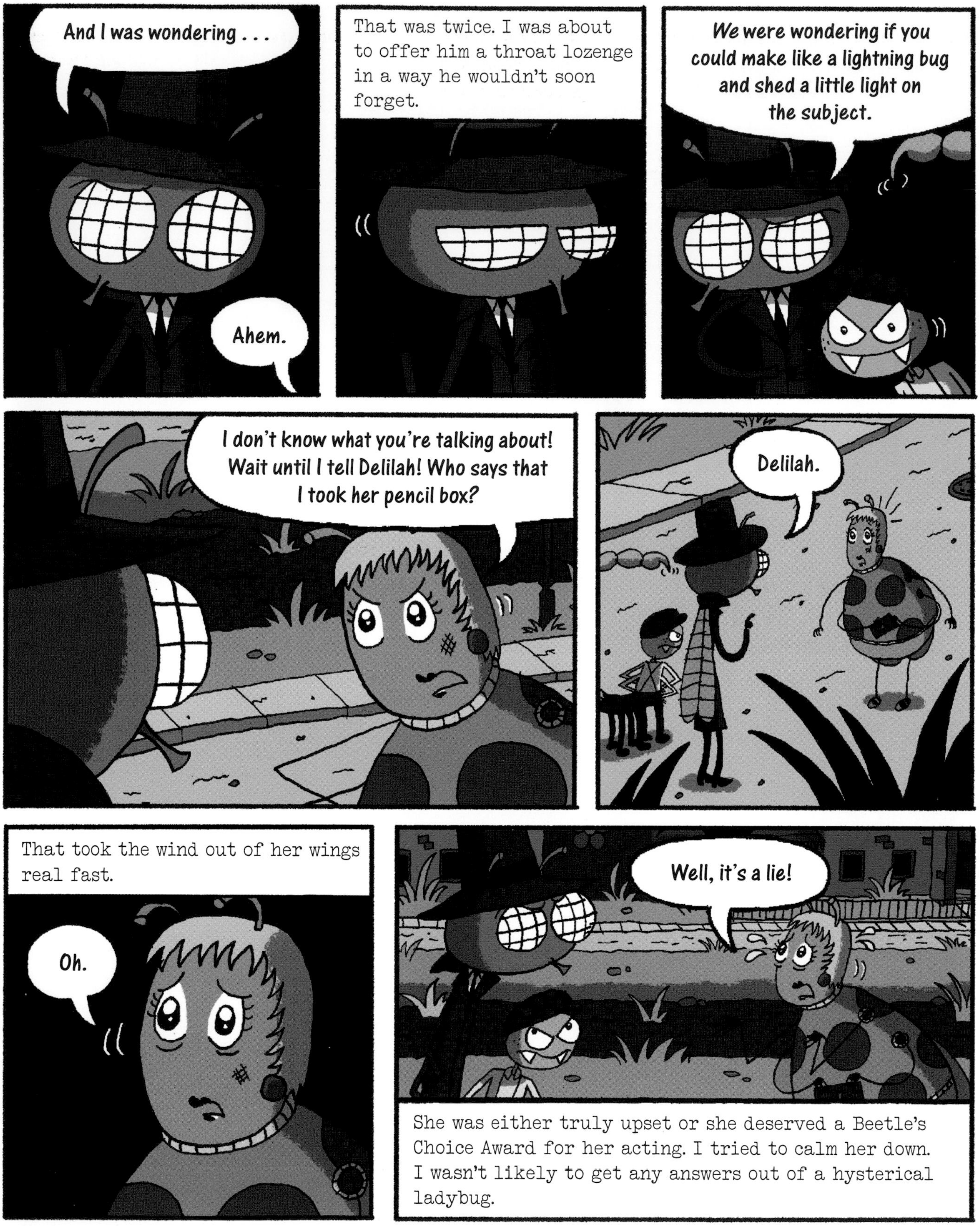
And I was wondering . . .
Ahem.
That was twice. I was about to offer him a throat lozenge in a way he wouldn't soon forget.
We were wondering if you could make like a lightning bug and shed a little light on the subject.
I don't know what you're talking about! Wait until I tell Delilah! Who says that I took her pencil box?
Delilah.
That took the wind out of her wings real fast.
Oh.
Well, it's a lie!
She was either truly upset or she deserved a Beetle's Choice Award for her acting. I tried to calm her down. I wasn't likely to get any answers out of a hysterical ladybug.

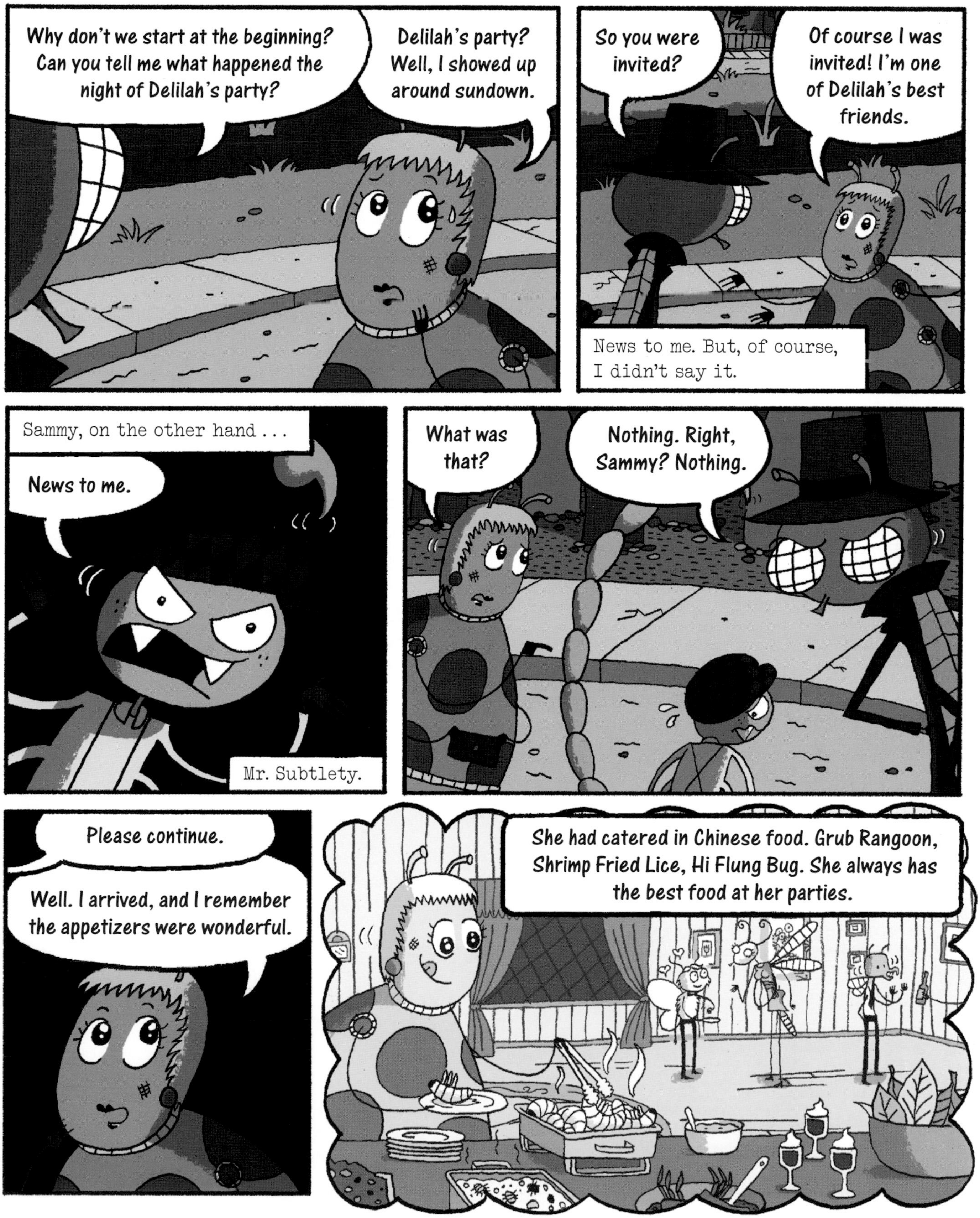
Why don't we start at the beginning? Can you tell me what happened the night of Delilah's party?
Delilah's party? Well, I showed up around sundown.
So you were invited?
Of course I was invited! I'm one of Delilah's best friends.
News to me. But, of course, I didn't say it.
Sammy, on the other hand . . .
News to me.
Mr. Subtlety.
What was that?
Nothing. Right, Sammy? Nothing.
Please continue.
Well. I arrived, and I remember the appetizers were wonderful.
She had catered in Chinese food. Grub Rangoon, Shrimp Fried Lice, Hi Flung Bug. She always has the best food at her parties.

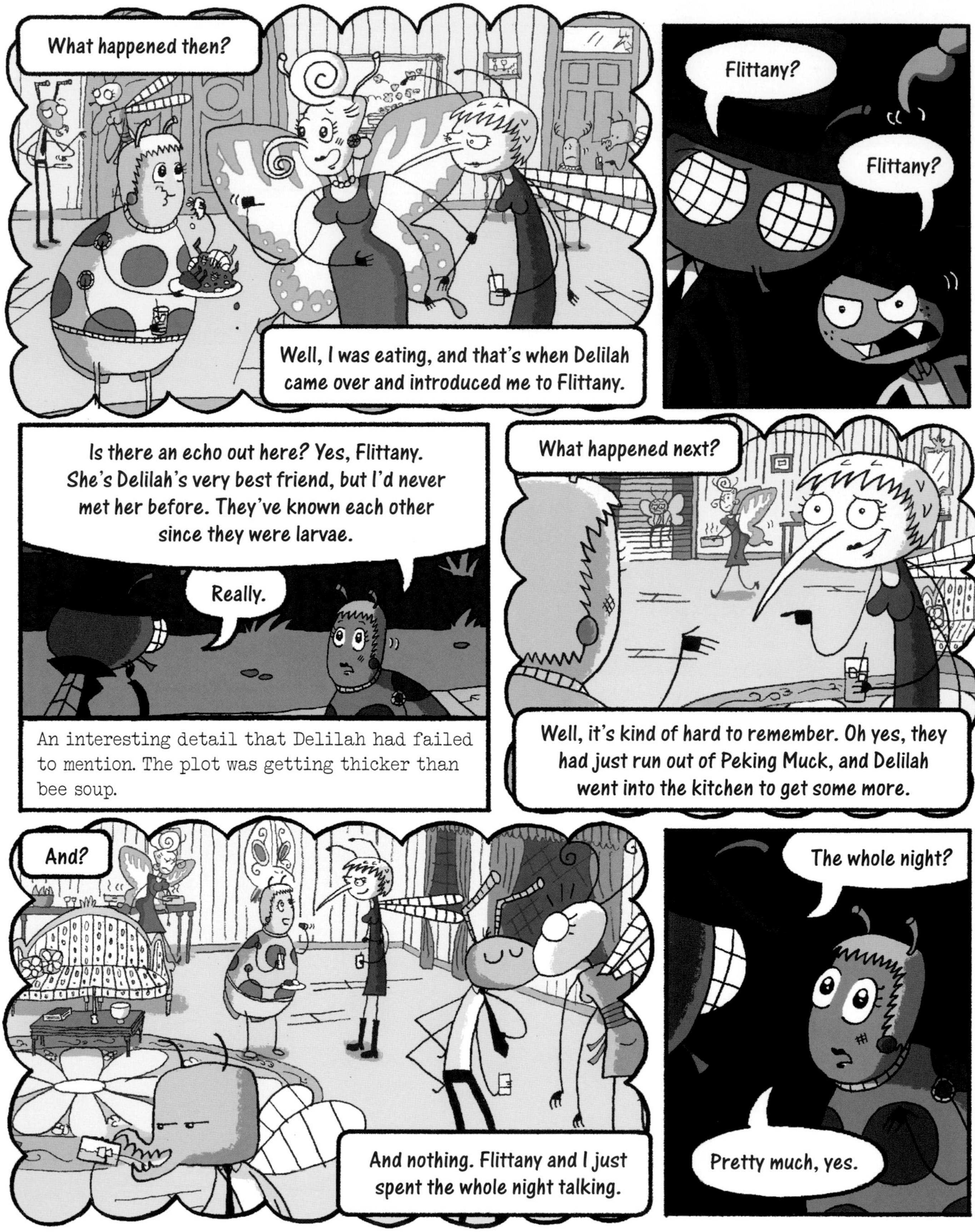
What happened then?
Well, I was eating, and that's when Delilah came over and introduced me to Flittany.
Flittany?
Flittany?
Is there an echo out here? Yes, Flittany. She's Delilah's very best friend, but I'd never met her before. They've known each other since they were larvae.
Really.
An interesting detail that Delilah had failed to mention. The plot was getting thicker than bee soup.
What happened next?
Well, it's kind of hard to remember. Oh yes, they had just run out of Peking Muck, and Delilah went into the kitchen to get some more.
And?
And nothing. Flittany and I just spent the whole night talking.
The whole night?
Pretty much, yes.

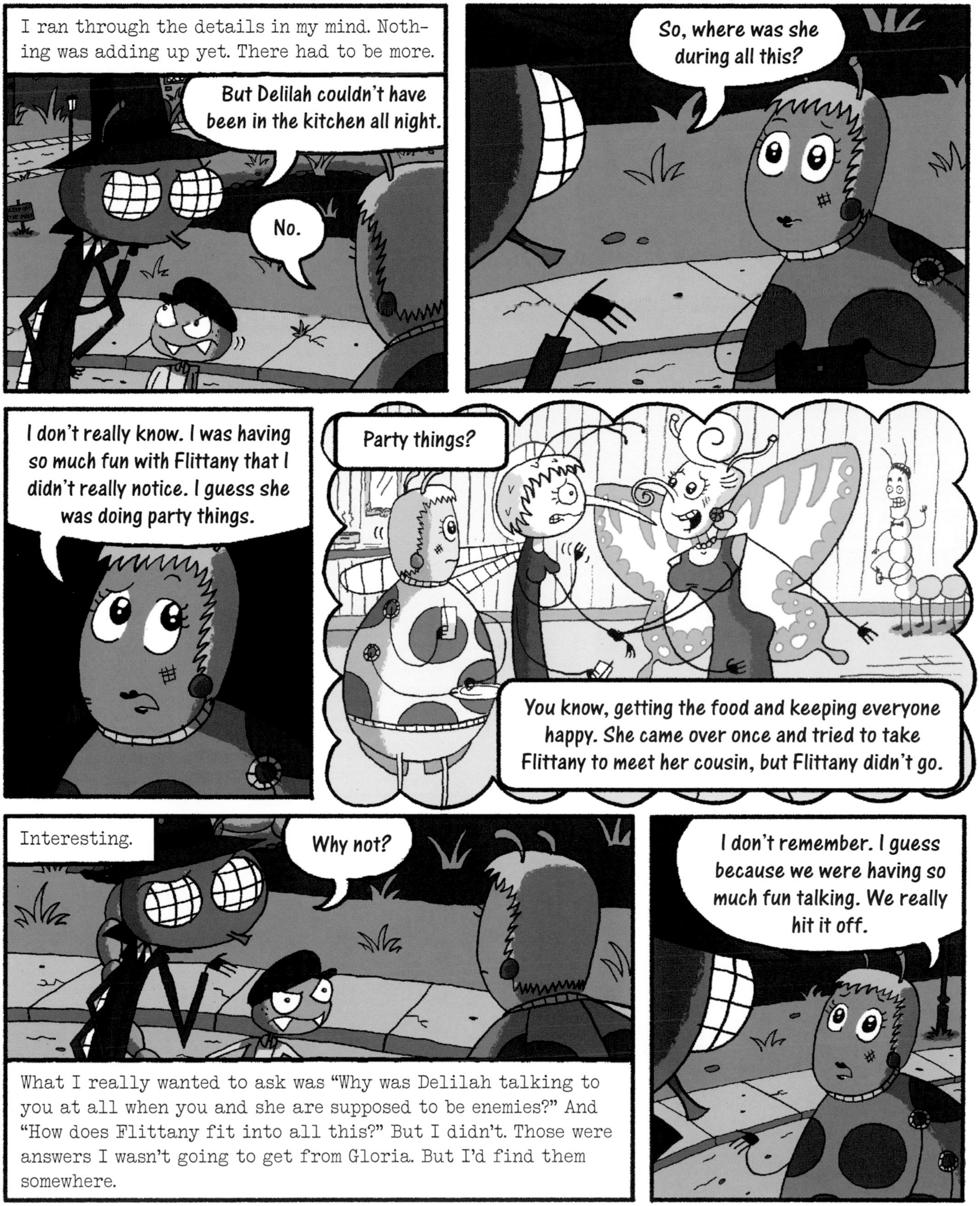
I ran through the details in my mind. Nothing was adding up yet. There had to be more.
But Delilah couldn't have been in the kitchen all night.
No.
So, where was she during all this?
I don't really know. I was having so much fun with Flittany that I didn't really notice. I guess she was doing party things.
Party things?
You know, getting the food and keeping everyone happy. She came over once and tried to take Flittany to meet her cousin, but Flittany didn't go.
Interesting.
Why not?
What I really wanted to ask was "Why was Delilah talking to you at all when you and she are supposed to be enemies?" And "How does Flittany fit into all this?" But I didn't. Those were answers I wasn't going to get from Gloria. But I'd find them somewhere.
I don't remember. I guess because we were having so much fun talking. We really hit it off.

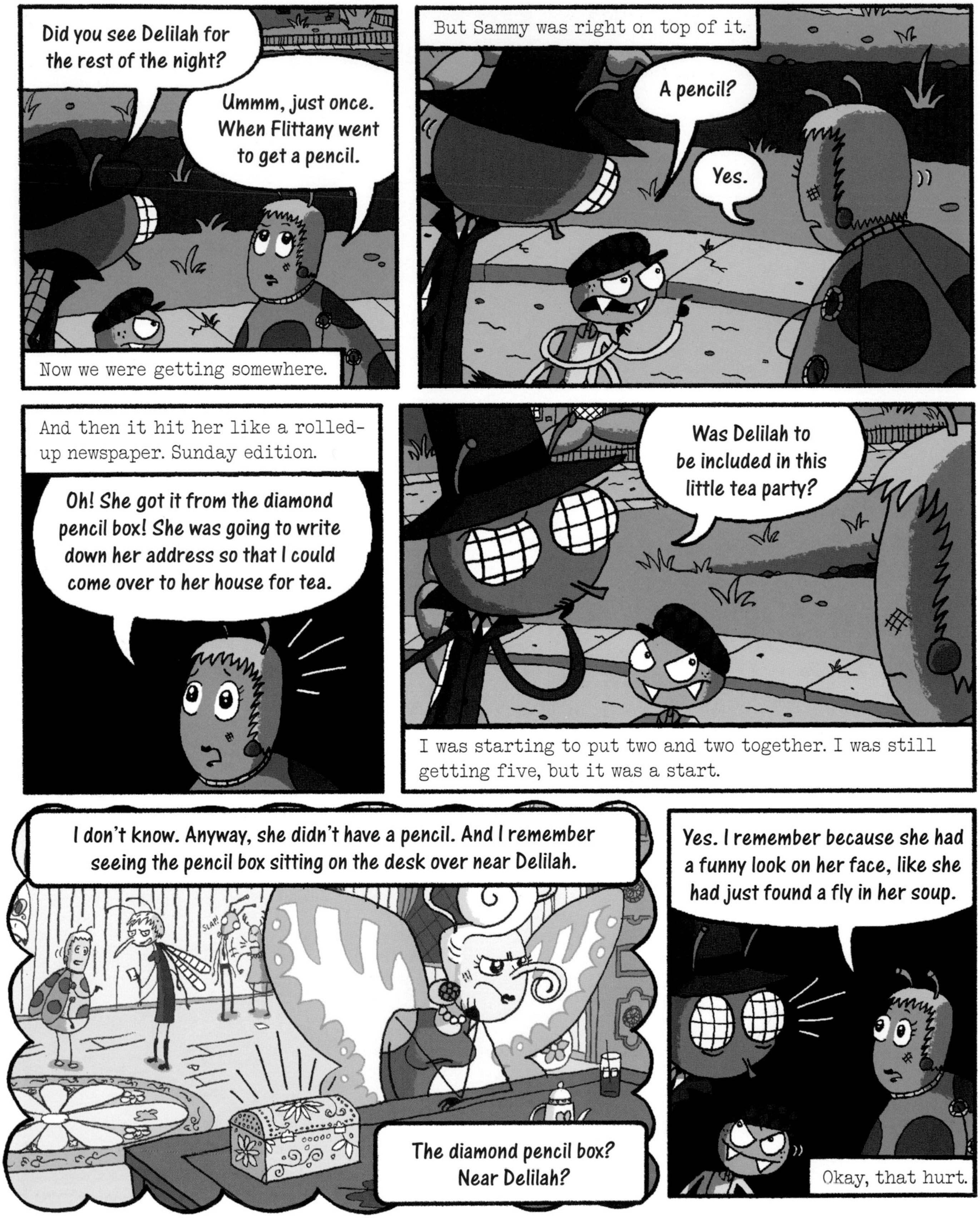
Did you see Delilah for the rest of the night?
Ummm, just once. When Flittany went to get a pencil.
Now we were getting somewhere.
But Sammy was right on top of it.
A pencil?
Yes.
And then it hit her like a rolled-up newspaper. Sunday edition.
Oh! She got it from the diamond pencil box! She was going to write down her address so that I could come over to her house for tea.
Was Delilah to be included in this little tea party?
I was starting to put two and two together. I was still getting five, but it was a start.
I don't know. Anyway, she didn't have a pencil. And I remember seeing the pencil box sitting on the desk over near Delilah.
The diamond pencil box? Near Delilah?
Yes. I remember because she had a funny look on her face, like she had just found a fly in her soup.
Okay, that hurt.

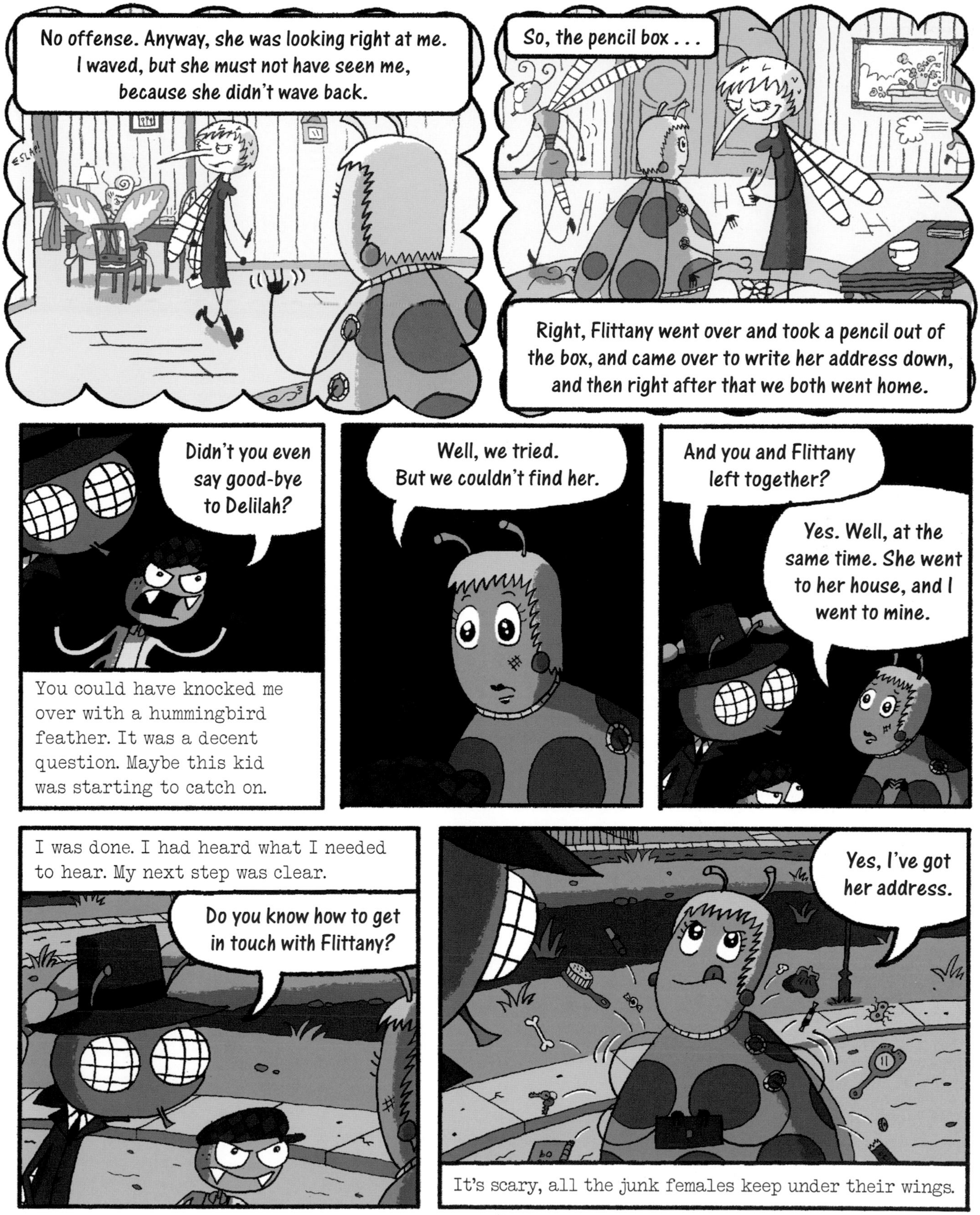
No offense. Anyway, she was looking right at me. I waved, but she must not have seen me, because she didn't wave back.
So, the pencil box . . .
Right, Flittany went over and took a pencil out of the box, and came over to write her address down, and then right after that we both went home.
Didn't you even say good-bye to Delilah?
You could have knocked me over with a hummingbird feather. It was a decent question. Maybe this kid was starting to catch on.
Well, we tried. But we couldn't find her.
And you and Flittany left together?
Yes. Well, at the same time. She went to her house, and I went to mine.
I was done. I had heard what I needed to hear. My next step was clear.
Do you know how to get in touch with Flittany?
Yes, I've got her address.
It's scary, all the junk females keep under their wings.

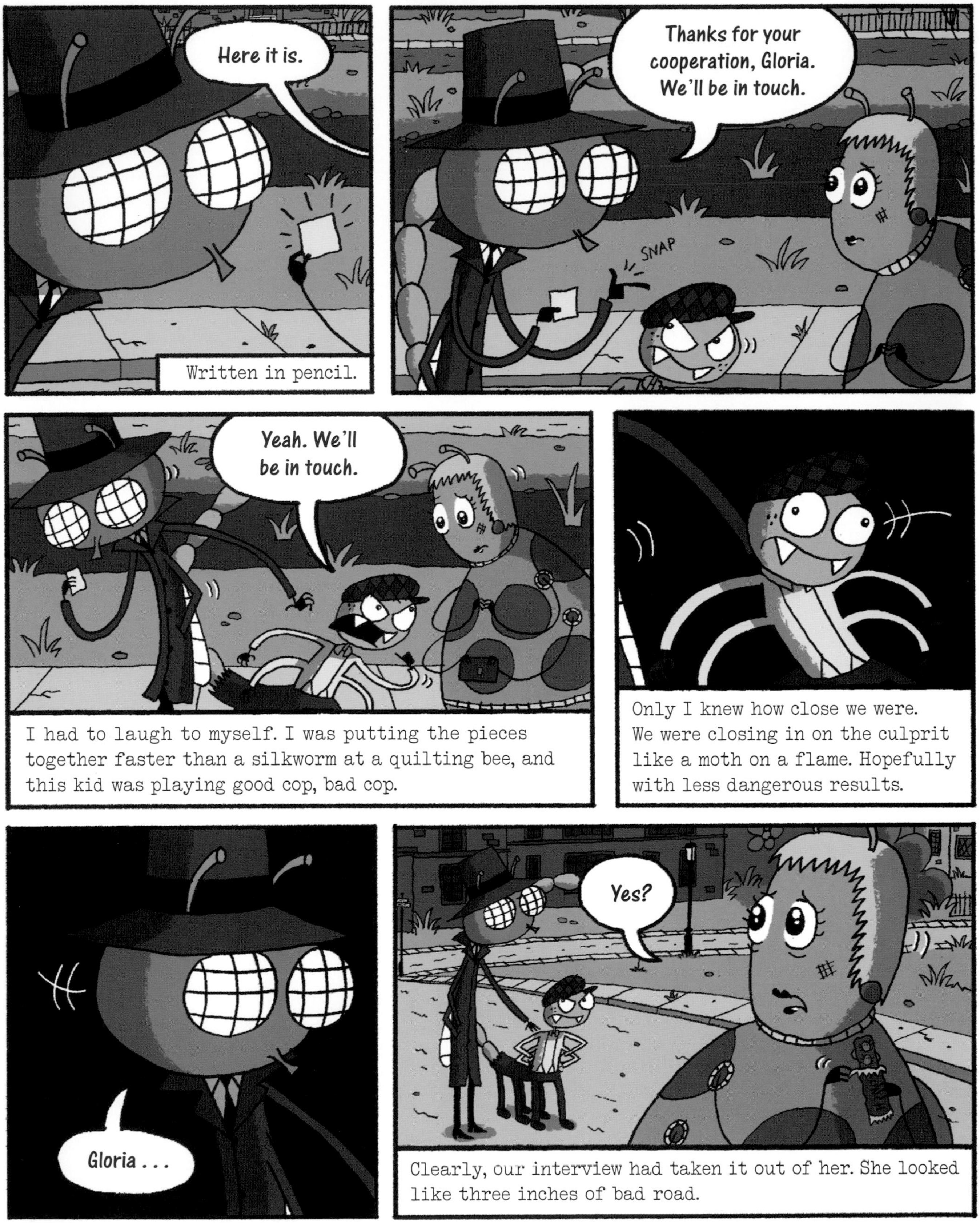
Here it is.
Written in pencil.
Thanks for your cooperation, Gloria. We'll be in touch.
SNAP
Yeah. We'll be in touch.
I had to laugh to myself. I was putting the pieces together faster than a silkworm at a quilting bee, and this kid was playing good cop, bad cop.
Only I knew how close we were. We were closing in on the culprit like a moth on a flame. Hopefully with less dangerous results.
Gloria . . .
Yes?
Clearly, our interview had taken it out of her. She looked like three inches of bad road.

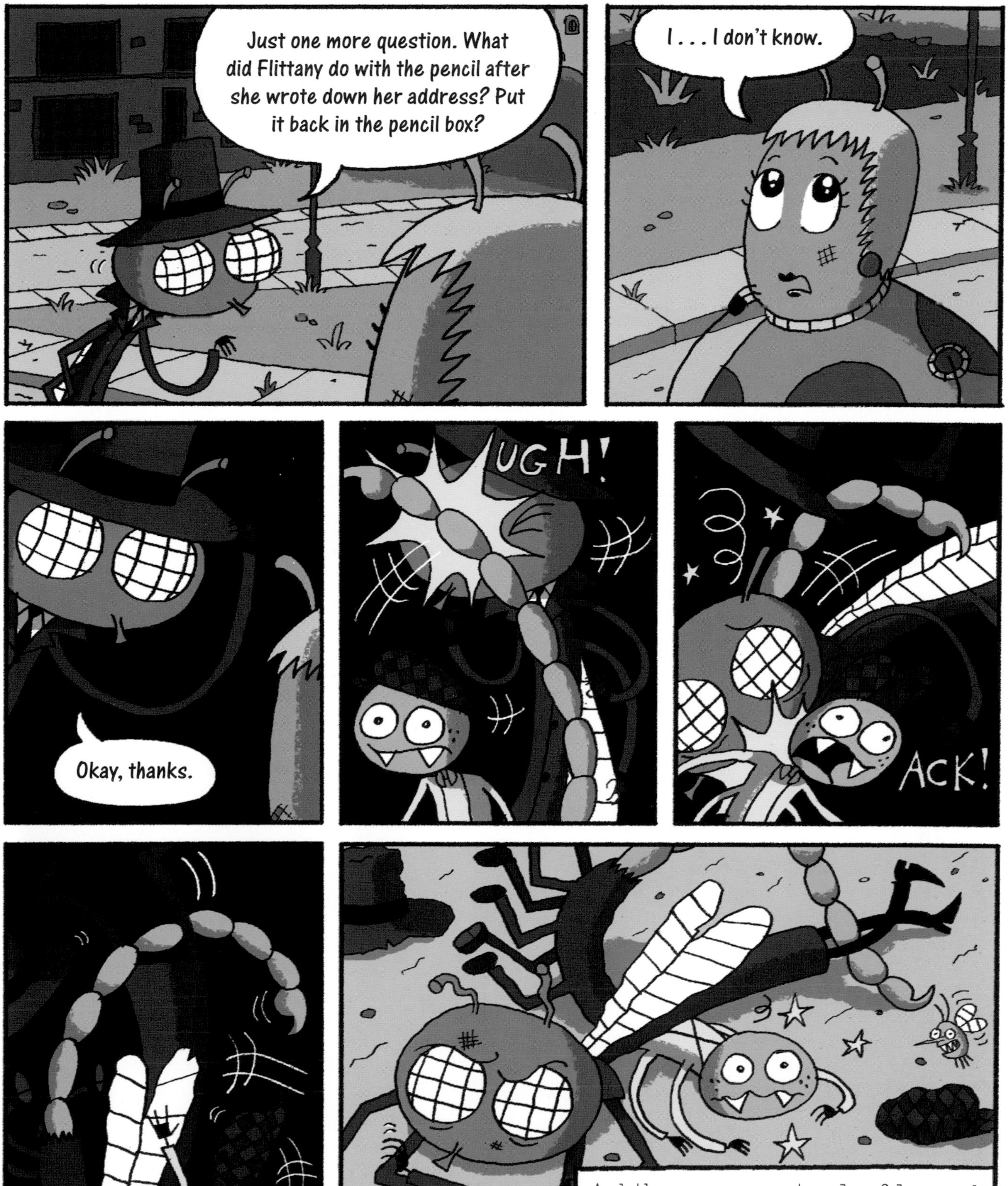
Just one more question. What did Flittany do with the pencil after she wrote down her address? Put it back in the pencil box?
I . . . I don't know.
Okay, thanks.
UGH!
ACK!
And there we were, a tangle of legs and antennae. So much for style.

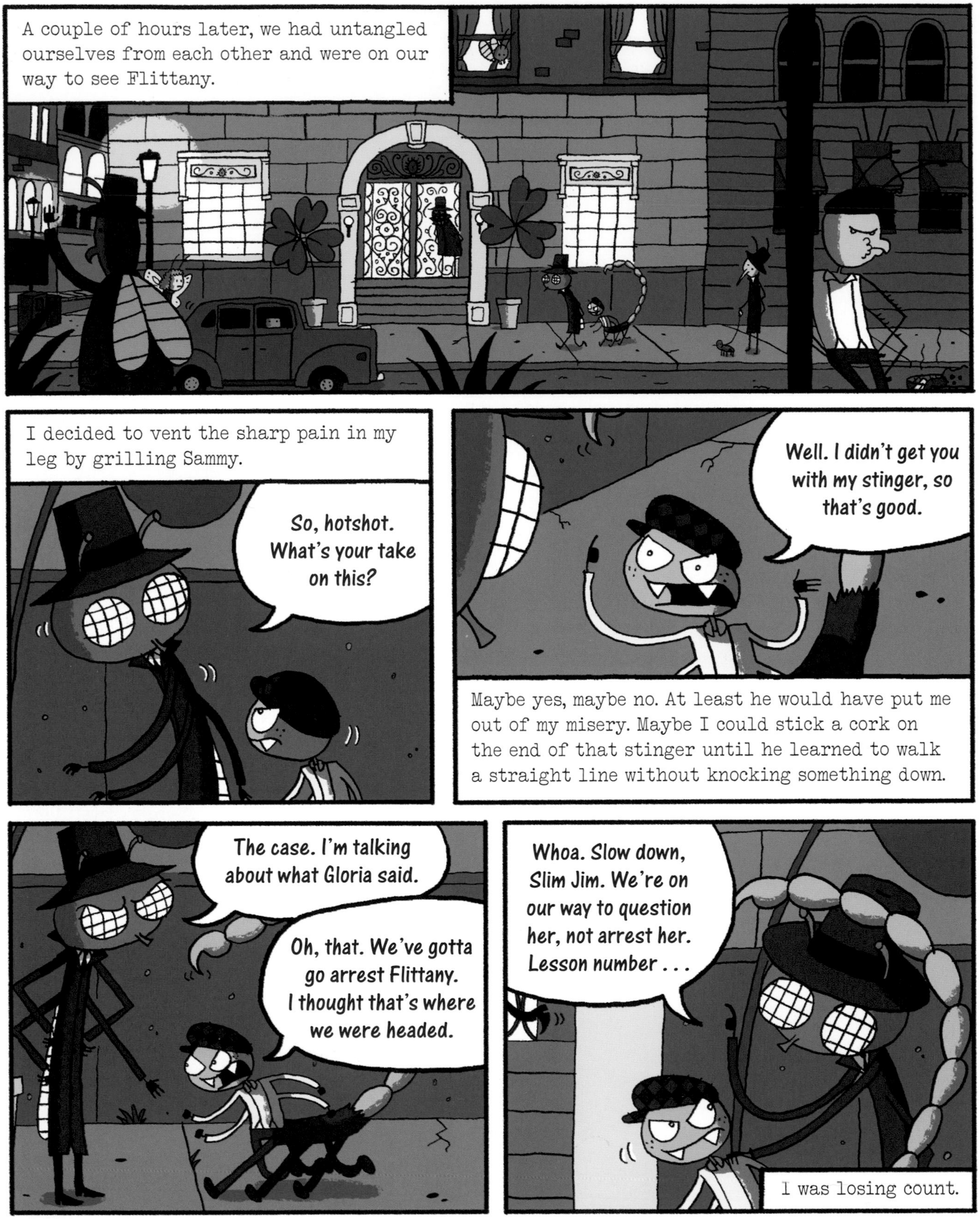
A couple of hours later, we had untangled ourselves from each other and were on our way to see Flittany.
I decided to vent the sharp pain in my leg by grilling Sammy.
So, hotshot. What's your take on this?
Well. I didn't get you with my stinger, so that's good.
Maybe yes, maybe no. At least he would have put me out of my misery. Maybe I could stick a cork on the end of that stinger until he learned to walk a straight line without knocking something down.
The case. I'm talking about what Gloria said.
Oh, that. We've gotta go arrest Flittany. I thought that's where we were headed.
Whoa. Slow down, Slim Jim. We're on our way to question her, not arrest her. Lesson number . . .
I was losing count.

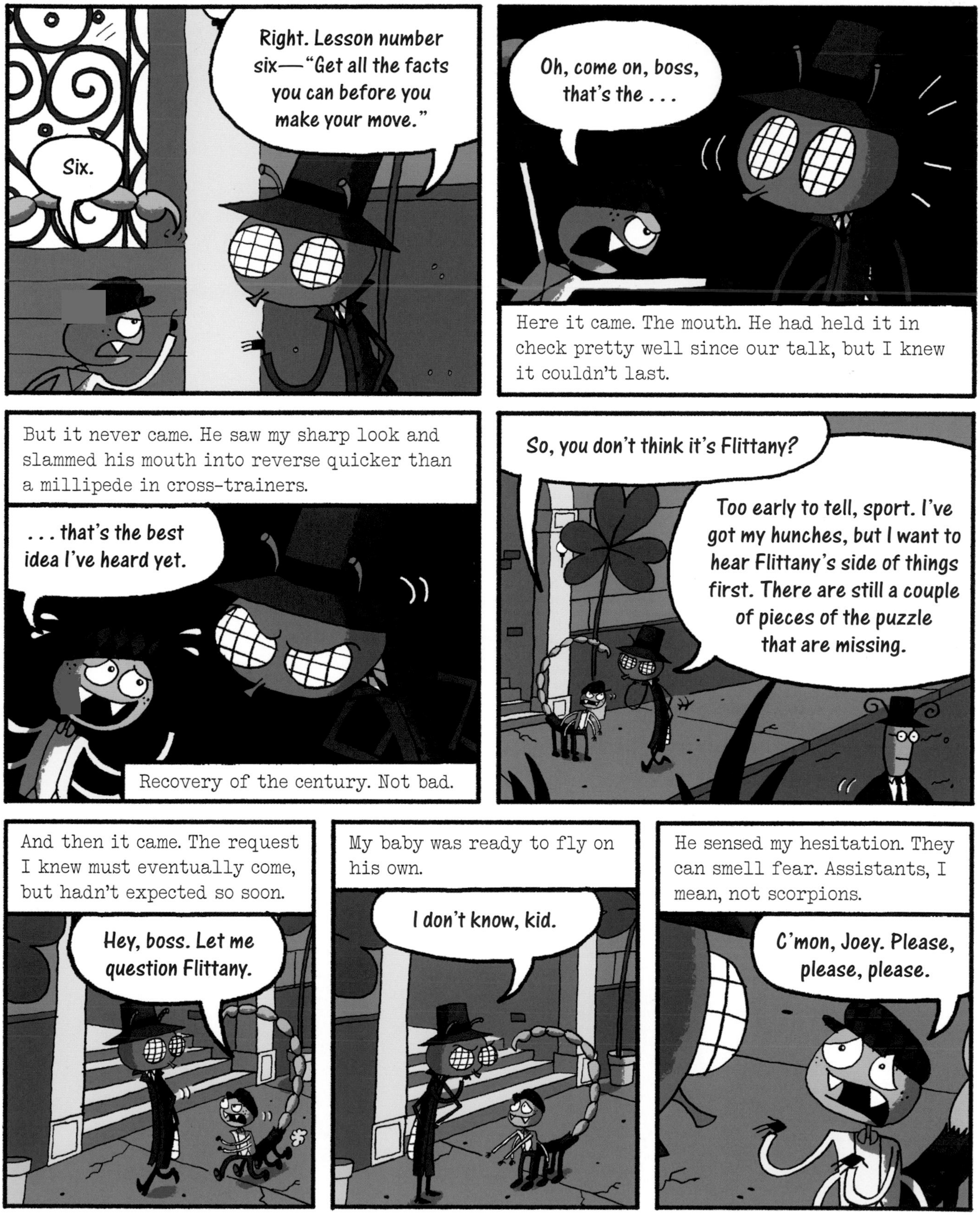
Right. Lesson number six—"Get all the facts you can before you make your move."
Six.
Oh, come on, boss, that's the . . .
Here it came. The mouth. He had held it in check pretty well since our talk, but I knew it couldn't last.
But it never came. He saw my sharp look and slammed his mouth into reverse quicker than a millipede in cross-trainers.
. . . that's the best idea I've heard yet.
Recovery of the century. Not bad.
So, you don't think it's Flittany?
Too early to tell, sport. I've got my hunches, but I want to hear Flittany's side of things first. There are still a couple of pieces of the puzzle that are missing.
And then it came. The request I knew must eventually come, but hadn't expected so soon.
Hey, boss. Let me question Flittany.
My baby was ready to fly on his own.
I don't know, kid.
He sensed my hesitation. They can smell fear. Assistants, I mean, not scorpions.
C'mon, Joey. Please, please, please.

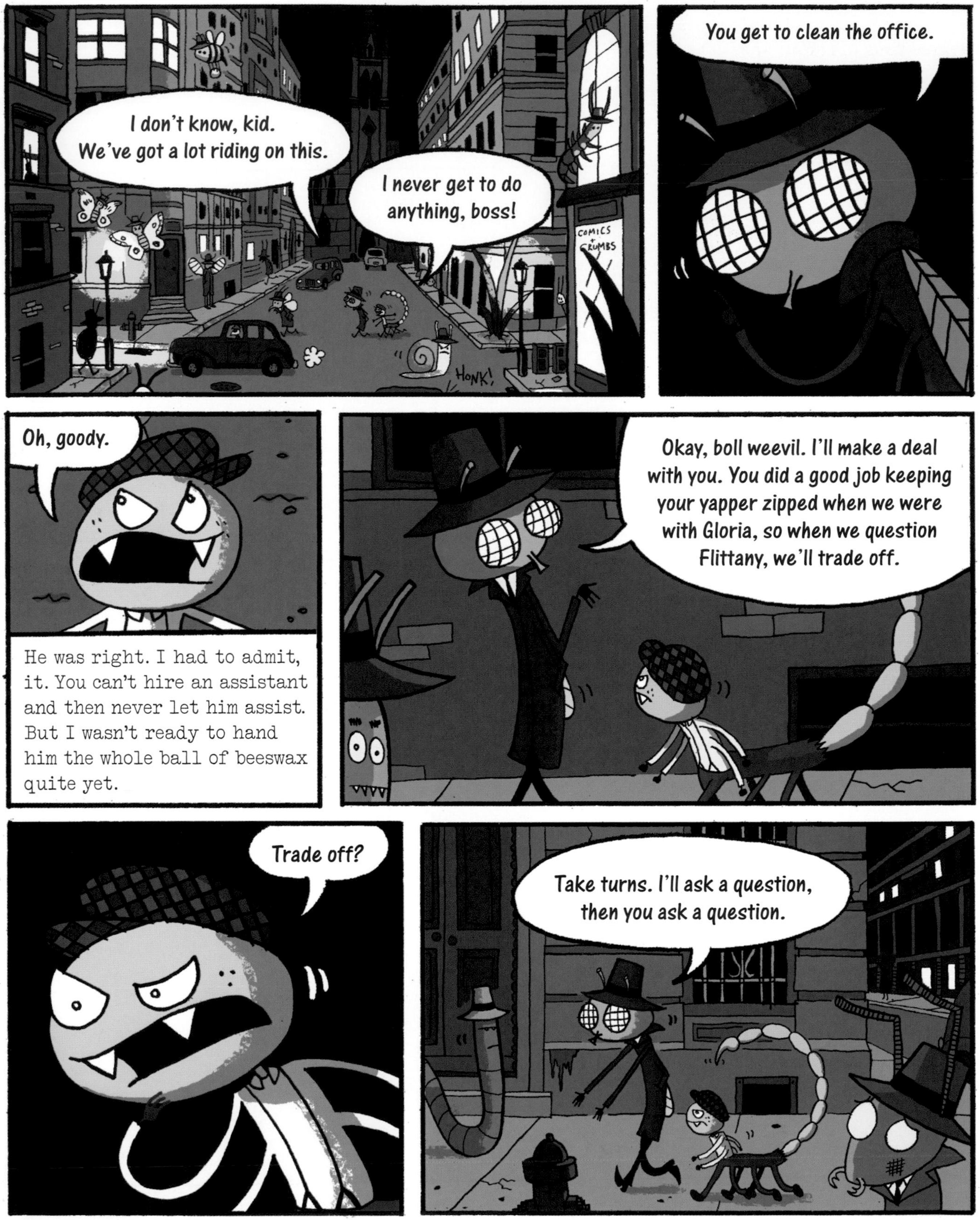
I don't know, kid. We've got a lot riding on this.
I never get to do anything, boss!
COMICS + CRUMBS
HONK!
You get to clean the office.
Oh, goody.
He was right. I had to admit, it. You can't hire an assistant and then never let him assist. But I wasn't ready to hand him the whole ball of beeswax quite yet.
Okay, boll weevil. I'll make a deal with you. You did a good job keeping your yapper zipped when we were with Gloria, so when we question Flittany, we'll trade off.
Trade off?
Take turns. I'll ask a question, then you ask a question.

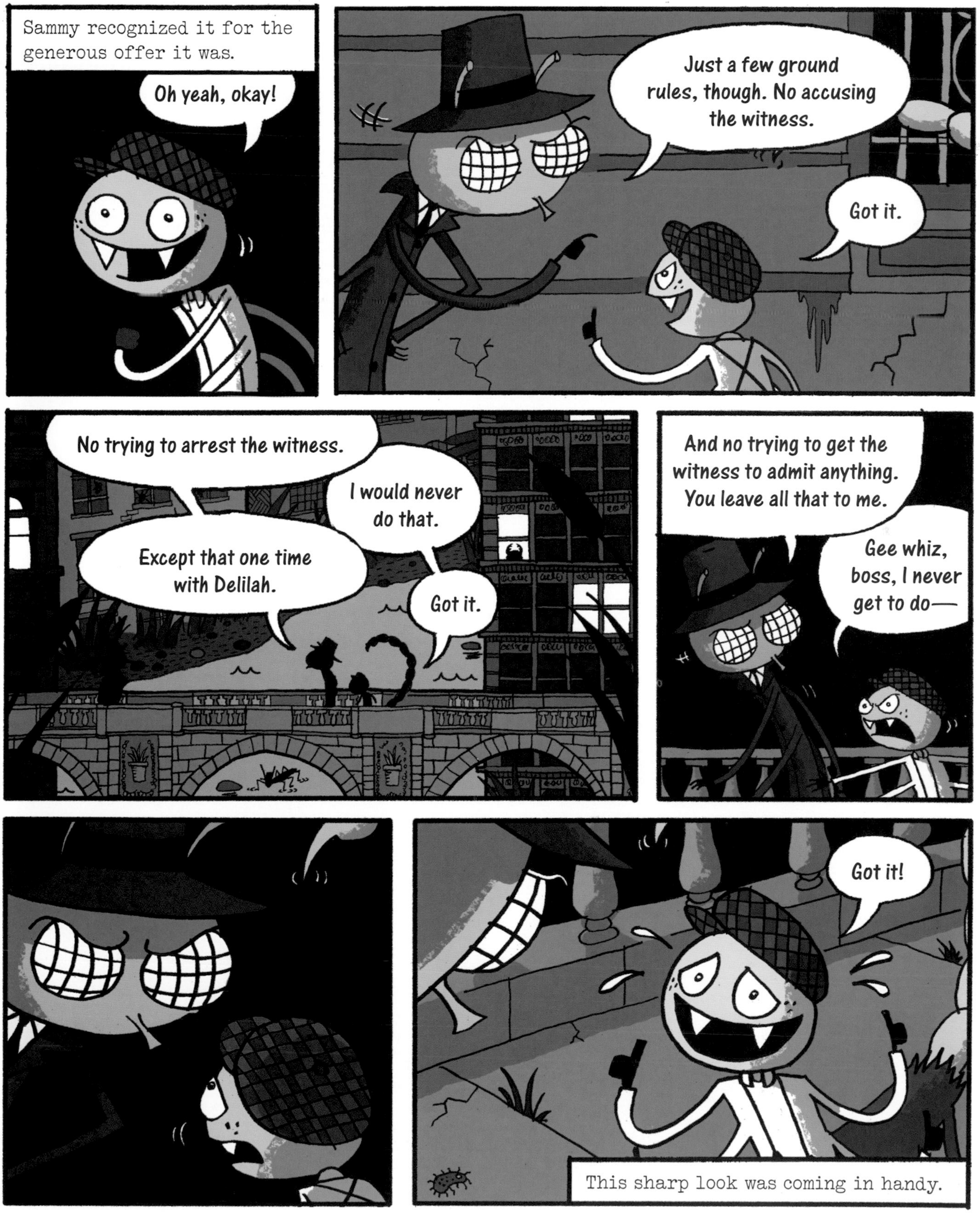

Sammy recognized it for the generous offer it was.
Oh yeah, okay!
Just a few ground rules, though. No accusing the witness.
Got it.
No trying to arrest the witness.
I would never do that.
Except that one time with Delilah.
Got it.
And no trying to get the witness to admit anything. You leave all that to me.
Gee whiz, boss, I never get to do—
Got it!
This sharp look was coming in handy.

We found ourselves outside Flittany's place. She lived in one of those skyscrapers on the east side of the city. The Cattail Apartments, right next to the stagnant puddle. What a view!

After several long inches of climbing, we found ourselves outside her door. Apartment P-U.

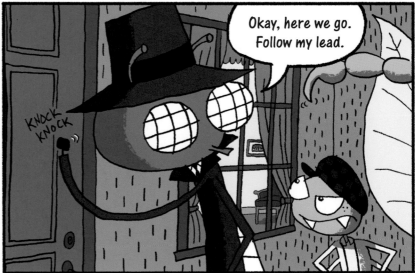

Okay, here we go. Follow my lead.

KNOCK KNOCK

THE CATTAIL APARTMENTS 143

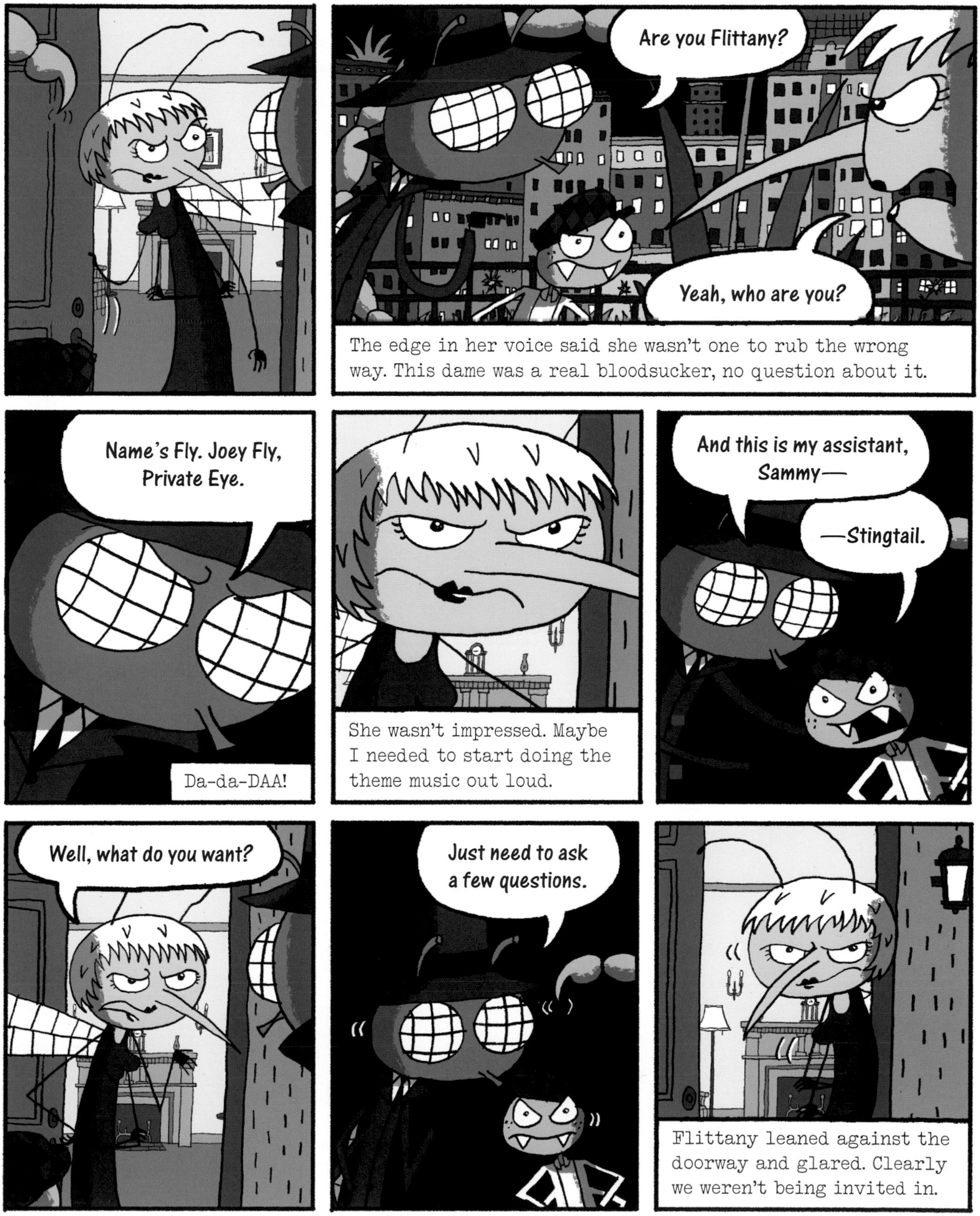
Are you Flittany?
Yeah, who are you?
The edge in her voice said she wasn't one to rub the wrong way. This dame was a real bloodsucker, no question about it.
Name's Fly. Joey Fly, Private Eye.
Da-da-DAA!
She wasn't impressed. Maybe I needed to start doing the theme music out loud.
And this is my assistant, Sammy—
—Stingtail.
Well, what do you want?
Just need to ask a few questions.
Flittany leaned against the doorway and glared. Clearly we weren't being invited in.

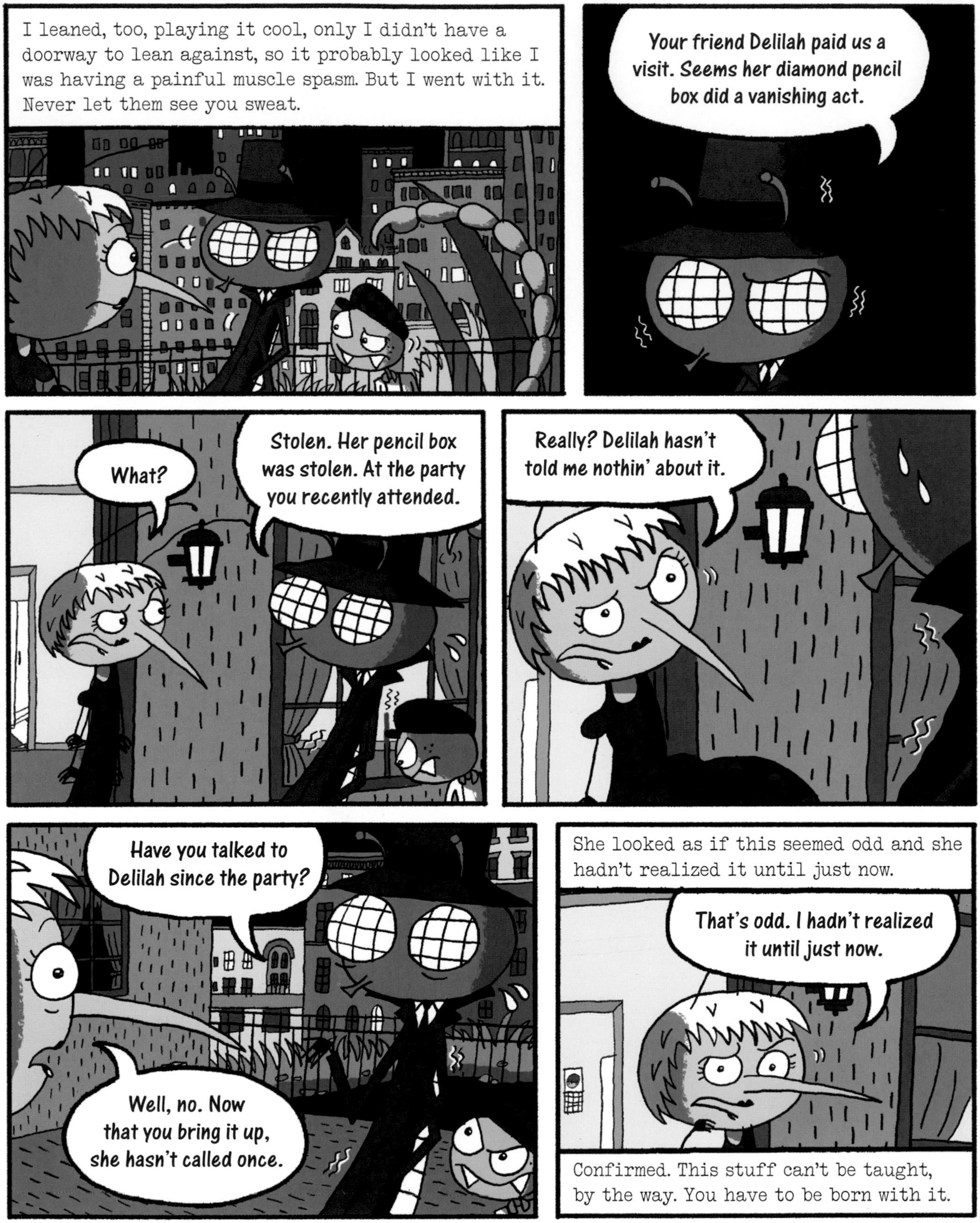
I leaned, too, playing it cool, only I didn't have a doorway to lean against, so it probably looked like I was having a painful muscle spasm. But I went with it. Never let them see you sweat.
Your friend Delilah paid us a visit. Seems her diamond pencil box did a vanishing act.
What?
Stolen. Her pencil box was stolen. At the party you recently attended.
Really? Delilah hasn't told me nothin' about it.
Have you talked to Delilah since the party?
Well, no. Now that you bring it up, she hasn't called once.
She looked as if this seemed odd and she hadn't realized it until just now.
That's odd. I hadn't realized it until just now.
Confirmed. This stuff can't be taught, by the way. You have to be born with it.

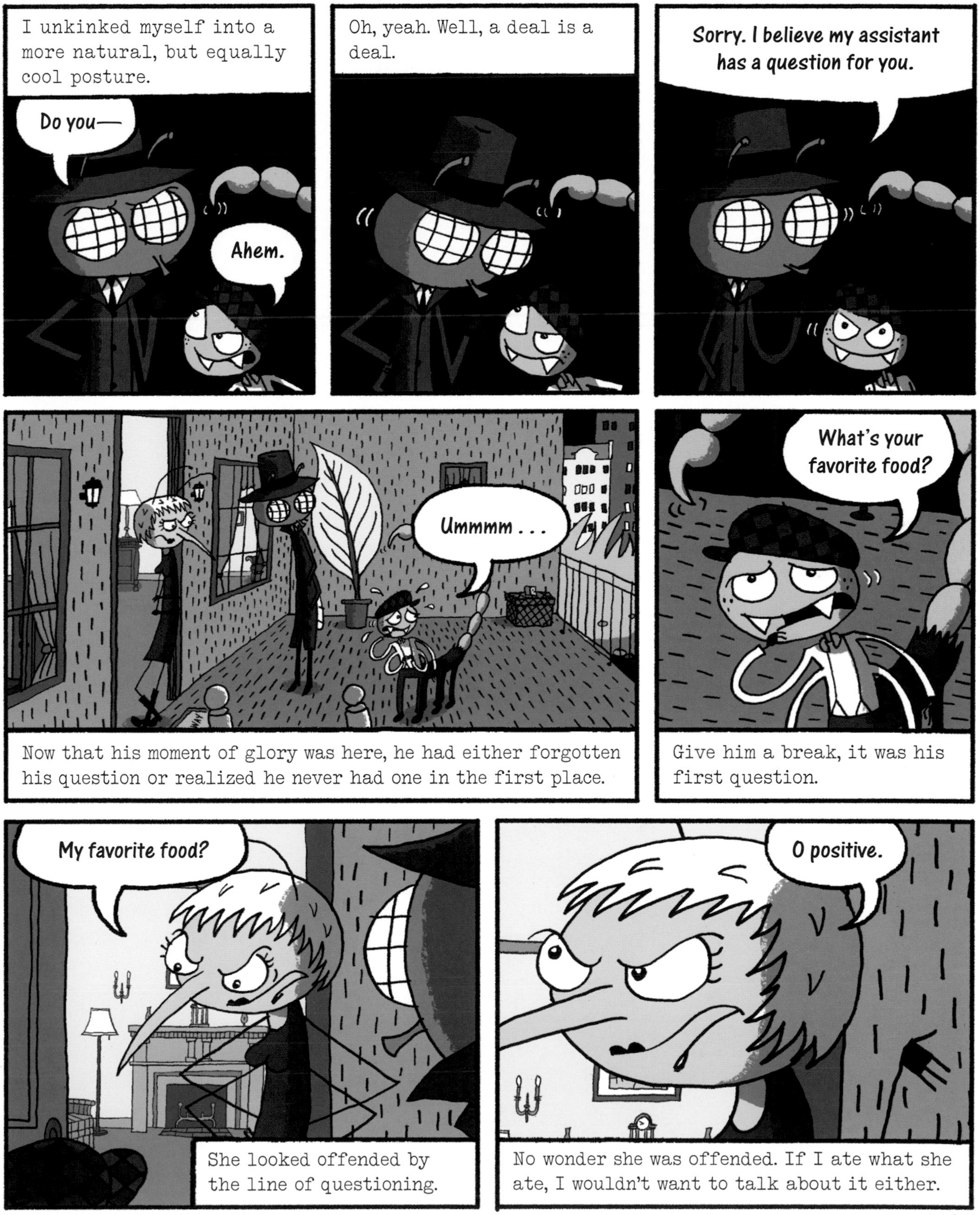
I unkinked myself into a more natural, but equally cool posture.
Do you—
Ahem.
Oh, yeah. Well, a deal is a deal.
Sorry. I believe my assistant has a question for you.
Ummmm . . .
Now that his moment of glory was here, he had either forgotten his question or realized he never had one in the first place.
What's your favorite food?
Give him a break, it was his first question.
My favorite food?
She looked offended by the line of questioning.
O positive.
No wonder she was offended. If I ate what she ate, I wouldn't want to talk about it either.

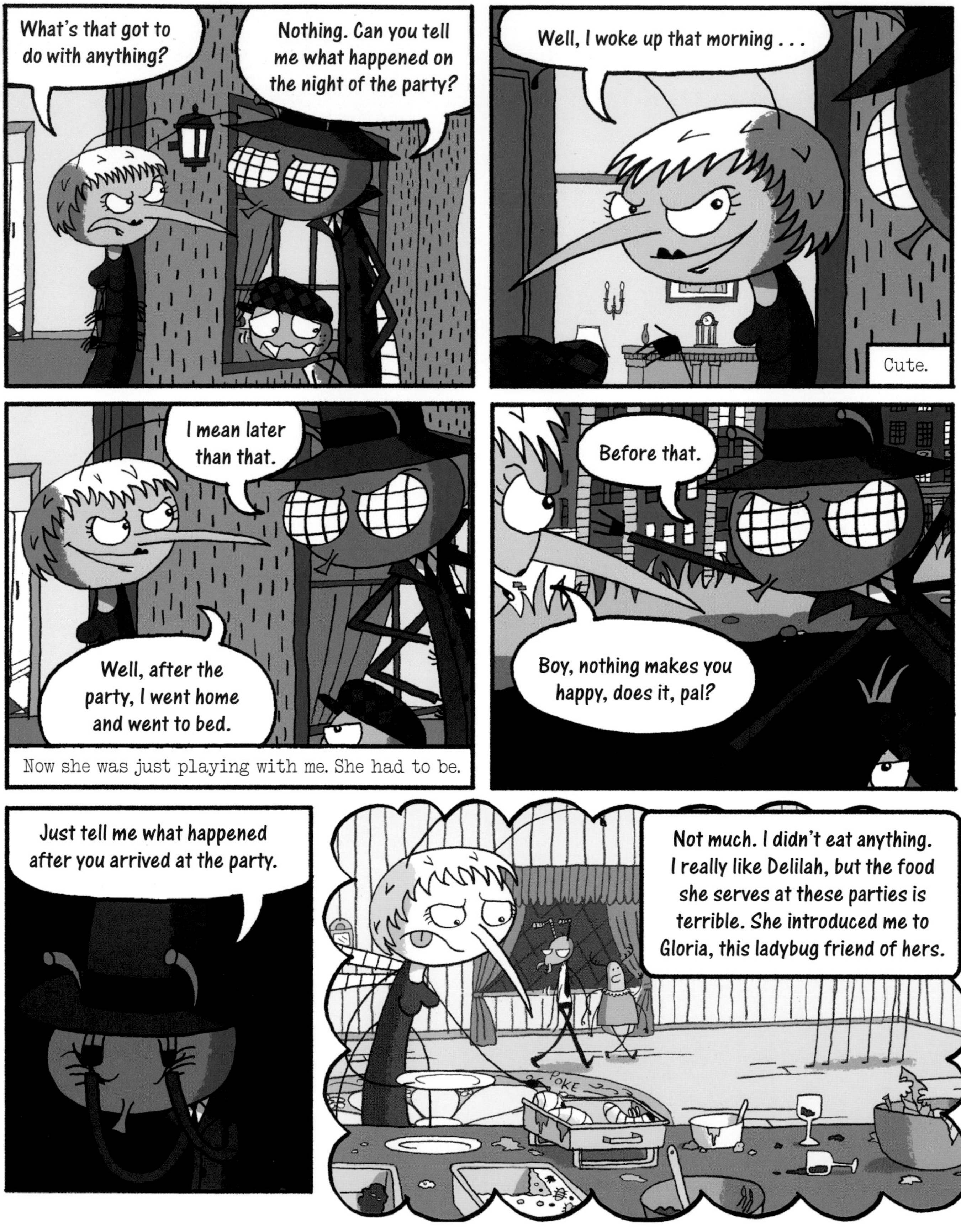
What's that got to do with anything?
Nothing. Can you tell me what happened on the night of the party?
Well, I woke up that morning . . .
Cute.
I mean later than that.
Well, after the party, I went home and went to bed.
Now she was just playing with me. She had to be.
Before that.
Boy, nothing makes you happy, does it, pal?
Just tell me what happened after you arrived at the party.
Not much. I didn't eat anything. I really like Delilah, but the food she serves at these parties is terrible. She introduced me to Gloria, this ladybug friend of hers.
POKE

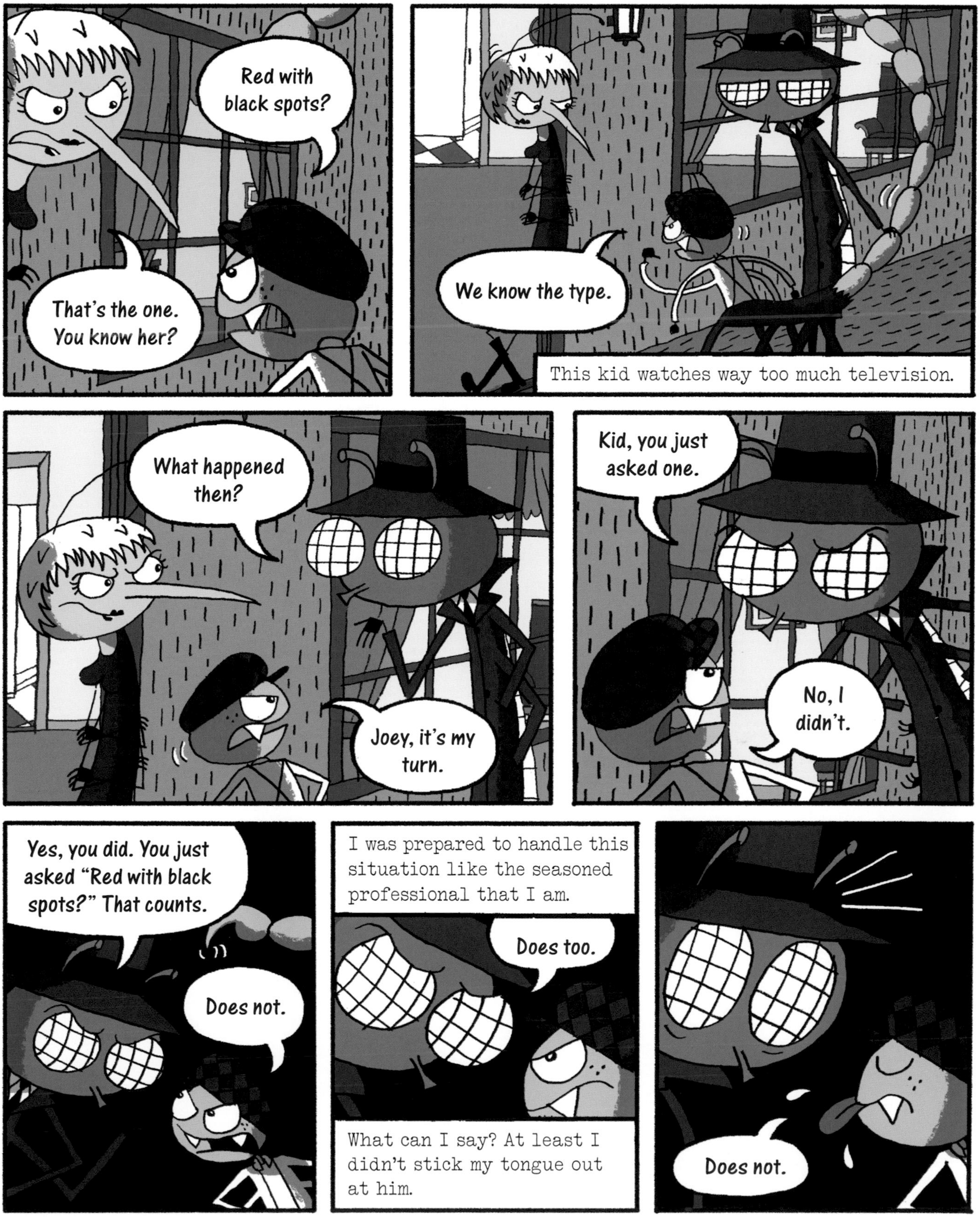
Red with black spots?
That's the one. You know her?
We know the type.
This kid watches way too much television.
What happened then?
Joey, it's my turn.
Kid, you just asked one.
No, I didn't.
Yes, you did. You just asked "Red with black spots?" That counts.
Does not.
I was prepared to handle this situation like the seasoned professional that I am.
Does too.
What can I say? At least I didn't stick my tongue out at him.
Does not.

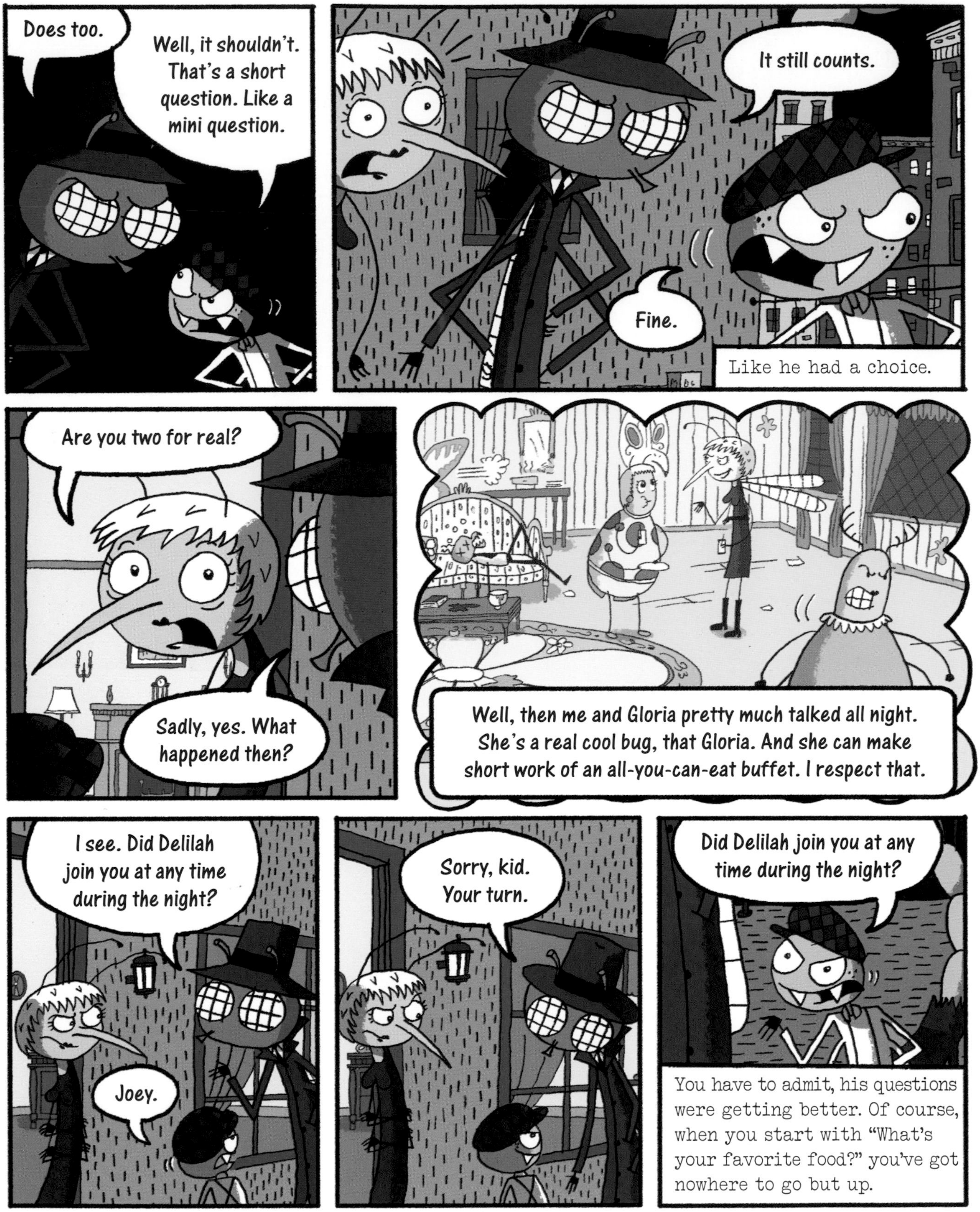
Does too.
Well, it shouldn't. That's a short question. Like a mini question.
It still counts.
Fine.
Like he had a choice.
Are you two for real?
Sadly, yes. What happened then?
Well, then me and Gloria pretty much talked all night. She's a real cool bug, that Gloria. And she can make short work of an all-you-can-eat buffet. I respect that.
I see. Did Delilah join you at any time during the night?
Joey.
Sorry, kid. Your turn.
Did Delilah join you at any time during the night?
You have to admit, his questions were getting better. Of course, when you start with "What's your favorite food?" you've got nowhere to go but up.

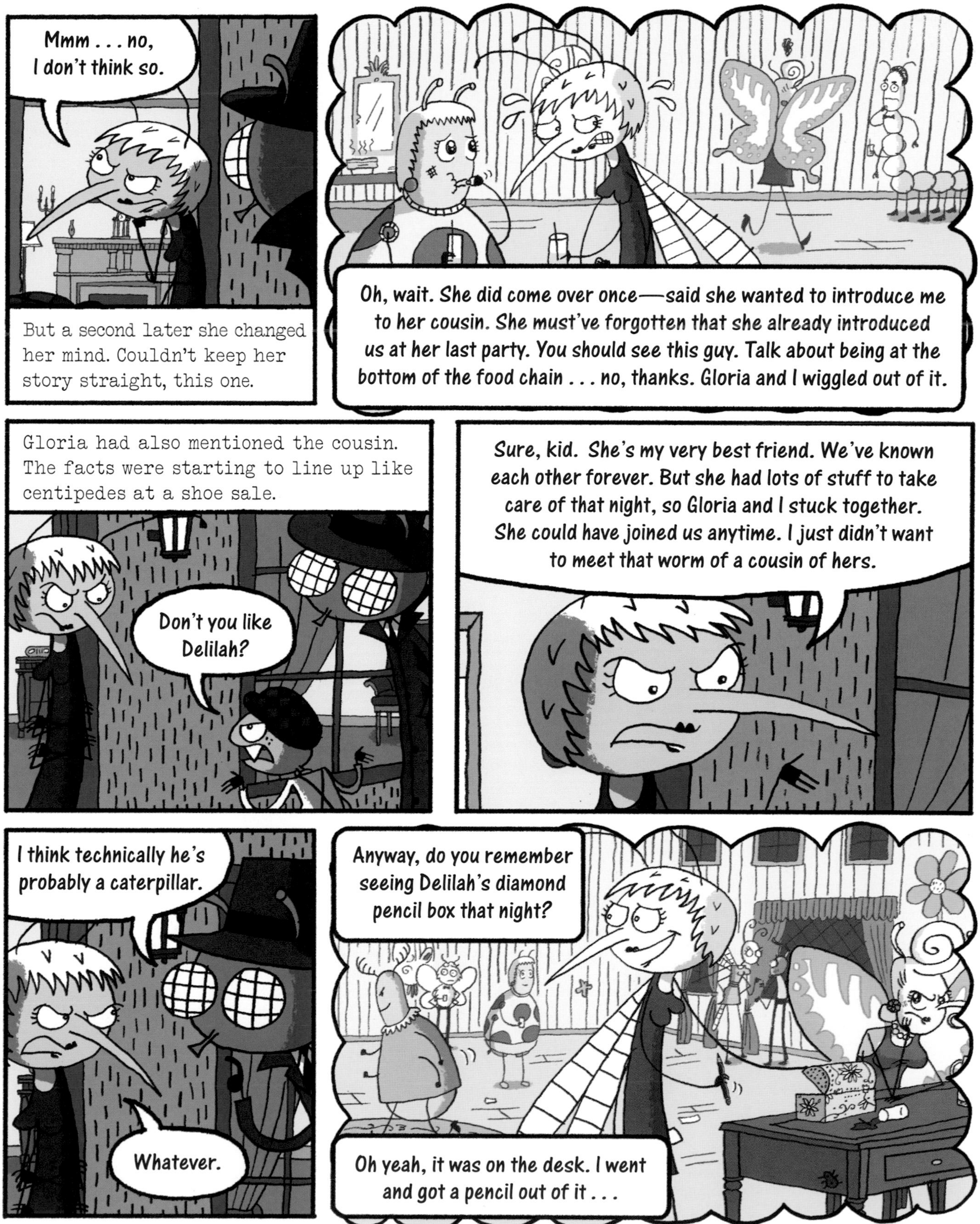
Mmm . . . no, I don't think so.
But a second later she changed her mind. Couldn't keep her story straight, this one.
Oh, wait. She did come over once—said she wanted to introduce me to her cousin. She must've forgotten that she already introduced us at her last party. You should see this guy. Talk about being at the bottom of the food chain . . . no, thanks. Gloria and I wiggled out of it.
Gloria had also mentioned the cousin. The facts were starting to line up like centipedes at a shoe sale.
Don't you like Delilah?
Sure, kid. She's my very best friend. We've known each other forever. But she had lots of stuff to take care of that night, so Gloria and I stuck together. She could have joined us anytime. I just didn't want to meet that worm of a cousin of hers.
I think technically he's probably a caterpillar.
Whatever.
Anyway, do you remember seeing Delilah's diamond pencil box that night?
Oh yeah, it was on the desk. I went and got a pencil out of it . . .

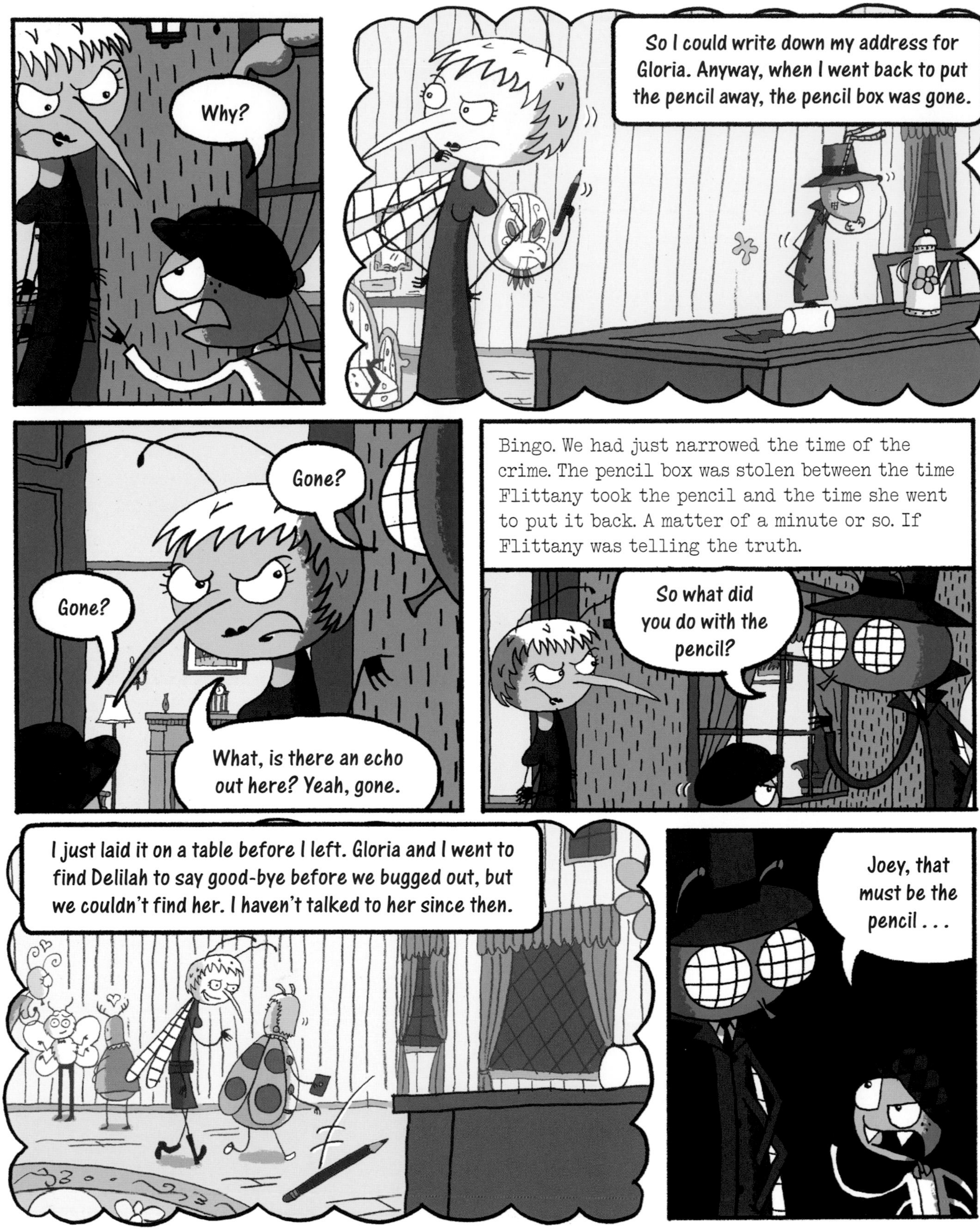

Why?
So I could write down my address for Gloria. Anyway, when I went back to put the pencil away, the pencil box was gone.
Gone?
Gone?
What, is there an echo out here? Yeah, gone.
Bingo. We had just narrowed the time of the crime. The pencil box was stolen between the time Flittany took the pencil and the time she went to put it back. A matter of a minute or so. If Flittany was telling the truth.
So what did you do with the pencil?
I just laid it on a table before I left. Gloria and I went to find Delilah to say good-bye before we bugged out, but we couldn't find her. I haven't talked to her since then.
Joey, that must be the pencil . . .

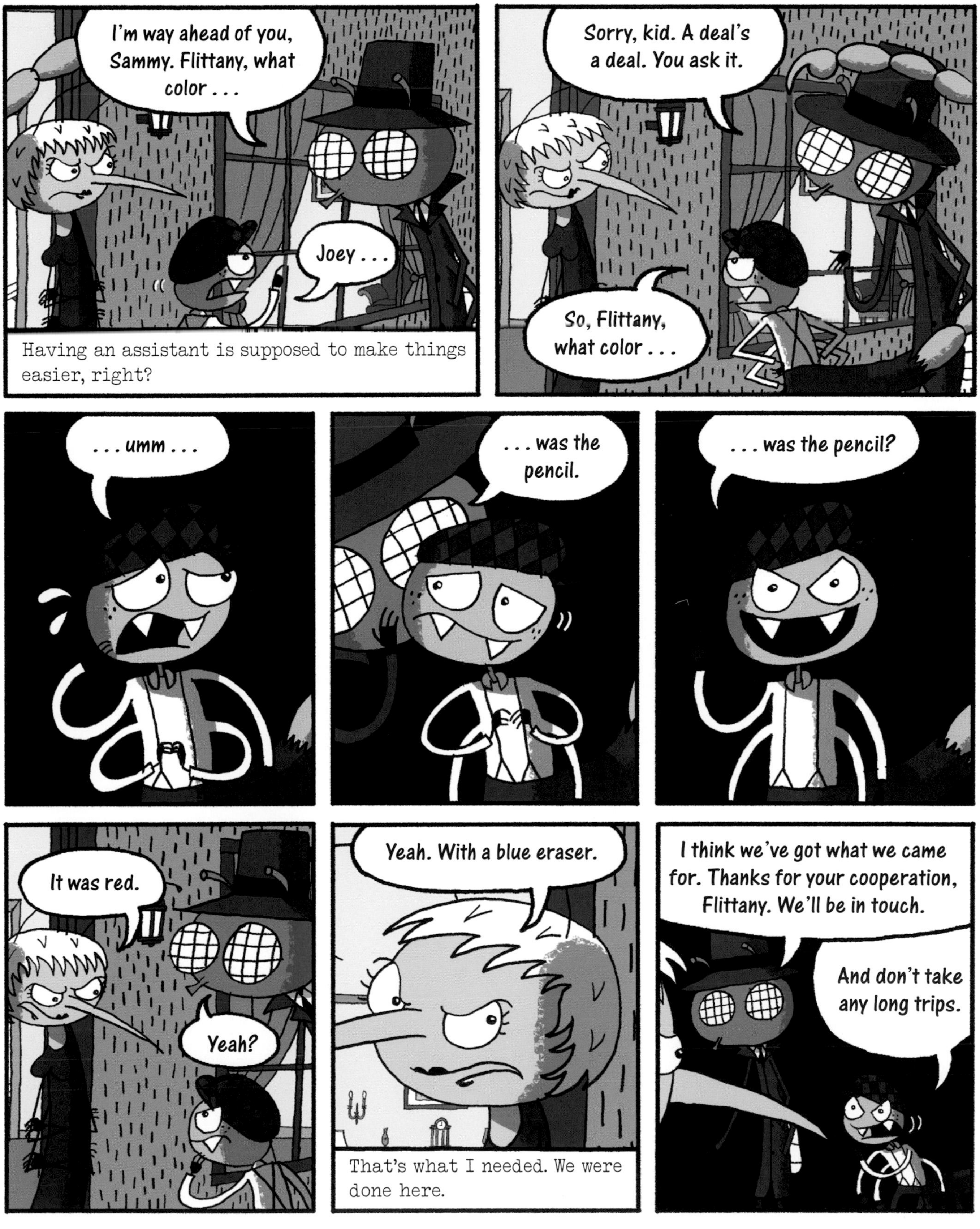
I'm way ahead of you, Sammy. Flittany, what color . . .
Joey . . .
Having an assistant is supposed to make things easier, right?
Sorry, kid. A deal's a deal. You ask it.
So, Flittany, what color . . .
. . . umm . . .
. . . was the pencil.
. . . was the pencil?
It was red.
Yeah?
Yeah. With a blue eraser.
That's what I needed. We were done here.
I think we've got what we came for. Thanks for your cooperation, Flittany. We'll be in touch.
And don't take any long trips.

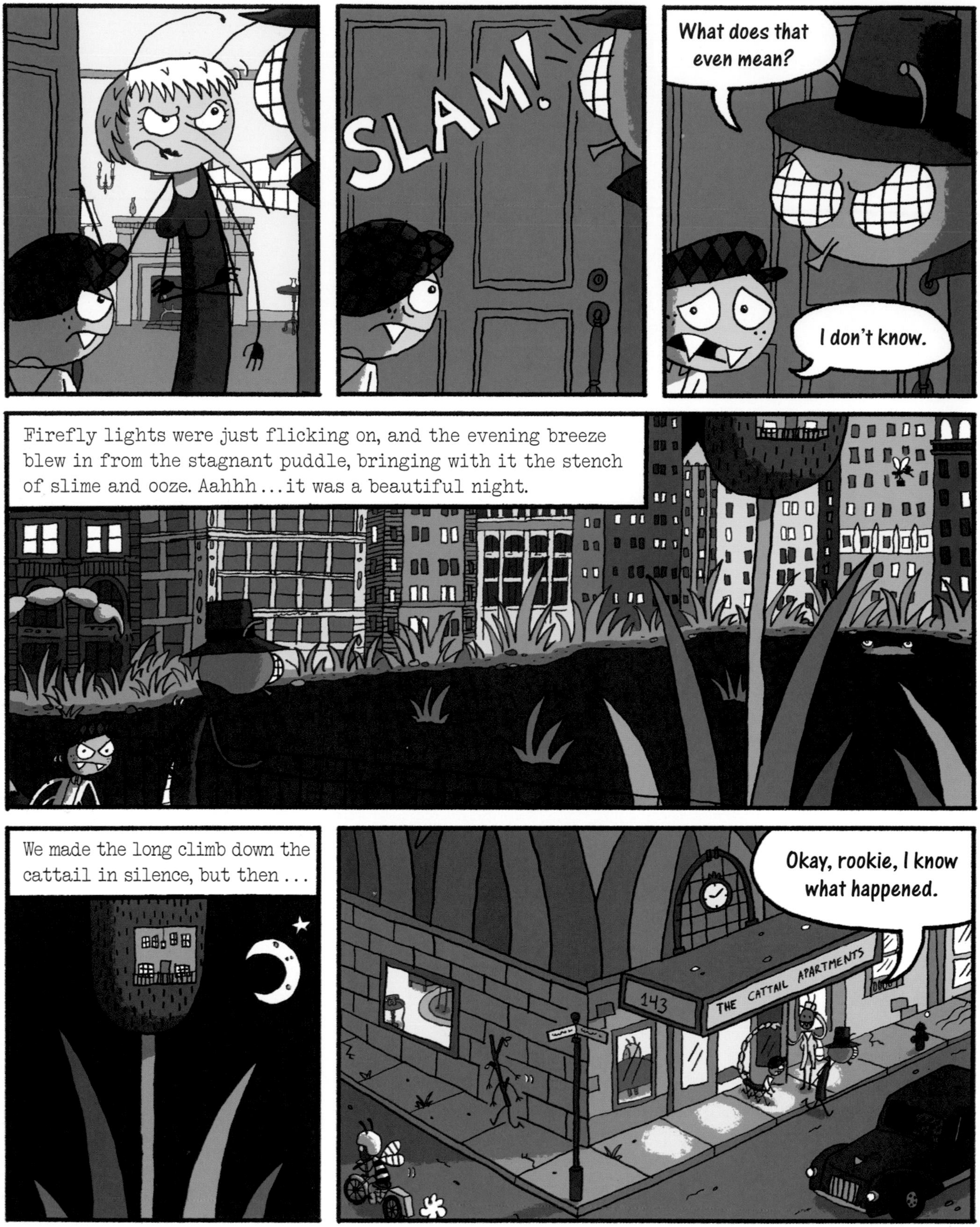
SLAM!
What does that even mean?
I don't know.
Firefly lights were just flicking on, and the evening breeze blew in from the stagnant puddle, bringing with it the stench of slime and ooze. Aahhh . . . it was a beautiful night.
We made the long climb down the cattail in silence, but then . . .
Okay, rookie, I know what happened.
143
THE CATTAIL APARTMENTS

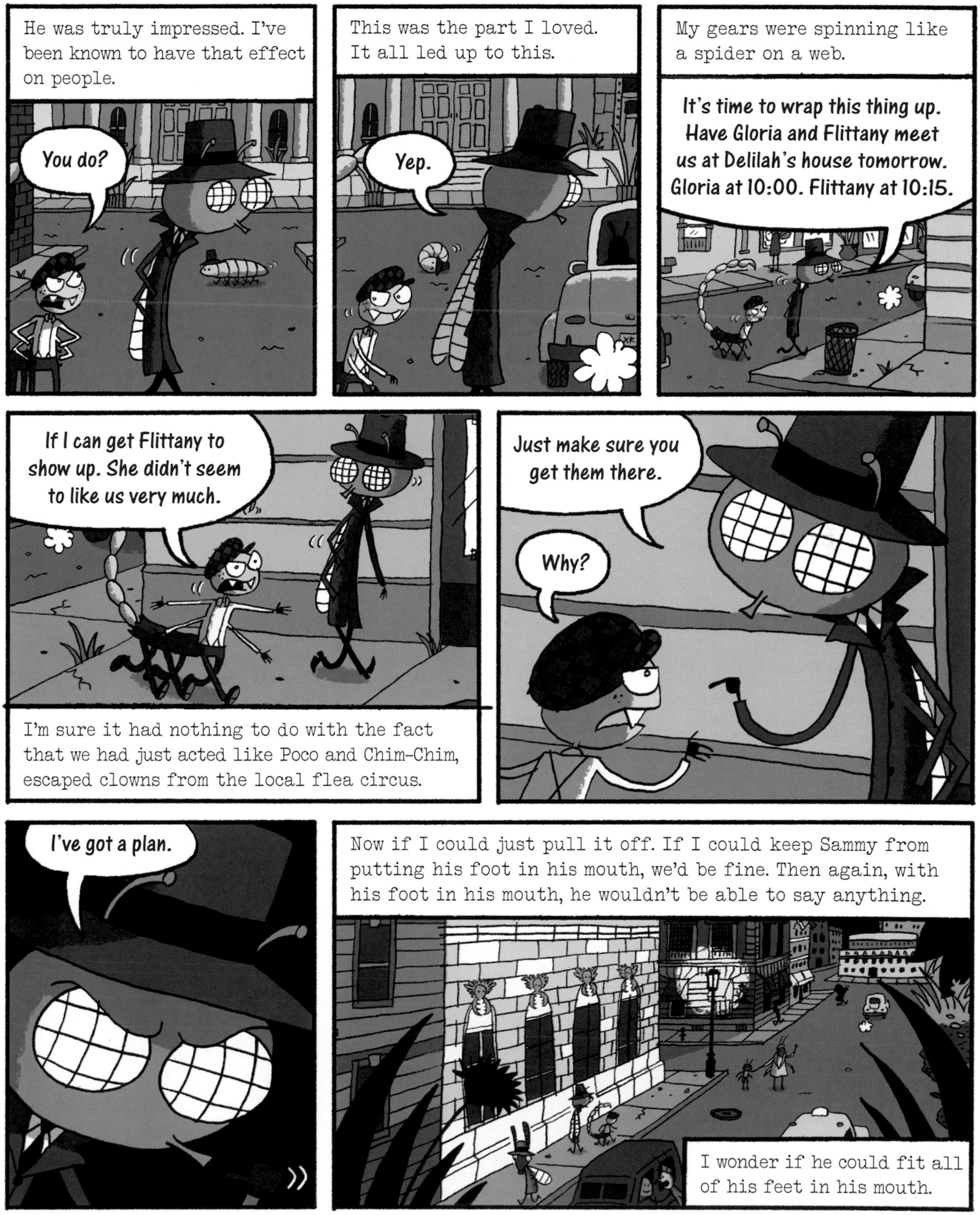

He was truly impressed. I've been known to have that effect on people.
You do?
This was the part I loved. It all led up to this.
Yep.
My gears were spinning like a spider on a web.
It's time to wrap this thing up. Have Gloria and Flittany meet us at Delilah's house tomorrow. Gloria at 10:00. Flittany at 10:15.
If I can get Flittany to show up. She didn't seem to like us very much.
I'm sure it had nothing to do with the fact that we had just acted like Poco and Chim-Chim, escaped clowns from the local flea circus.
Just make sure you get them there.
Why?
I've got a plan.
Now if I could just pull it off. If I could keep Sammy from putting his foot in his mouth, we'd be fine. Then again, with his foot in his mouth, he wouldn't be able to say anything.
I wonder if he could fit all of his feet in his mouth.

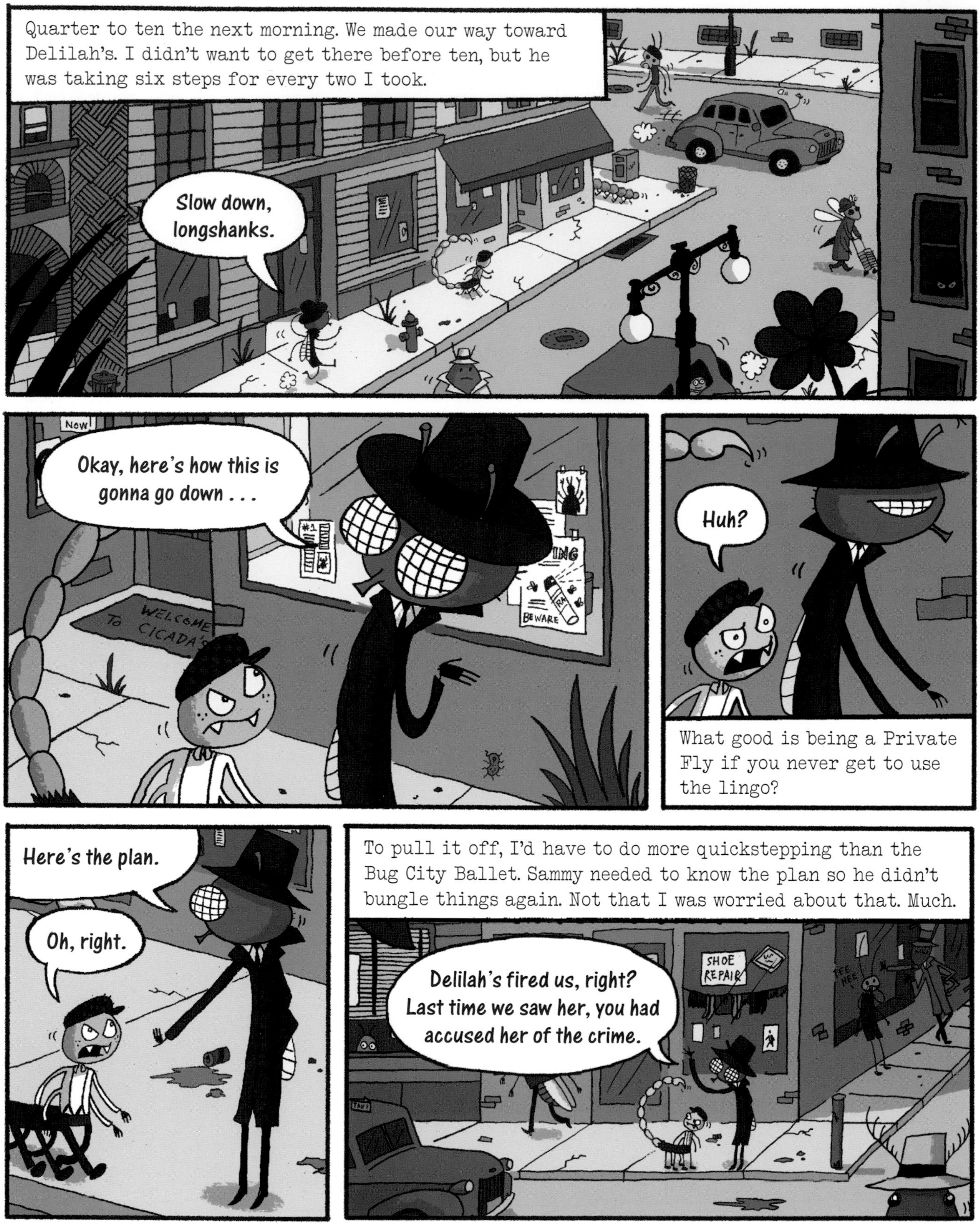
Quarter to ten the next morning. We made our way toward Delilah's. I didn't want to get there before ten, but he was taking six steps for every two I took.
Slow down, longshanks.
NOW
Okay, here's how this is gonna go down . . .
WELCOME TO CICADA'S
BEWARE
Huh?
What good is being a Private Fly if you never get to use the lingo?
Here's the plan.
Oh, right.
To pull it off, I'd have to do more quickstepping than the Bug City Ballet. Sammy needed to know the plan so he didn't bungle things again. Not that I was worried about that. Much.
SHOE REPAIR
TEE HEE
Delilah's fired us, right? Last time we saw her, you had accused her of the crime.
TAXI

Way to rub it in.

I'm not rubbing it in.

And I wasn't. Much.

Take us to Fifth and Frogway. And put your wings into it.

YELLOW JACKET

All I'm saying is she's not going to be too pleased to see us. That's why I've got Gloria meeting us outside at 10:00. She's our ticket in.

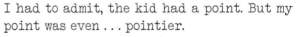

But Delilah won't want to see Gloria either, will she? She thinks that Gloria took the pencil box.

I had to admit, the kid had a point. But my point was even . . . pointier.

Right . . .

But wait a minute.

Uh-oh. I could see his wheels turning as he tried to put it all together in his mind. I was sure smoke would be wafting from his ears any minute.

Gloria says that she and Delilah are great friends.

Right . . .

Just put down the brain and nobody will get hurt.

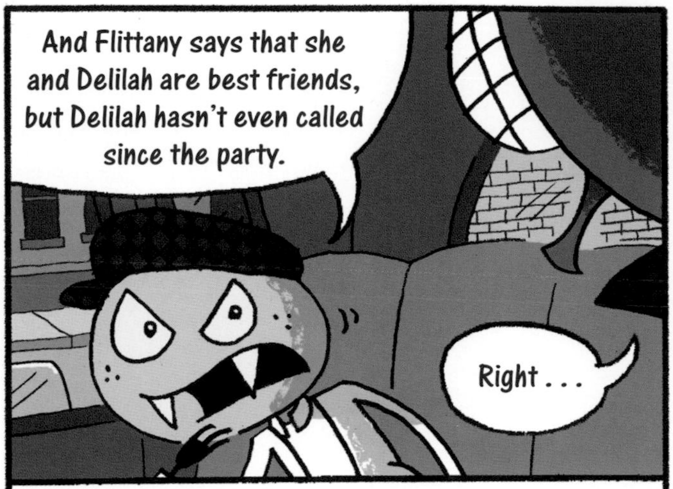
And Flittany says that she and Delilah are best friends, but Delilah hasn't even called since the party.
Right . . .

I'm glad I wasn't paying this kid by the minute.

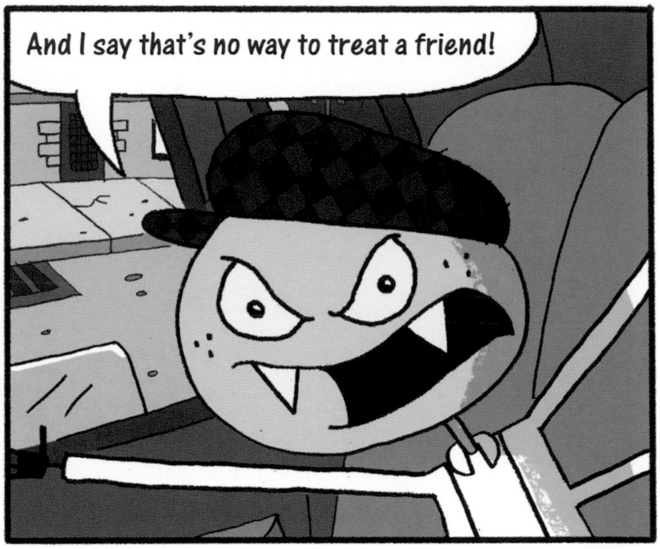
And I say that's no way to treat a friend!

Okay, remember the version of the plan where I explain everything to him? Forget that.

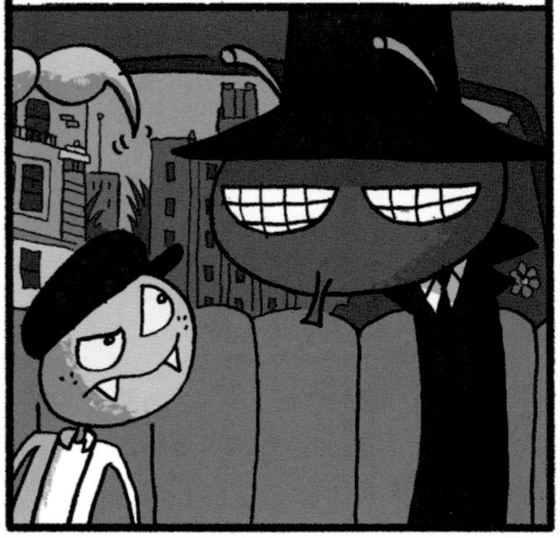

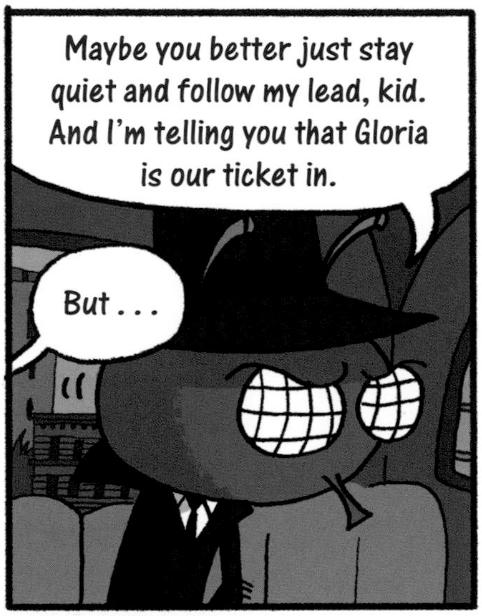
Maybe you better just stay quiet and follow my lead, kid. And I'm telling you that Gloria is our ticket in.
But . . .

"But" nothing.

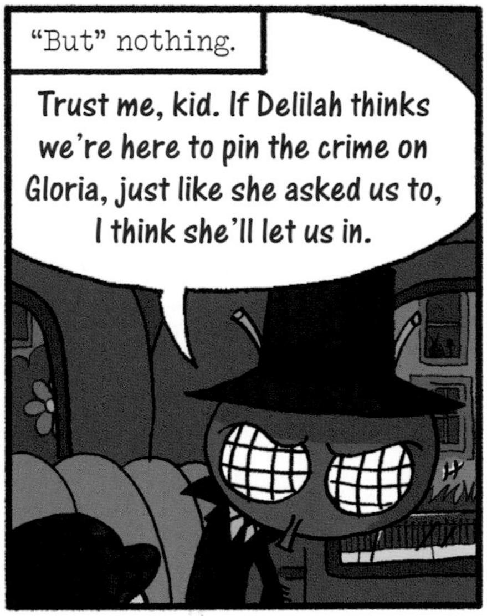
Trust me, kid. If Delilah thinks we're here to pin the crime on Gloria, just like she asked us to, I think she'll let us in.

I waited for an argument, a comment, a brain spasm, something.

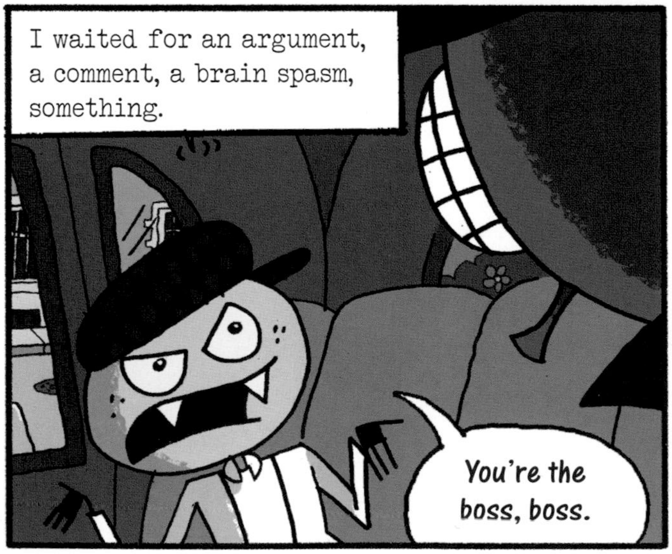
You're the boss, boss.

I was shocked. He just sat there, waiting for my next move. I wanted to say something, but it was possible I had just suffered a brain spasm of my own.

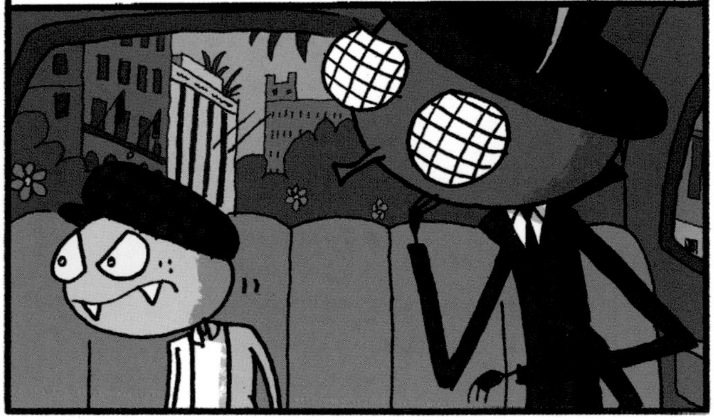

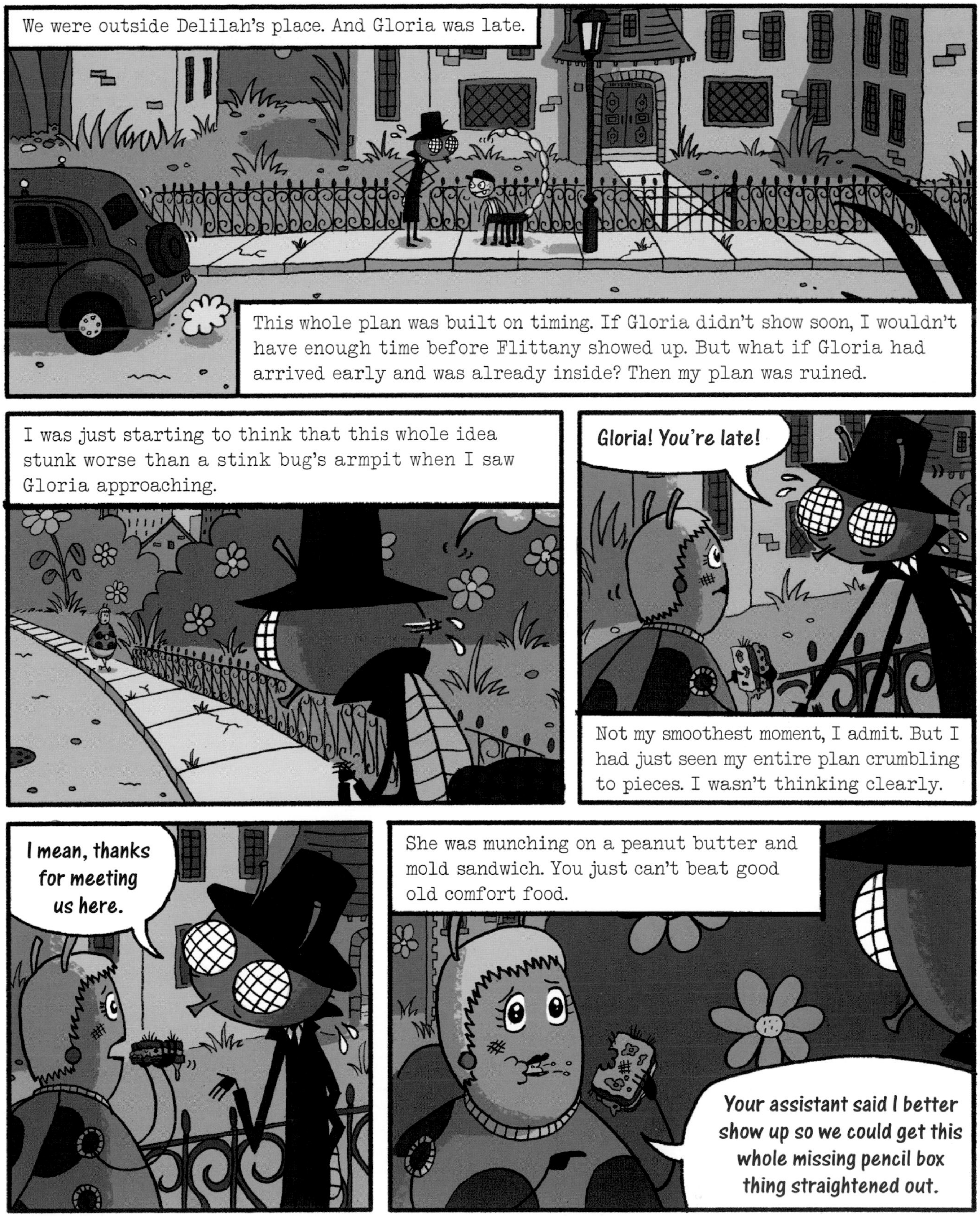
We were outside Delilah's place. And Gloria was late.
This whole plan was built on timing. If Gloria didn't show soon, I wouldn't have enough time before Flittany showed up. But what if Gloria had arrived early and was already inside? Then my plan was ruined.
I was just starting to think that this whole idea stunk worse than a stink bug's armpit when I saw Gloria approaching.
Gloria! You're late!
Not my smoothest moment, I admit. But I had just seen my entire plan crumbling to pieces. I wasn't thinking clearly.
I mean, thanks for meeting us here.
She was munching on a peanut butter and mold sandwich. You just can't beat good old comfort food.
Your assistant said I better show up so we could get this whole missing pencil box thing straightened out.

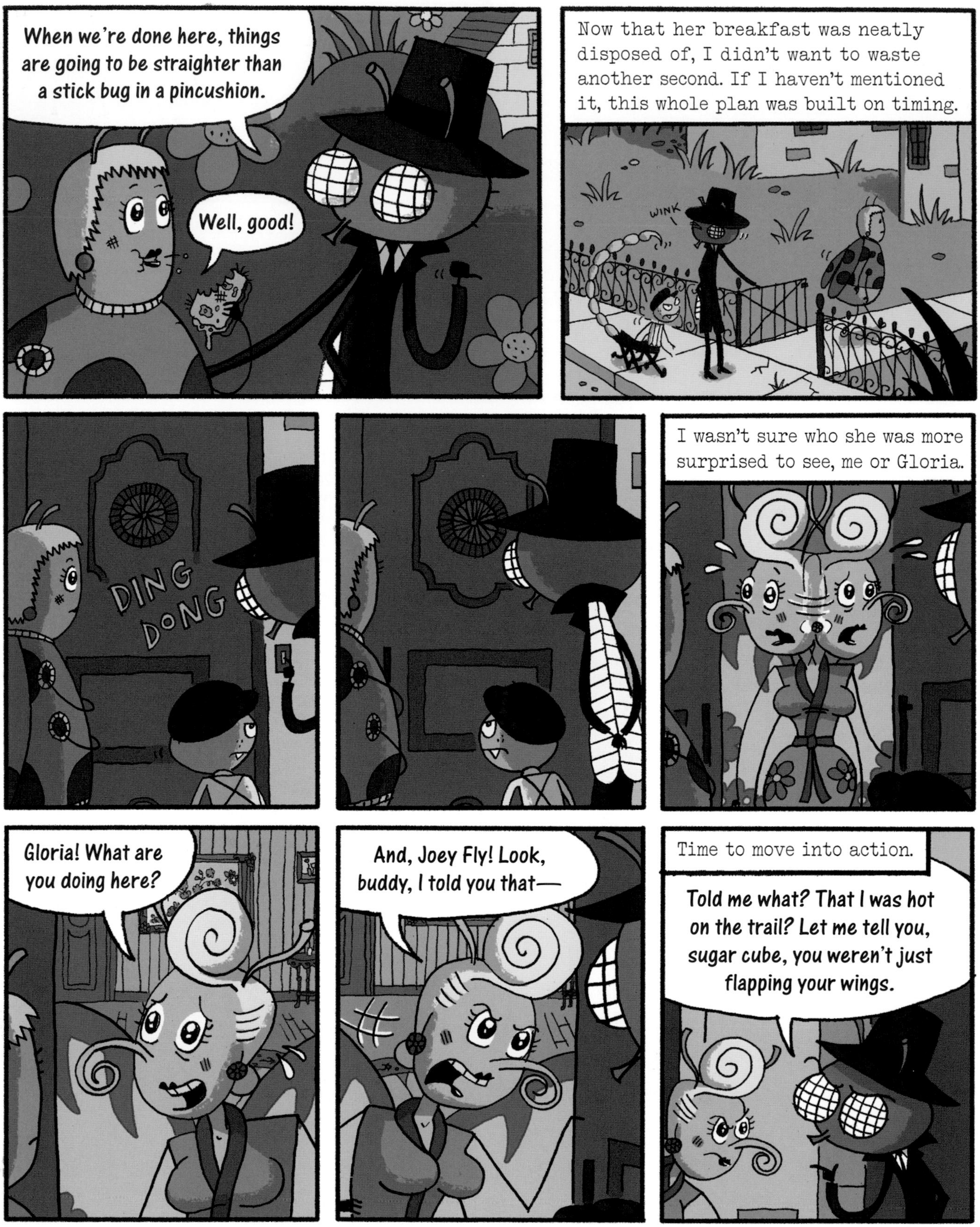
When we're done here, things are going to be straighter than a stick bug in a pincushion.
Well, good!
Now that her breakfast was neatly disposed of, I didn't want to waste another second. If I haven't mentioned it, this whole plan was built on timing.
WINK
DING DONG
I wasn't sure who she was more surprised to see, me or Gloria.
Gloria! What are you doing here?
And, Joey Fly! Look, buddy, I told you that—
Time to move into action.
Told me what? That I was hot on the trail? Let me tell you, sugar cube, you weren't just flapping your wings.

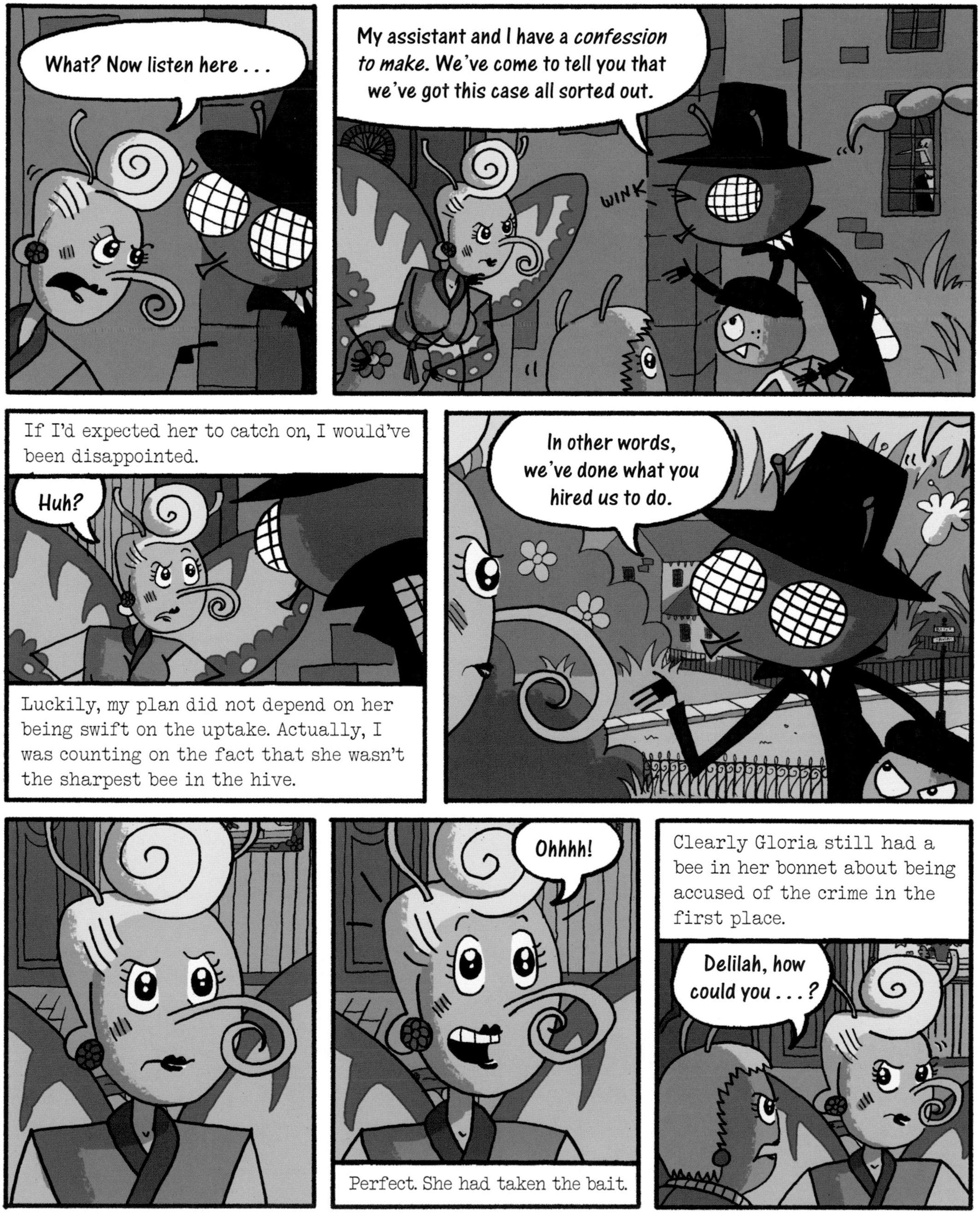
What? Now listen here . . .
My assistant and I have a *confession to make*. We've come to tell you that we've got this case all sorted out.
WINK
If I'd expected her to catch on, I would've been disappointed.
Huh?
Luckily, my plan did not depend on her being swift on the uptake. Actually, I was counting on the fact that she wasn't the sharpest bee in the hive.
In other words, we've done what you hired us to do.
Ohhhh!
Perfect. She had taken the bait.
Clearly Gloria still had a bee in her bonnet about being accused of the crime in the first place.
Delilah, how could you . . . ?

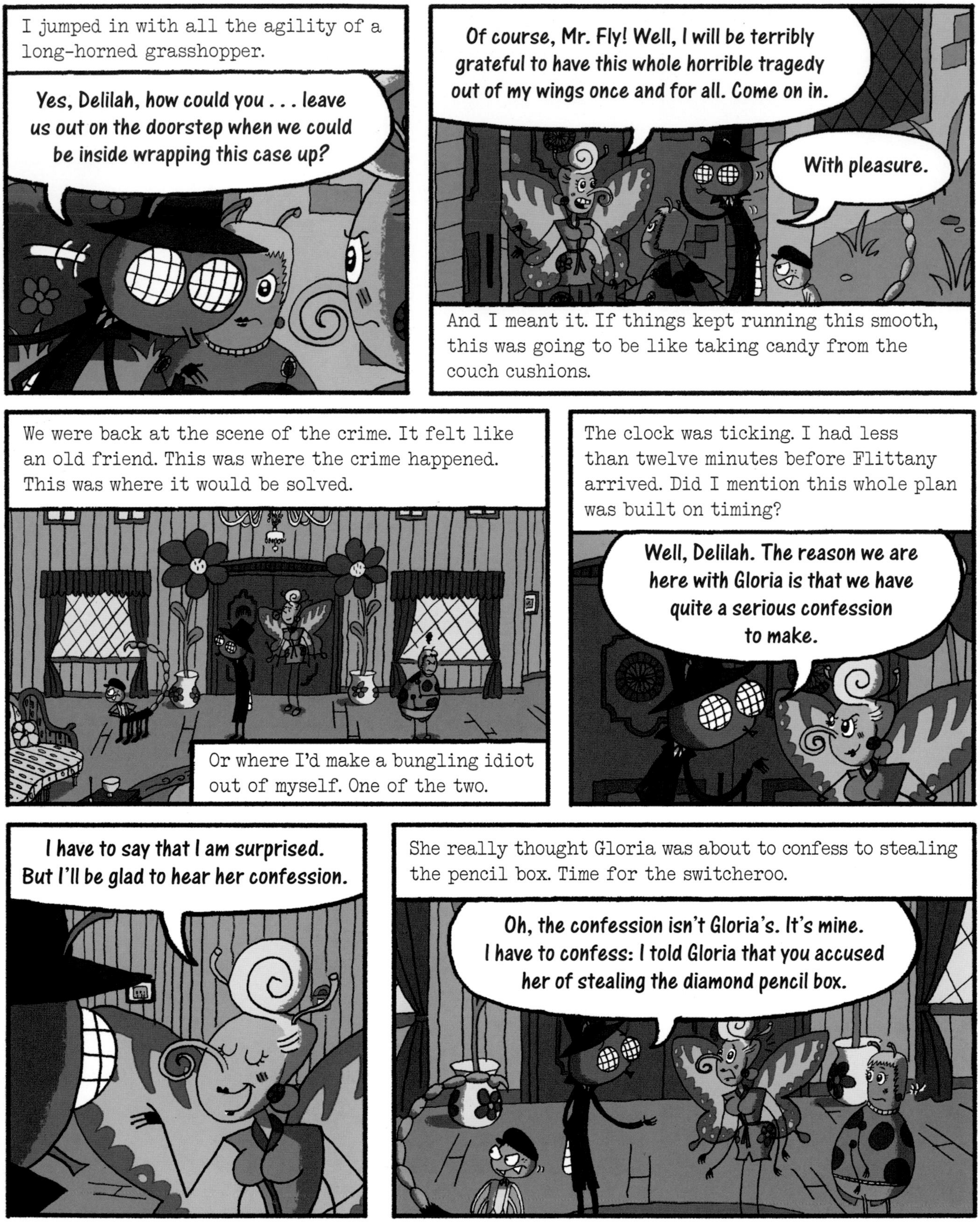

I jumped in with all the agility of a long-horned grasshopper.
Yes, Delilah, how could you . . . leave us out on the doorstep when we could be inside wrapping this case up?
Of course, Mr. Fly! Well, I will be terribly grateful to have this whole horrible tragedy out of my wings once and for all. Come on in.
With pleasure.
And I meant it. If things kept running this smooth, this was going to be like taking candy from the couch cushions.
We were back at the scene of the crime. It felt like an old friend. This was where the crime happened. This was where it would be solved.
Or where I'd make a bungling idiot out of myself. One of the two.
The clock was ticking. I had less than twelve minutes before Flittany arrived. Did I mention this whole plan was built on timing?
Well, Delilah. The reason we are here with Gloria is that we have quite a serious confession to make.
I have to say that I am surprised. But I'll be glad to hear her confession.
She really thought Gloria was about to confess to stealing the pencil box. Time for the switcheroo.
Oh, the confession isn't Gloria's. It's mine. I have to confess: I told Gloria that you accused her of stealing the diamond pencil box.

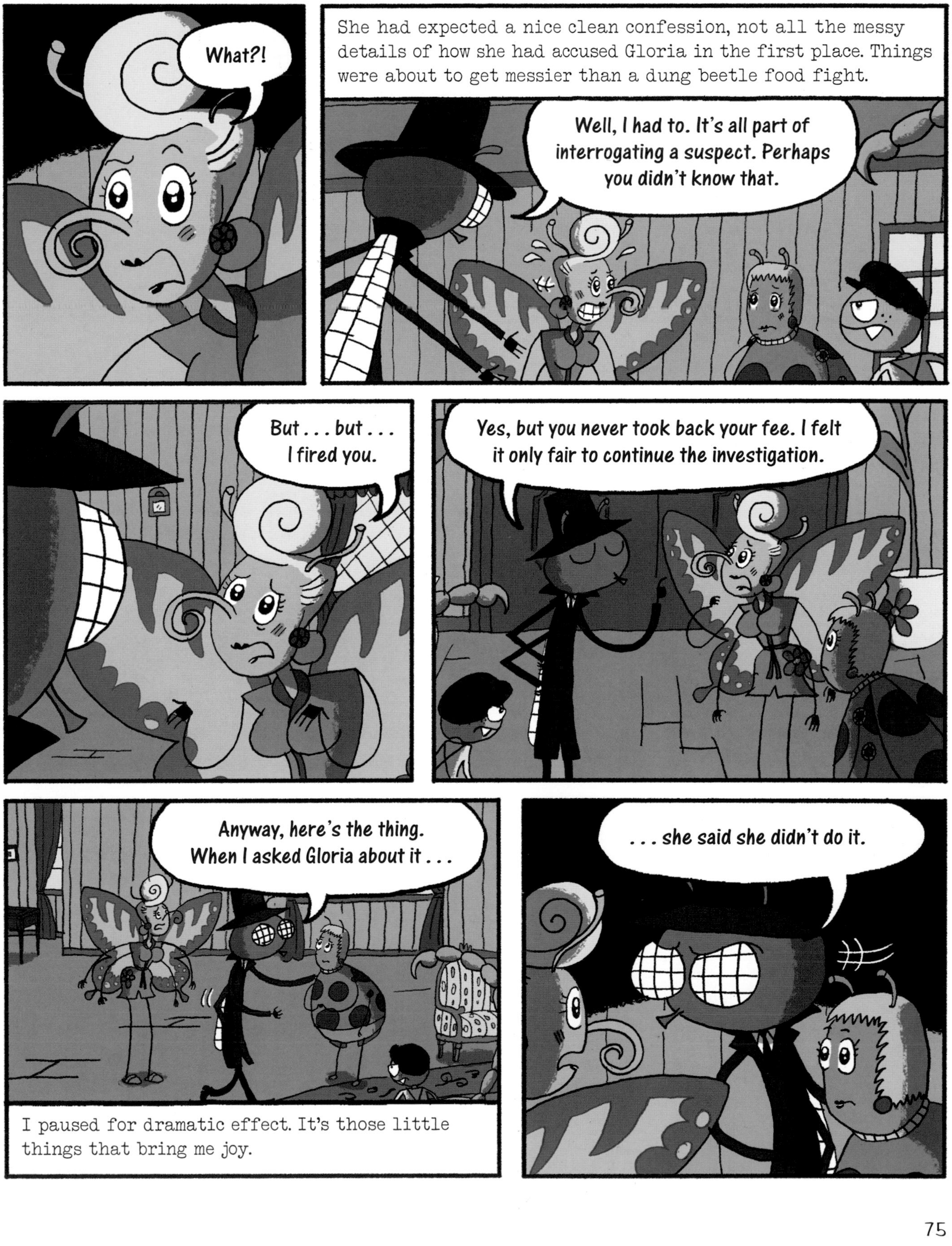
What?!
She had expected a nice clean confession, not all the messy details of how she had accused Gloria in the first place. Things were about to get messier than a dung beetle food fight.
Well, I had to. It's all part of interrogating a suspect. Perhaps you didn't know that.
But . . . but . . . I fired you.
Yes, but you never took back your fee. I felt it only fair to continue the investigation.
Anyway, here's the thing. When I asked Gloria about it . . .
I paused for dramatic effect. It's those little things that bring me joy.
. . . she said she didn't do it.

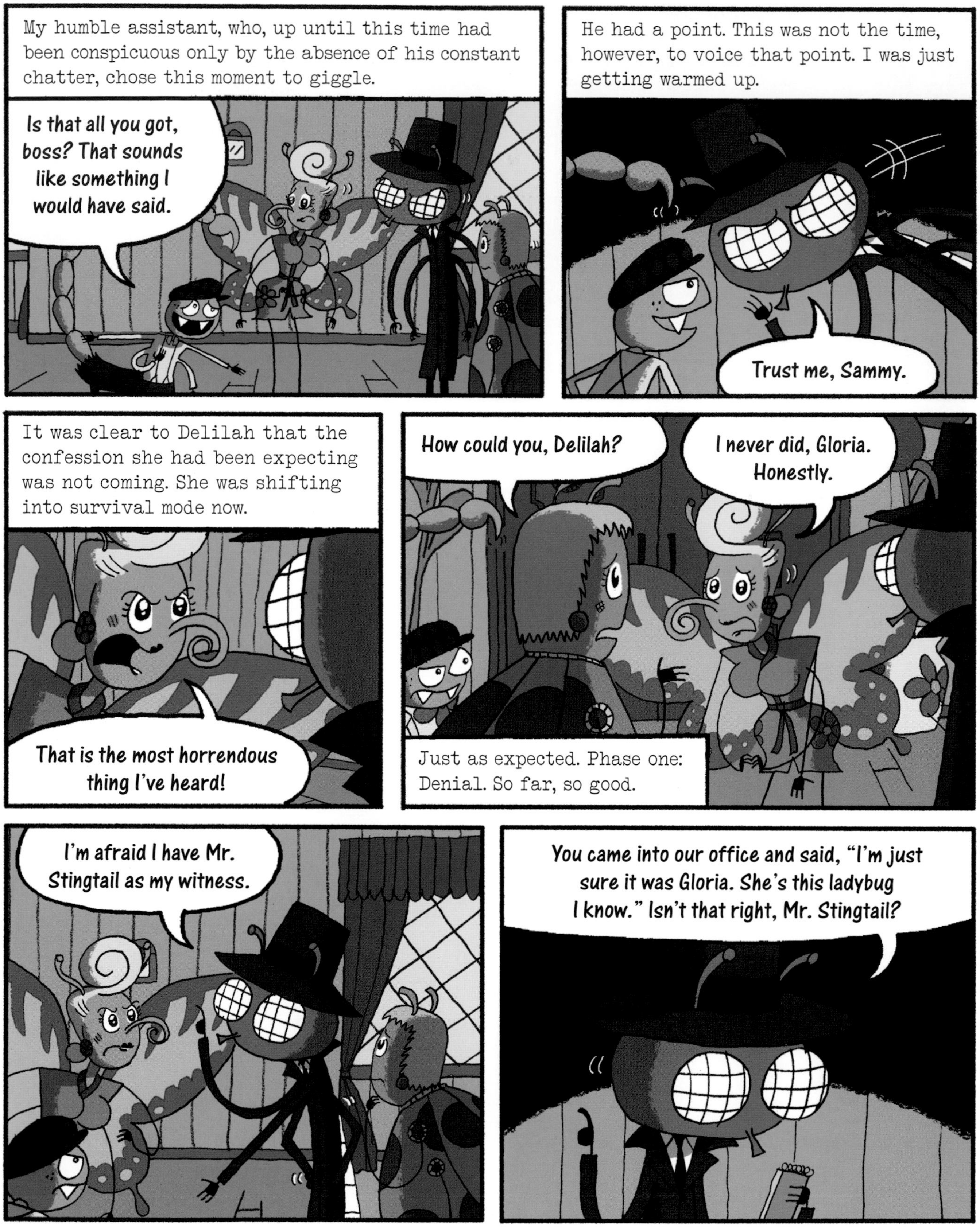

My humble assistant, who, up until this time had been conspicuous only by the absence of his constant chatter, chose this moment to giggle.
Is that all you got, boss? That sounds like something I would have said.
He had a point. This was not the time, however, to voice that point. I was just getting warmed up.
Trust me, Sammy.
It was clear to Delilah that the confession she had been expecting was not coming. She was shifting into survival mode now.
That is the most horrendous thing I've heard!
How could you, Delilah?
I never did, Gloria. Honestly.
Just as expected. Phase one: Denial. So far, so good.
I'm afraid I have Mr. Stingtail as my witness.
You came into our office and said, "I'm just sure it was Gloria. She's this ladybug I know." Isn't that right, Mr. Stingtail?

That's right, Mr. . . .

. . . Joey.

What he lacked in style, he made up for in . . . well, I haven't figured that out yet.

I . . . well . . . all right, fine. I didn't want to say it in front of her, but you've forced me to it.

Yes, you took it, Gloria. You always were jealous of my diamond pencil box, and of me, even though I've never liked you.

Ouch. But that was typical phase two: Move to the offensive. Like a queen bee trapped in the hive.

What?! We've been friends for over a year!

Ha! That's her story.

Gloria was gathering steam now. Her hands worked feverishly on the wrapper of a cicada cluster.

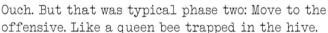

And besides, I couldn't have taken your pencil box. I was nowhere near it that night.

You have no proof of that.

I was talking to Flittany all night! You introduced her to me.

You have no witnesses to that.

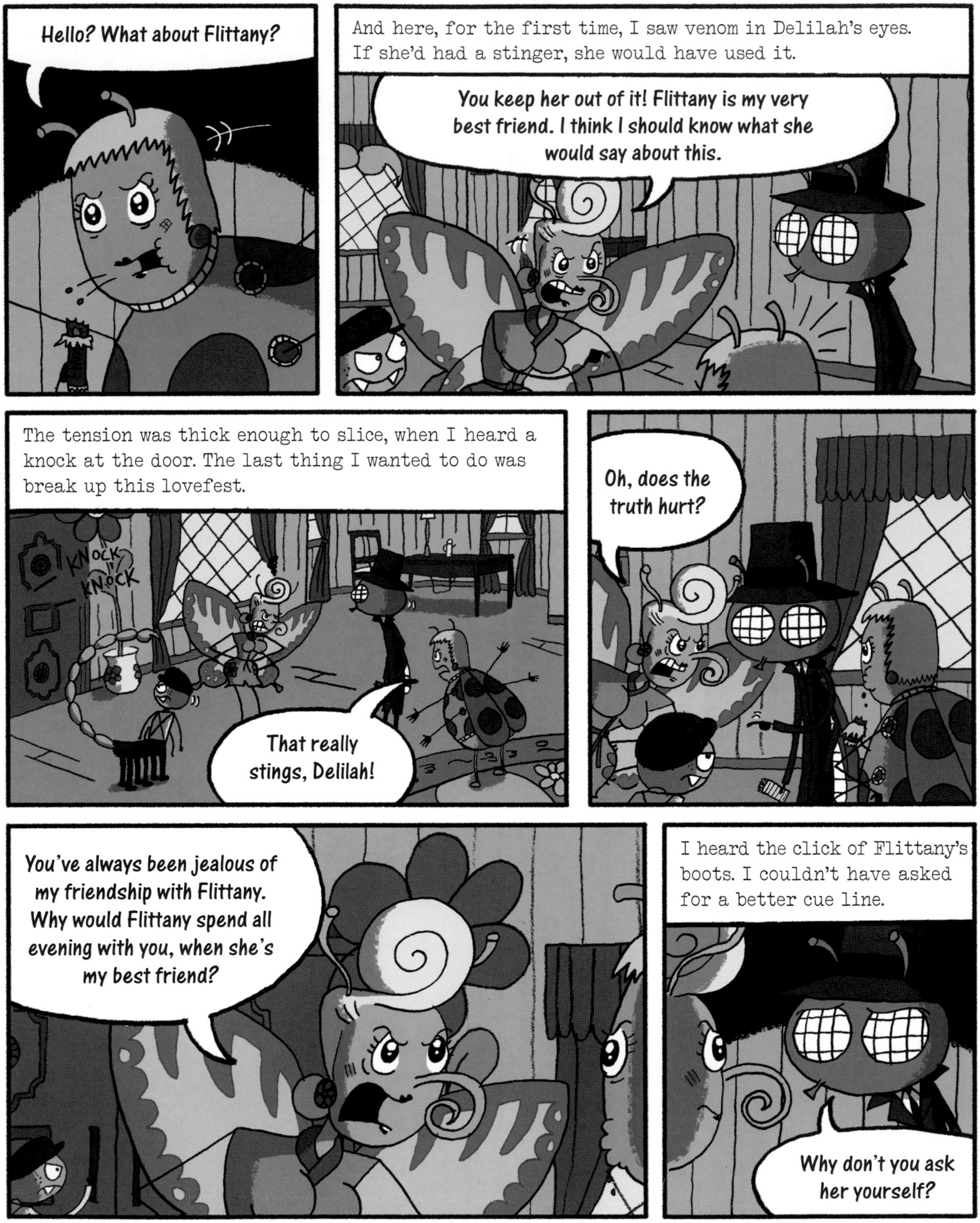
Hello? What about Flittany?
And here, for the first time, I saw venom in Delilah's eyes. If she'd had a stinger, she would have used it.
You keep her out of it! Flittany is my very best friend. I think I should know what she would say about this.
The tension was thick enough to slice, when I heard a knock at the door. The last thing I wanted to do was break up this lovefest.
KNOCK KNOCK
That really stings, Delilah!
Oh, does the truth hurt?
You've always been jealous of my friendship with Flittany. Why would Flittany spend all evening with you, when she's my best friend?
I heard the click of Flittany's boots. I couldn't have asked for a better cue line.
Why don't you ask her yourself?

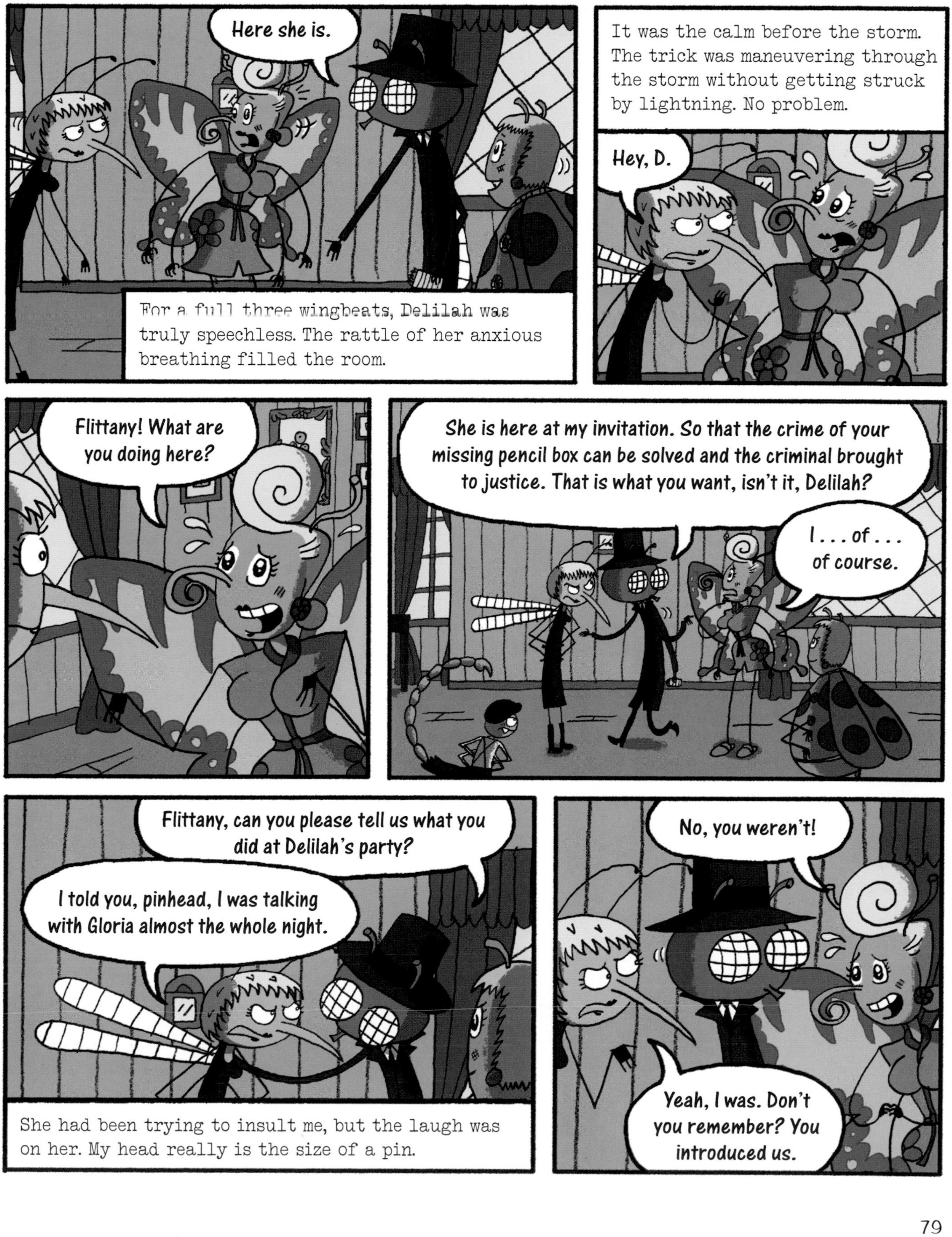
Here she is.
For a full three wingbeats, Delilah was truly speechless. The rattle of her anxious breathing filled the room.
It was the calm before the storm. The trick was maneuvering through the storm without getting struck by lightning. No problem.
Hey, D.
Flittany! What are you doing here?
She is here at my invitation. So that the crime of your missing pencil box can be solved and the criminal brought to justice. That is what you want, isn't it, Delilah?
I . . . of . . . of course.
Flittany, can you please tell us what you did at Delilah's party?
I told you, pinhead, I was talking with Gloria almost the whole night.
She had been trying to insult me, but the laugh was on her. My head really is the size of a pin.
No, you weren't!
Yeah, I was. Don't you remember? You introduced us.

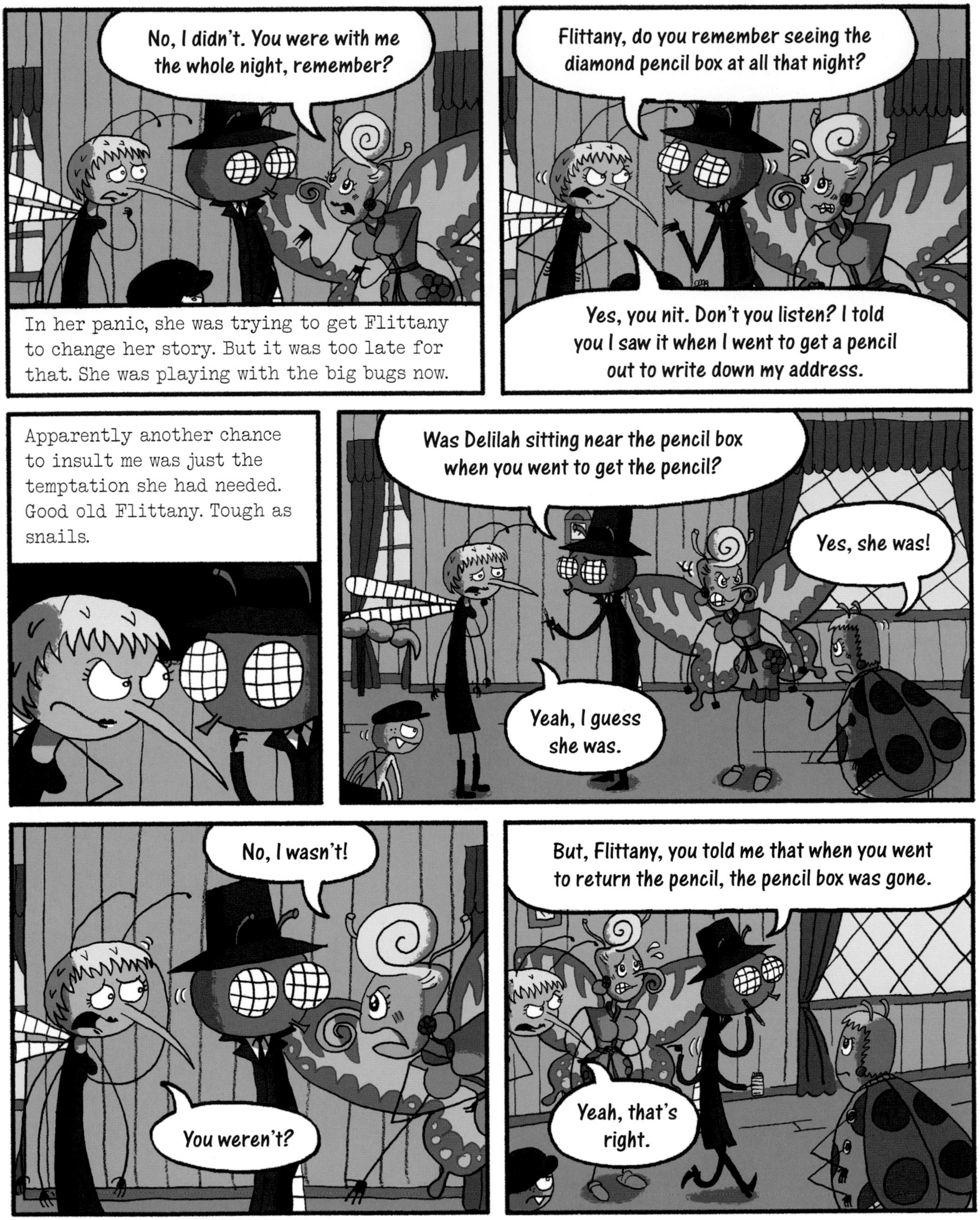
No, I didn't. You were with me the whole night, remember?
In her panic, she was trying to get Flittany to change her story. But it was too late for that. She was playing with the big bugs now.
Flittany, do you remember seeing the diamond pencil box at all that night?
Yes, you nit. Don't you listen? I told you I saw it when I went to get a pencil out to write down my address.
Apparently another chance to insult me was just the temptation she had needed. Good old Flittany. Tough as snails.
Was Delilah sitting near the pencil box when you went to get the pencil?
Yes, she was!
Yeah, I guess she was.
No, I wasn't!
You weren't?
But, Flittany, you told me that when you went to return the pencil, the pencil box was gone.
Yeah, that's right.

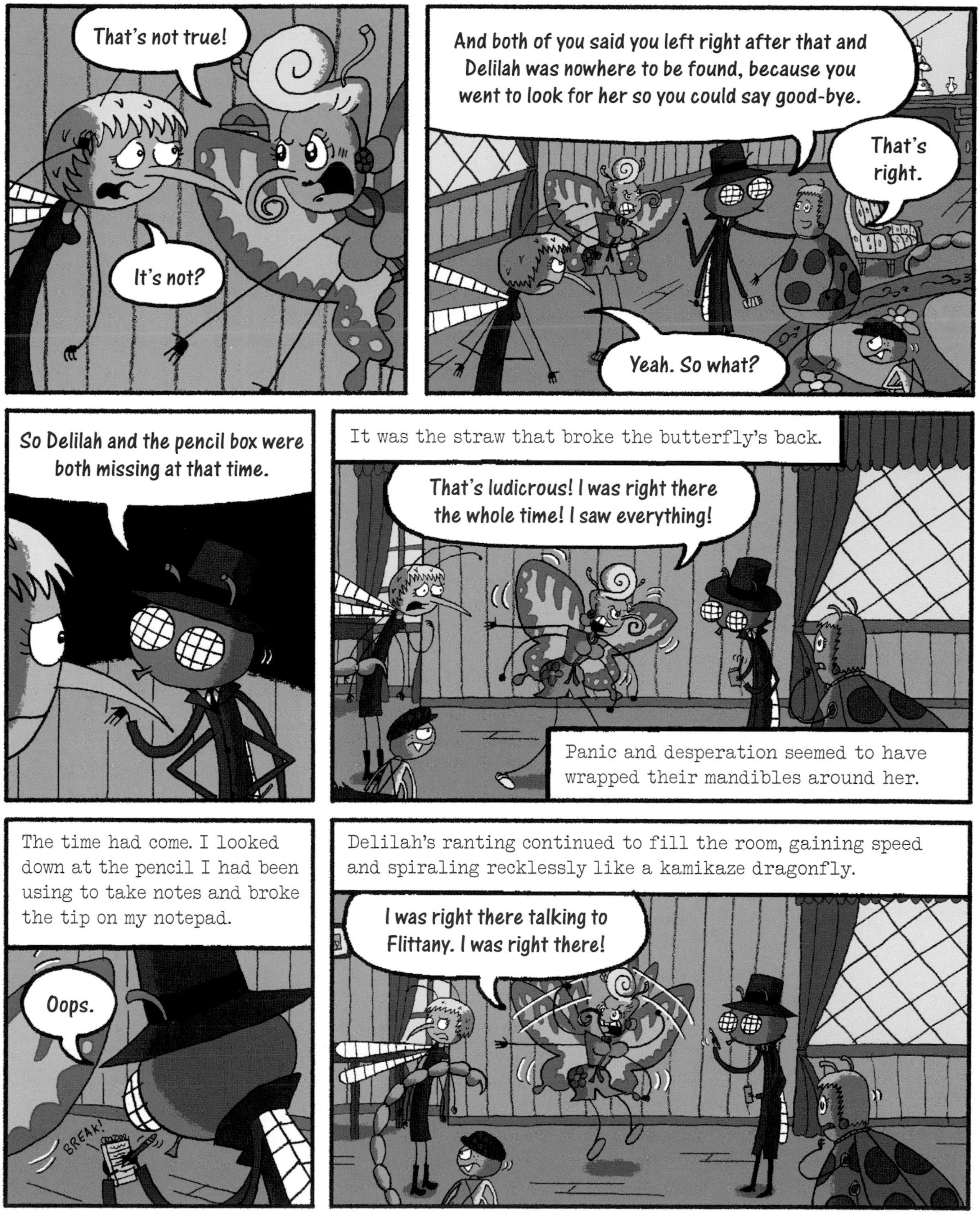

That's not true!
It's not?
And both of you said you left right after that and Delilah was nowhere to be found, because you went to look for her so you could say good-bye.
That's right.
Yeah. So what?
So Delilah and the pencil box were both missing at that time.
It was the straw that broke the butterfly's back.
That's ludicrous! I was right there the whole time! I saw everything!
Panic and desperation seemed to have wrapped their mandibles around her.
The time had come. I looked down at the pencil I had been using to take notes and broke the tip on my notepad.
Oops.
BREAK!
Delilah's ranting continued to fill the room, gaining speed and spiraling recklessly like a kamikaze dragonfly.
I was right there talking to Flittany. I was right there!

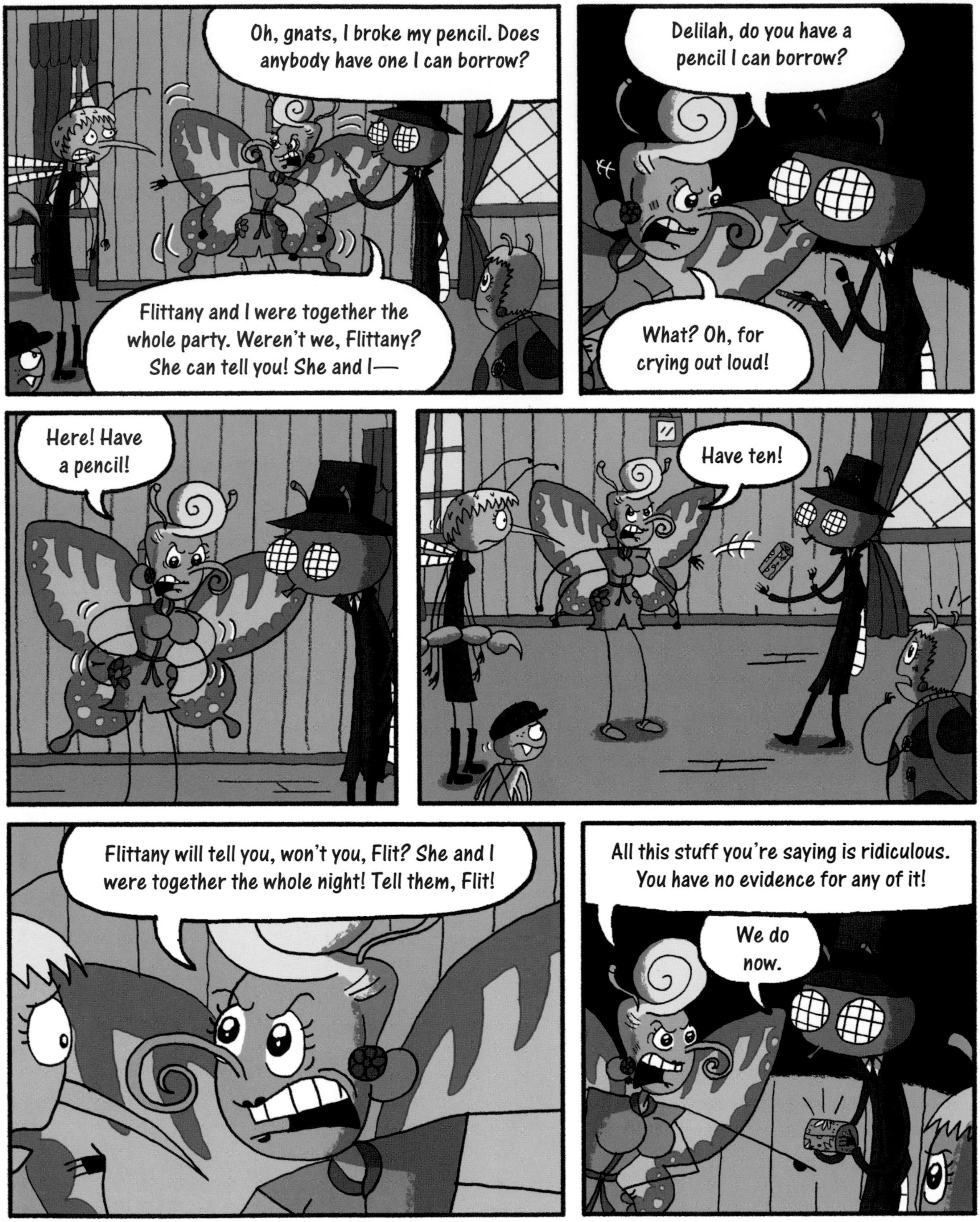
Oh, gnats, I broke my pencil. Does anybody have one I can borrow?
Flittany and I were together the whole party. Weren't we, Flittany? She can tell you! She and I—
Delilah, do you have a pencil I can borrow?
What? Oh, for crying out loud!
Here! Have a pencil!
Have ten!
Flittany will tell you, won't you, Flit? She and I were together the whole night! Tell them, Flit!
All this stuff you're saying is ridiculous. You have no evidence for any of it!
We do now.

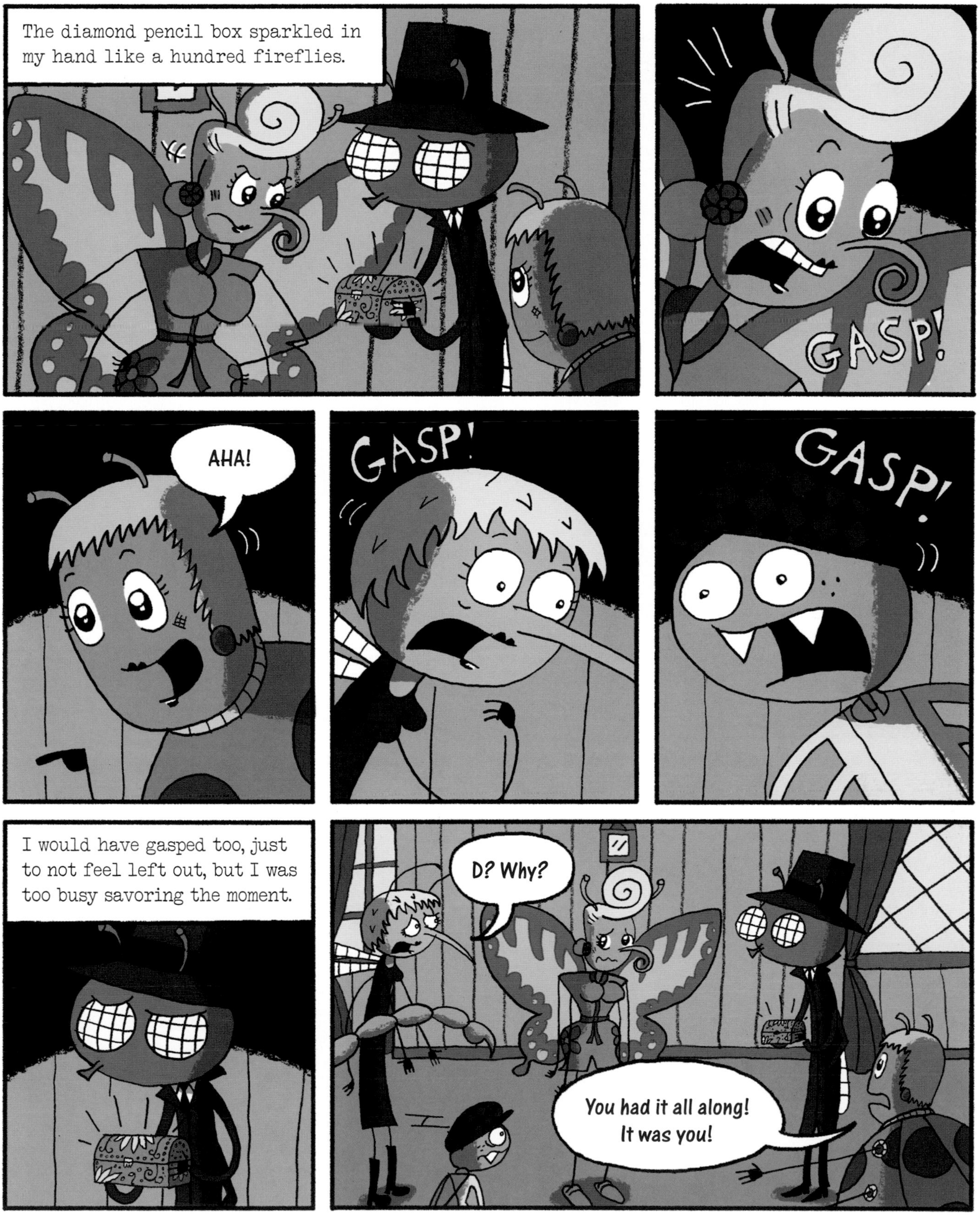
The diamond pencil box sparkled in my hand like a hundred fireflies.
GASP!
AHA!
GASP!
GASP!
I would have gasped too, just to not feel left out, but I was too busy savoring the moment.
D? Why?
You had it all along! It was you!

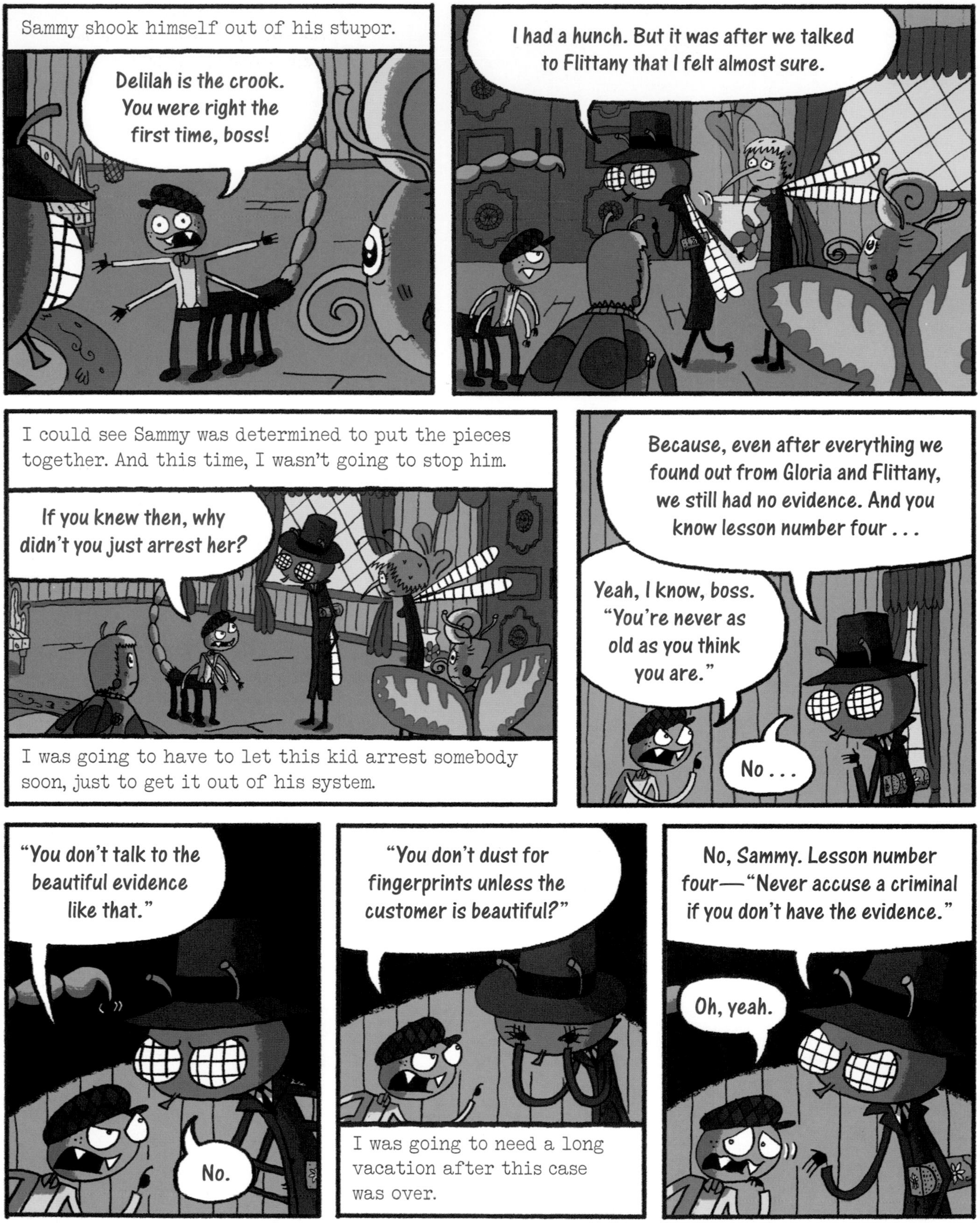
Sammy shook himself out of his stupor.
Delilah is the crook. You were right the first time, boss!
I had a hunch. But it was after we talked to Flittany that I felt almost sure.
I could see Sammy was determined to put the pieces together. And this time, I wasn't going to stop him.
If you knew then, why didn't you just arrest her?
I was going to have to let this kid arrest somebody soon, just to get it out of his system.
Because, even after everything we found out from Gloria and Flittany, we still had no evidence. And you know lesson number four . . .
Yeah, I know, boss. "You're never as old as you think you are."
No . . .
"You don't talk to the beautiful evidence like that."
No.
"You don't dust for fingerprints unless the customer is beautiful?"
I was going to need a long vacation after this case was over.
No, Sammy. Lesson number four—"Never accuse a criminal if you don't have the evidence."
Oh, yeah.

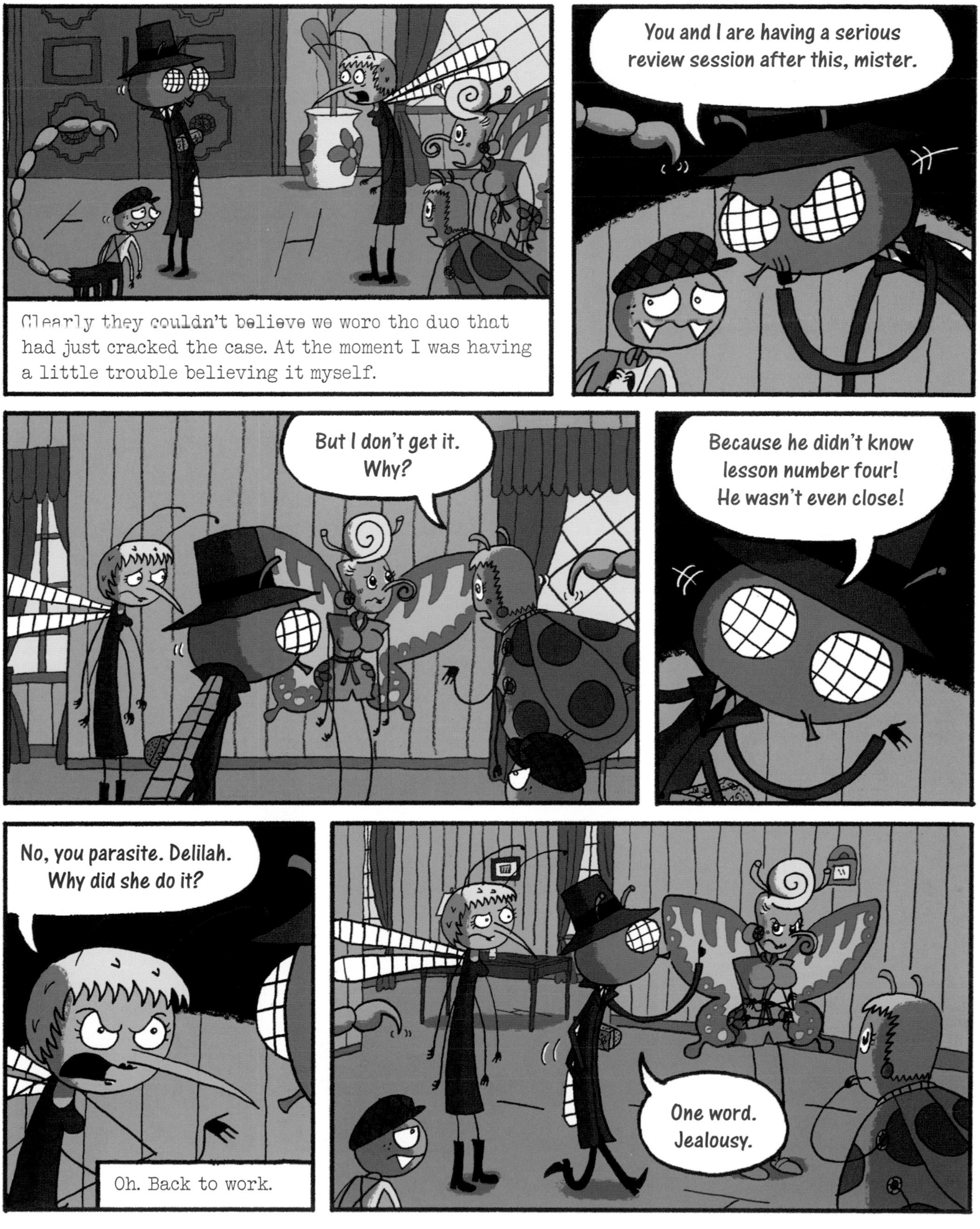
Clearly they couldn't believe we were the duo that had just cracked the case. At the moment I was having a little trouble believing it myself.
You and I are having a serious review session after this, mister.
But I don't get it. Why?
Because he didn't know lesson number four! He wasn't even close!
No, you parasite. Delilah. Why did she do it?
Oh. Back to work.
One word. Jealousy.

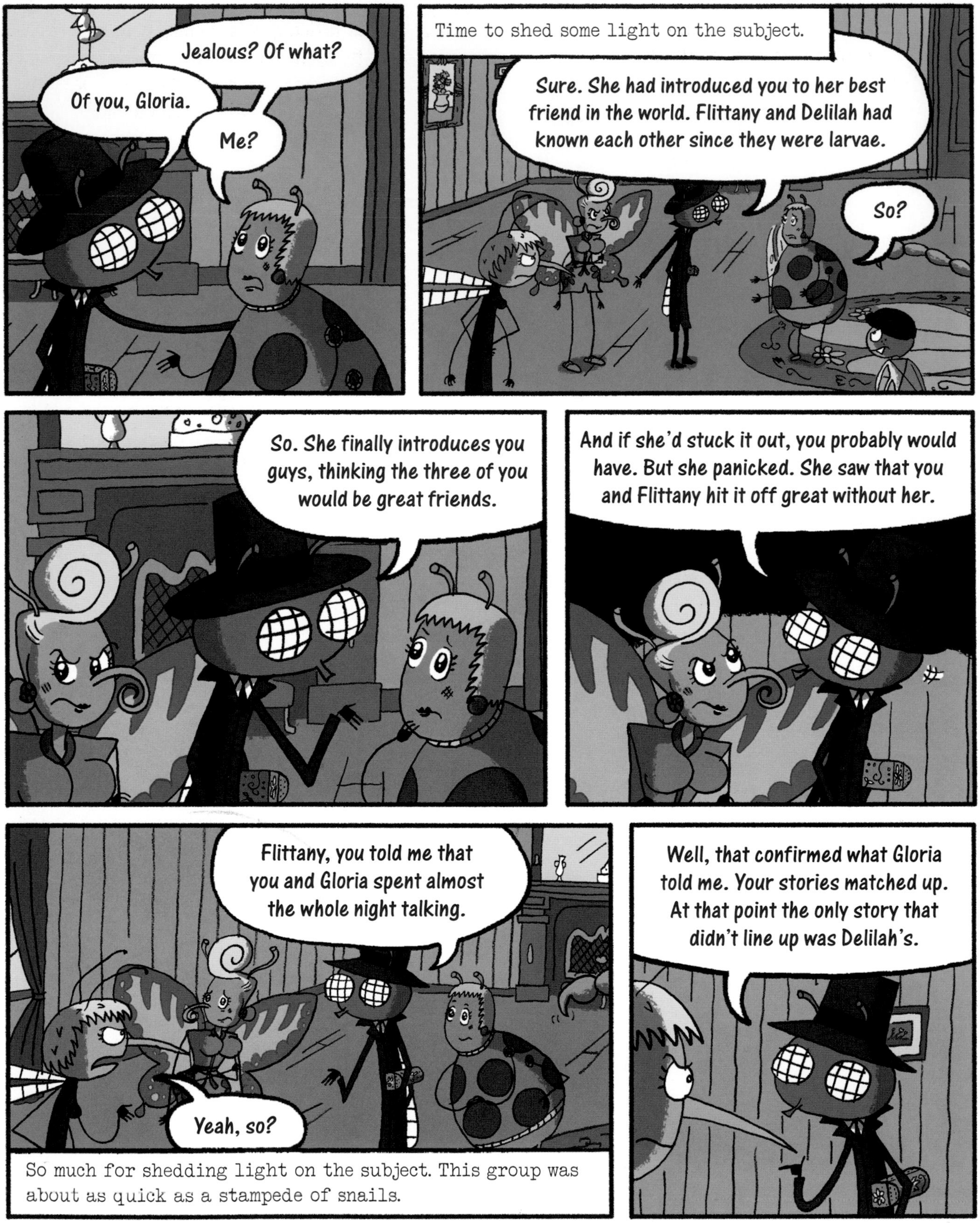
Jealous? Of what?
Of you, Gloria.
Me?
Time to shed some light on the subject.
Sure. She had introduced you to her best friend in the world. Flittany and Delilah had known each other since they were larvae.
So?
So. She finally introduces you guys, thinking the three of you would be great friends.
And if she'd stuck it out, you probably would have. But she panicked. She saw that you and Flittany hit it off great without her.
Flittany, you told me that you and Gloria spent almost the whole night talking.
Yeah, so?
So much for shedding light on the subject. This group was about as quick as a stampede of snails.
Well, that confirmed what Gloria told me. Your stories matched up. At that point the only story that didn't line up was Delilah's.

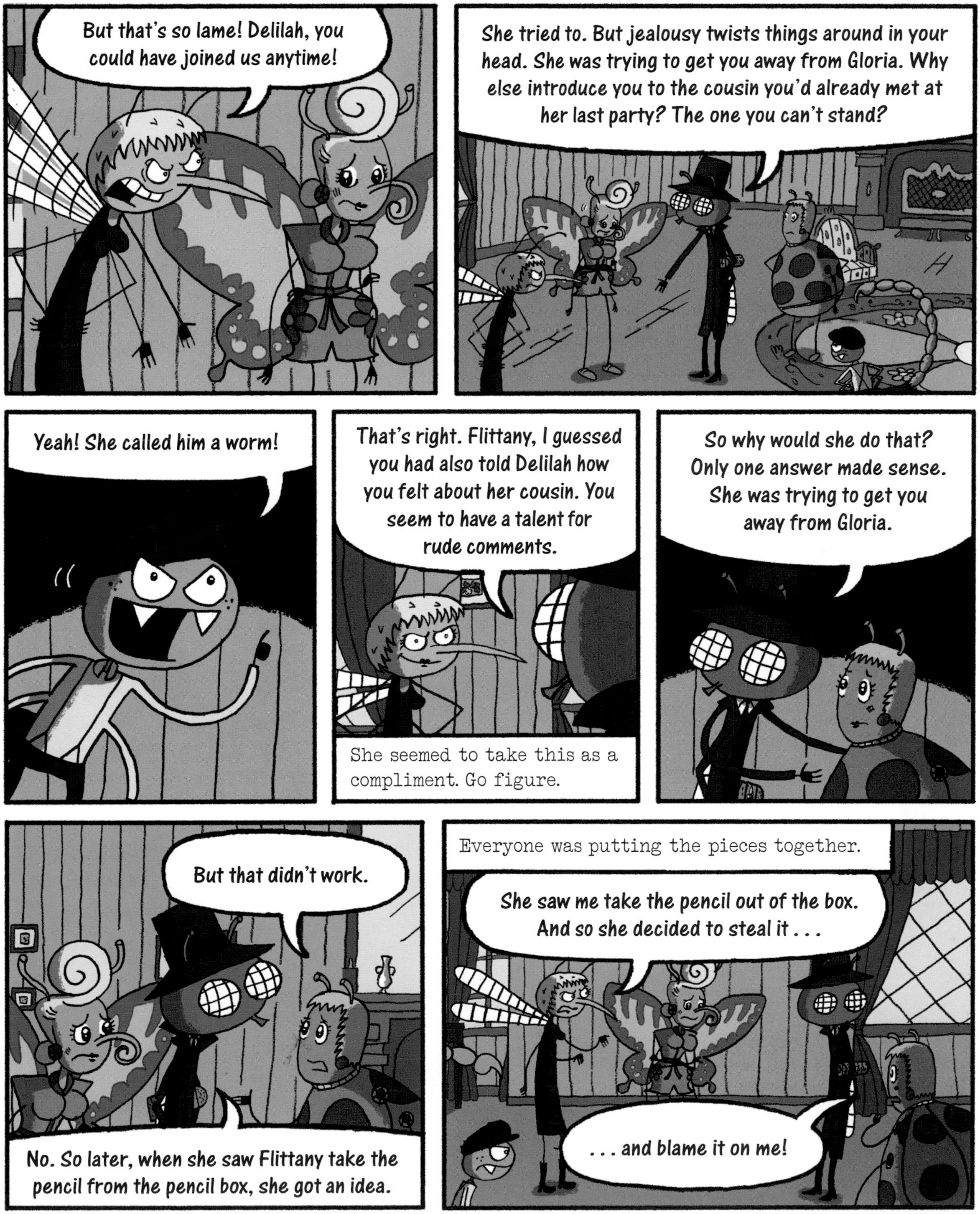
But that's so lame! Delilah, you could have joined us anytime!
She tried to. But jealousy twists things around in your head. She was trying to get you away from Gloria. Why else introduce you to the cousin you'd already met at her last party? The one you can't stand?
Yeah! She called him a worm!
That's right. Flittany, I guessed you had also told Delilah how you felt about her cousin. You seem to have a talent for rude comments.
She seemed to take this as a compliment. Go figure.
So why would she do that? Only one answer made sense. She was trying to get you away from Gloria.
But that didn't work.
No. So later, when she saw Flittany take the pencil from the pencil box, she got an idea.
Everyone was putting the pieces together.
She saw me take the pencil out of the box. And so she decided to steal it . . .
. . . and blame it on me!

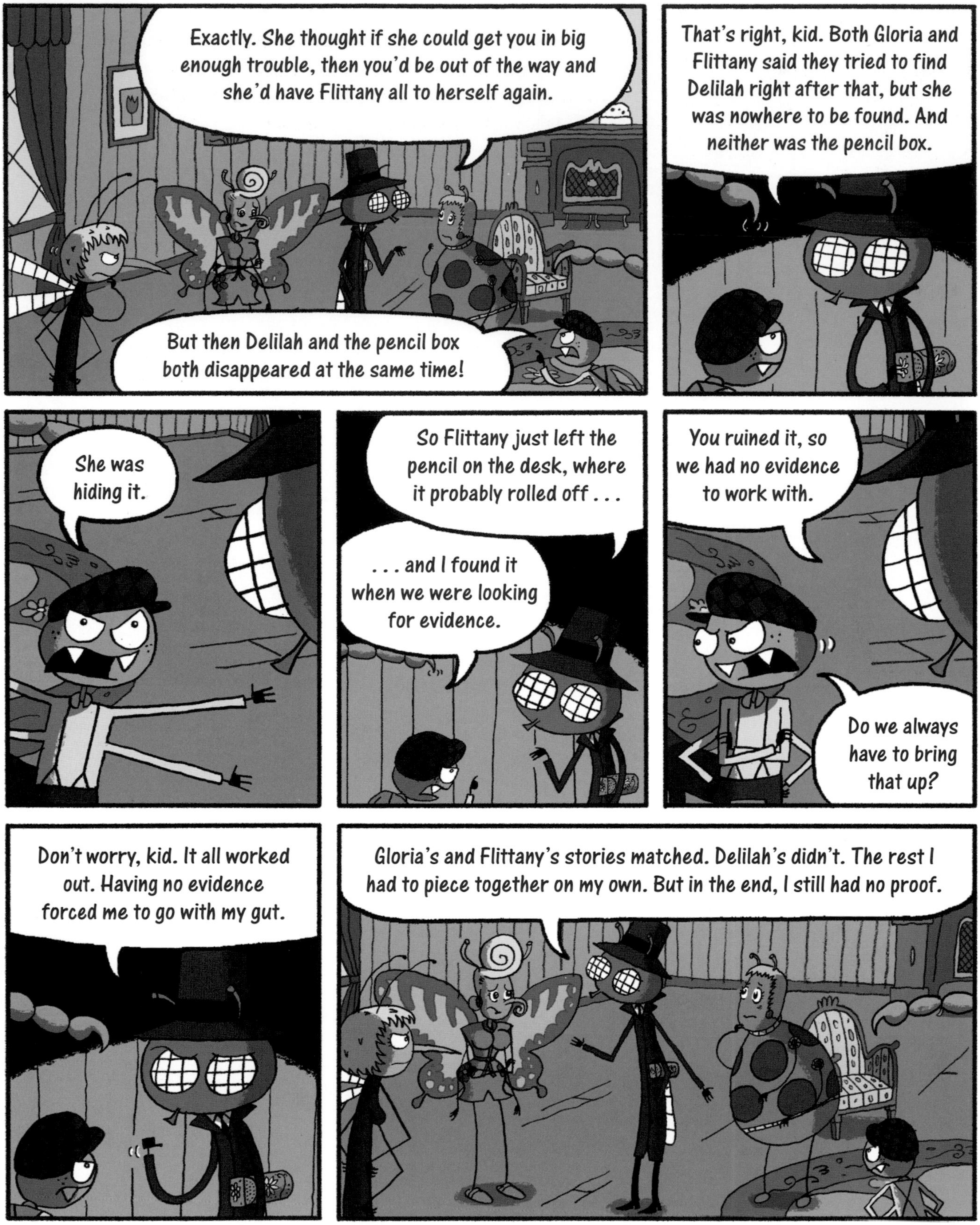
Exactly. She thought if she could get you in big enough trouble, then you'd be out of the way and she'd have Flittany all to herself again.
But then Delilah and the pencil box both disappeared at the same time!
That's right, kid. Both Gloria and Flittany said they tried to find Delilah right after that, but she was nowhere to be found. And neither was the pencil box.
She was hiding it.
So Flittany just left the pencil on the desk, where it probably rolled off . . .
. . . and I found it when we were looking for evidence.
You ruined it, so we had no evidence to work with.
Do we always have to bring that up?
Don't worry, kid. It all worked out. Having no evidence forced me to go with my gut.
Gloria's and Flittany's stories matched. Delilah's didn't. The rest I had to piece together on my own. But in the end, I still had no proof.

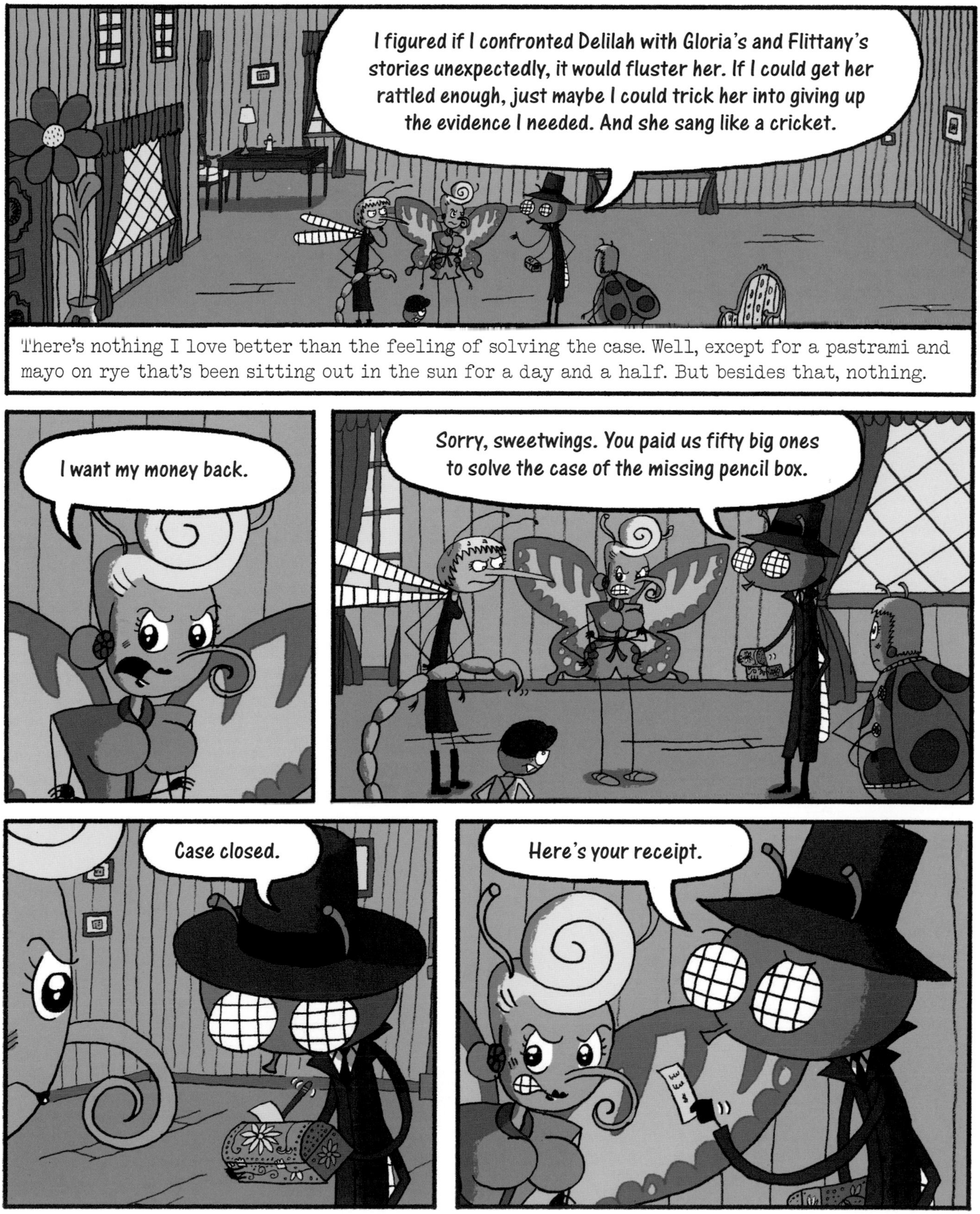
I figured if I confronted Delilah with Gloria's and Flittany's stories unexpectedly, it would fluster her. If I could get her rattled enough, just maybe I could trick her into giving up the evidence I needed. And she sang like a cricket.
There's nothing I love better than the feeling of solving the case. Well, except for a pastrami and mayo on rye that's been sitting out in the sun for a day and a half. But besides that, nothing.
I want my money back.
Sorry, sweetwings. You paid us fifty big ones to solve the case of the missing pencil box.
Case closed.
Here's your receipt.

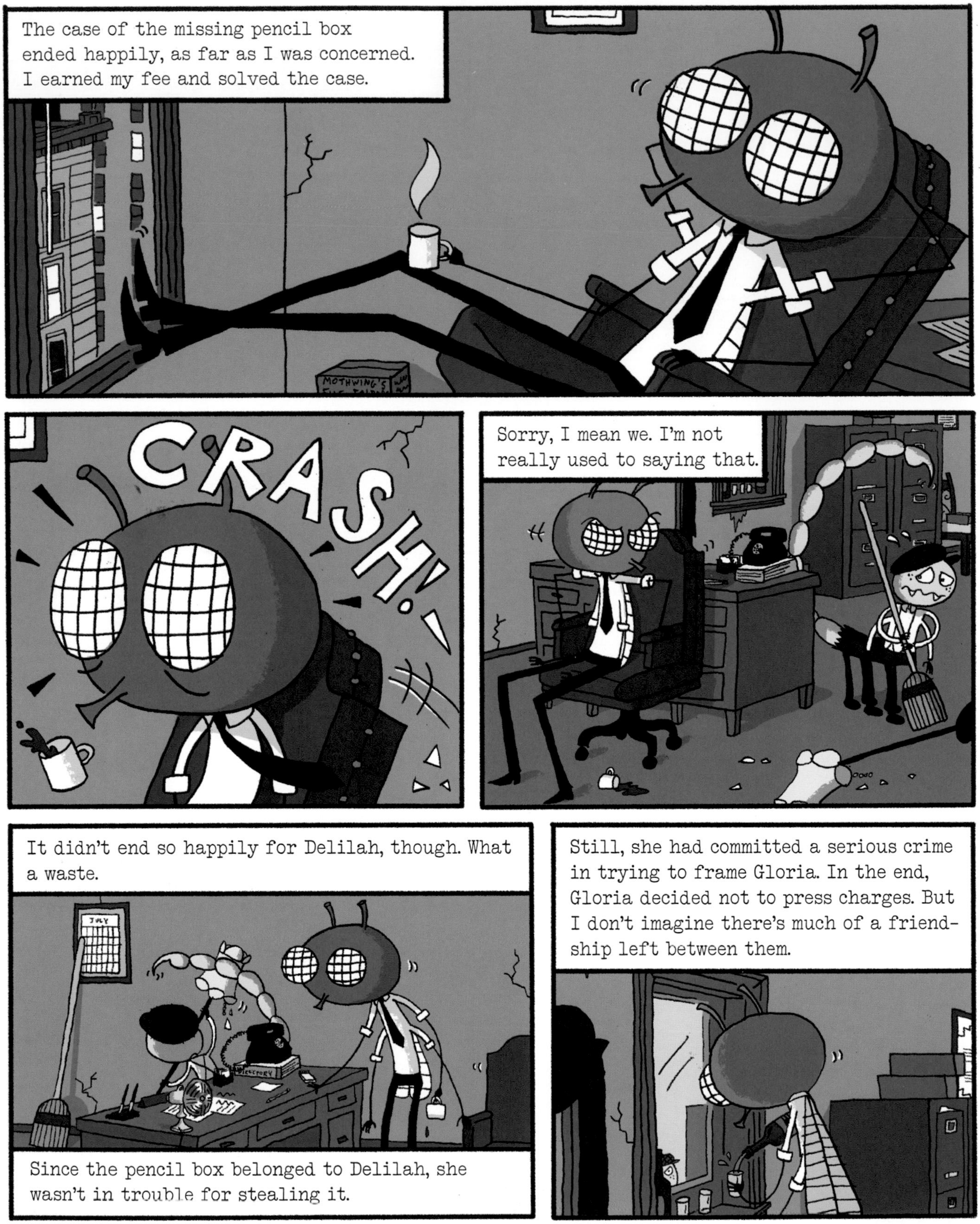
The case of the missing pencil box ended happily, as far as I was concerned. I earned my fee and solved the case.
CRASH!
Sorry, I mean we. I'm not really used to saying that.
It didn't end so happily for Delilah, though. What a waste.
Since the pencil box belonged to Delilah, she wasn't in trouble for stealing it.
Still, she had committed a serious crime in trying to frame Gloria. In the end, Gloria decided not to press charges. But I don't imagine there's much of a friendship left between them.

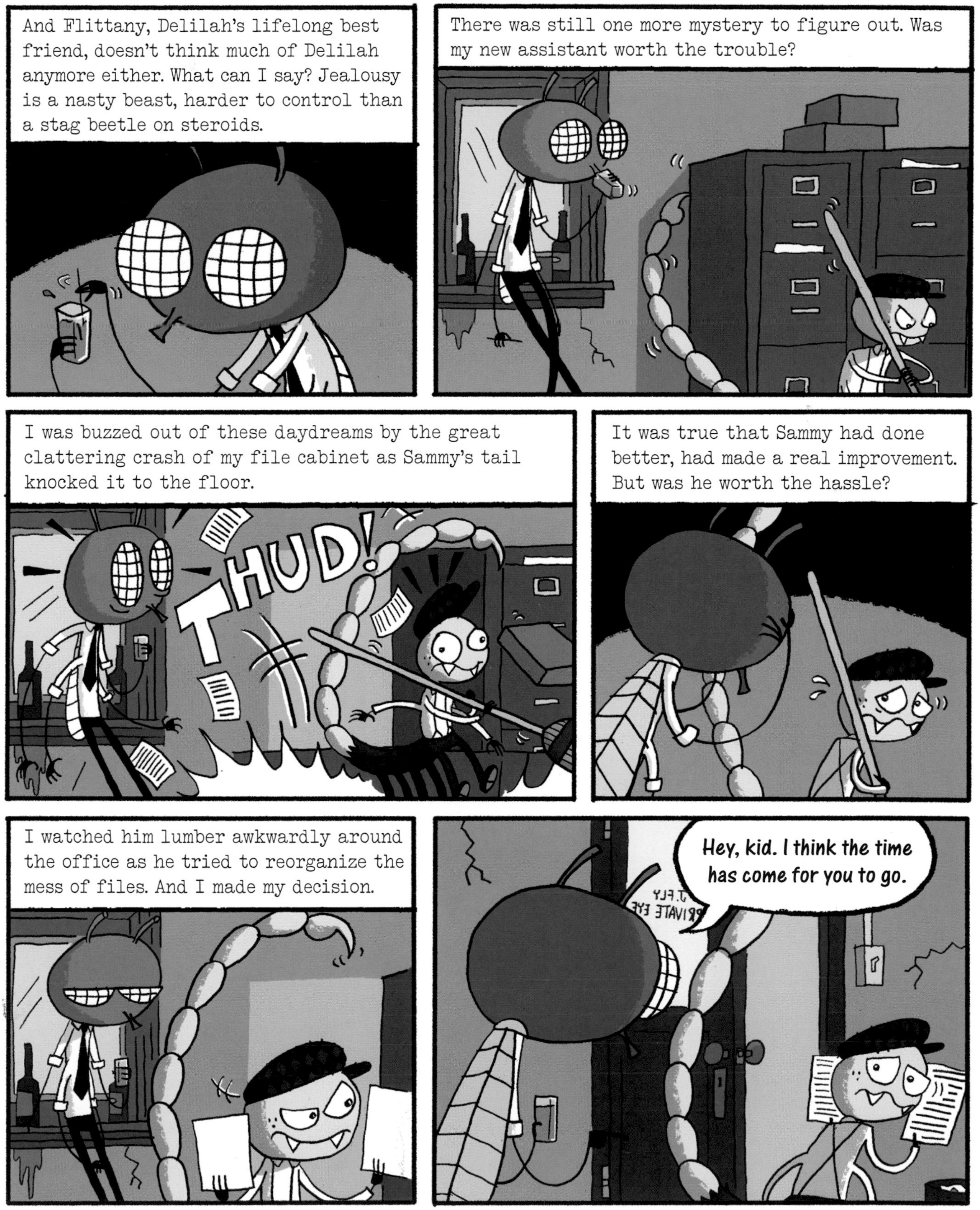
And Flittany, Delilah's lifelong best friend, doesn't think much of Delilah anymore either. What can I say? Jealousy is a nasty beast, harder to control than a stag beetle on steroids.
There was still one more mystery to figure out. Was my new assistant worth the trouble?
I was buzzed out of these daydreams by the great clattering crash of my file cabinet as Sammy's tail knocked it to the floor.
THUD!
It was true that Sammy had done better, had made a real improvement. But was he worth the hassle?
I watched him lumber awkwardly around the office as he tried to reorganize the mess of files. And I made my decision.
Hey, kid. I think the time has come for you to go.

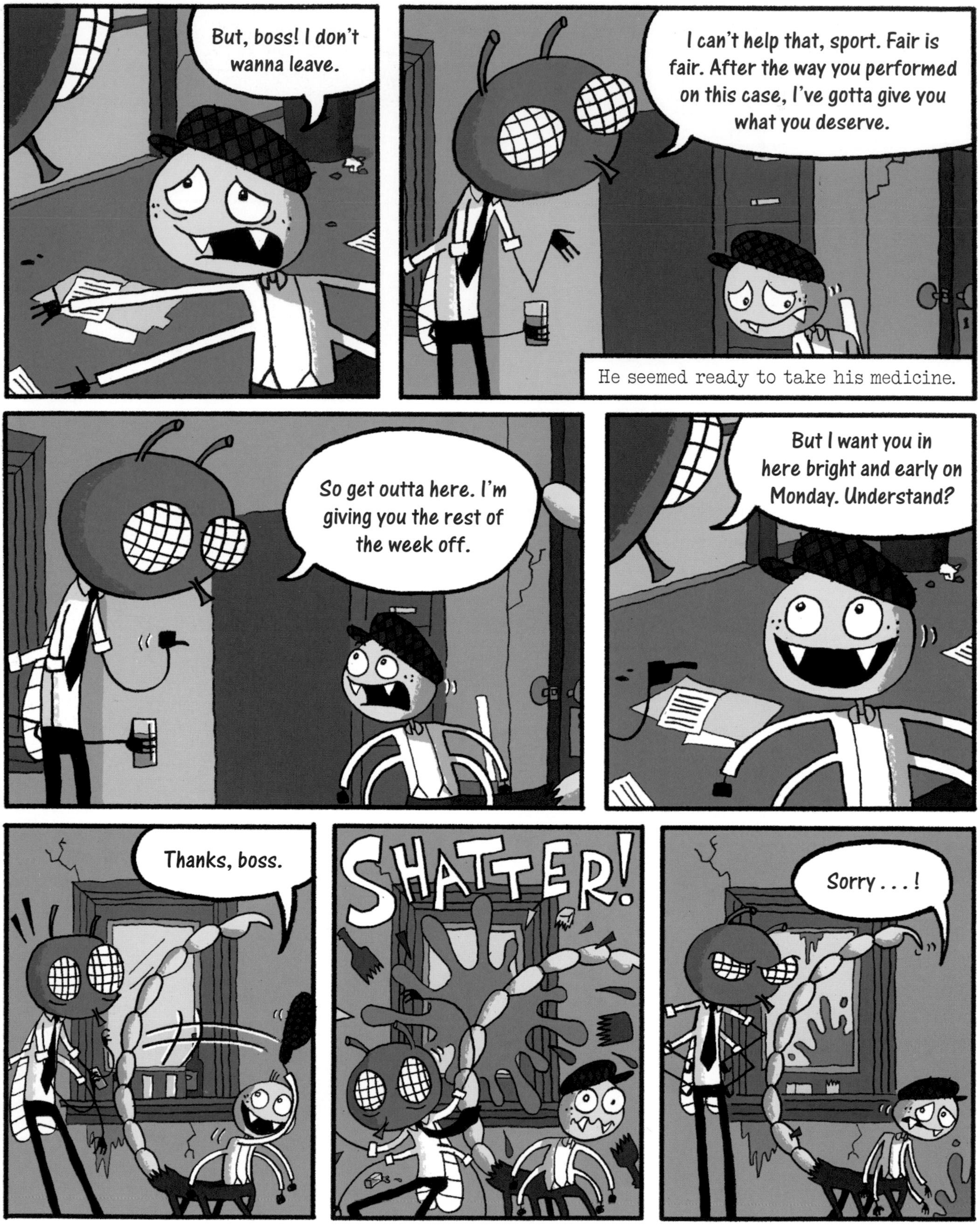
But, boss! I don't wanna leave.
I can't help that, sport. Fair is fair. After the way you performed on this case, I've gotta give you what you deserve.
He seemed ready to take his medicine.
So get outta here. I'm giving you the rest of the week off.
But I want you in here bright and early on Monday. Understand?
Thanks, boss.
SHATTER!
Sorry . . . !

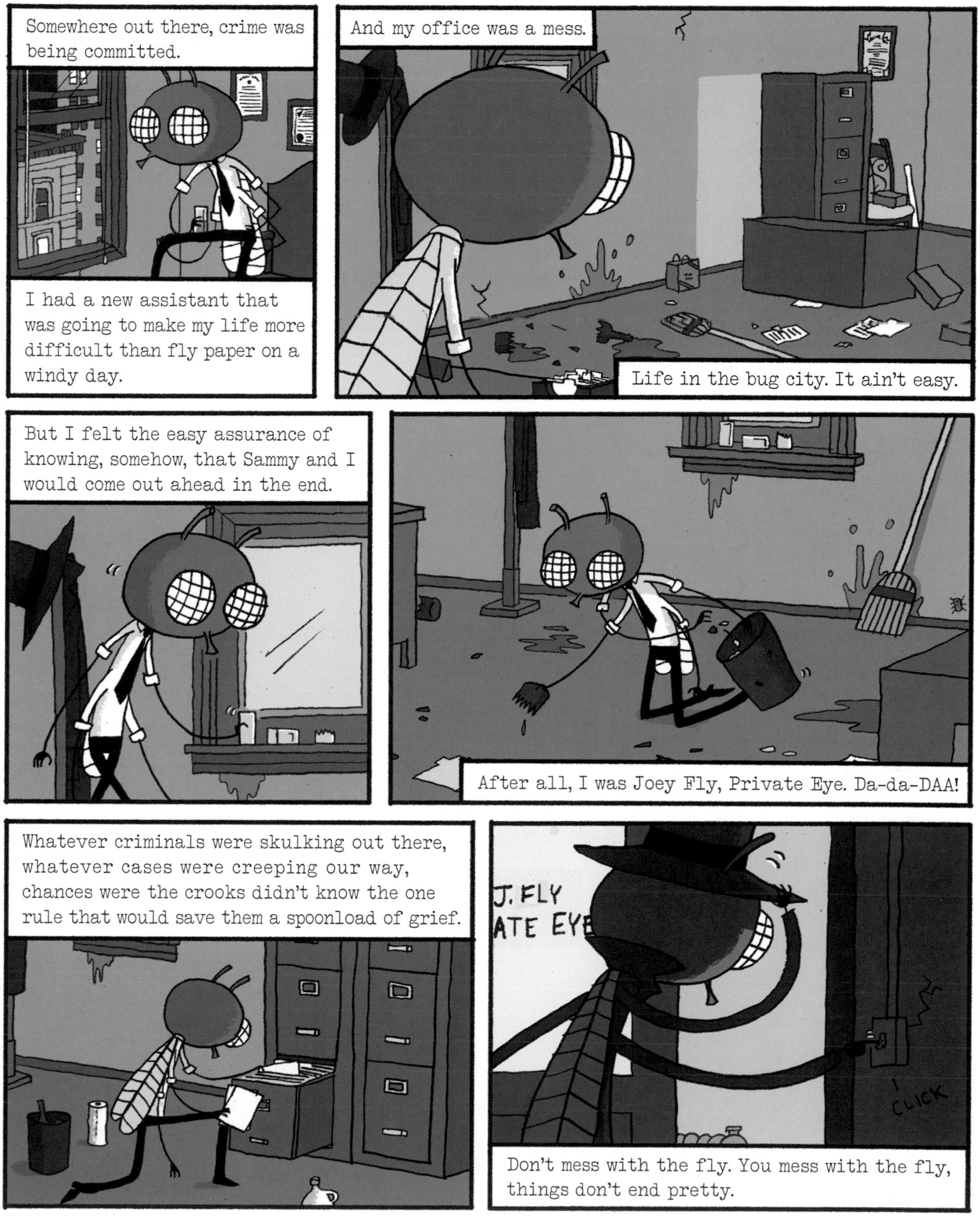
Somewhere out there, crime was being committed.
I had a new assistant that was going to make my life more difficult than fly paper on a windy day.
And my office was a mess.
Life in the bug city. It ain't easy.
But I felt the easy assurance of knowing, somehow, that Sammy and I would come out ahead in the end.
After all, I was Joey Fly, Private Eye. Da-da-DAA!
Whatever criminals were skulking out there, whatever cases were creeping our way, chances were the crooks didn't know the one rule that would save them a spoonload of grief.
J. FLY
ATE EYE
CLICK
Don't mess with the fly. You mess with the fly, things don't end pretty.

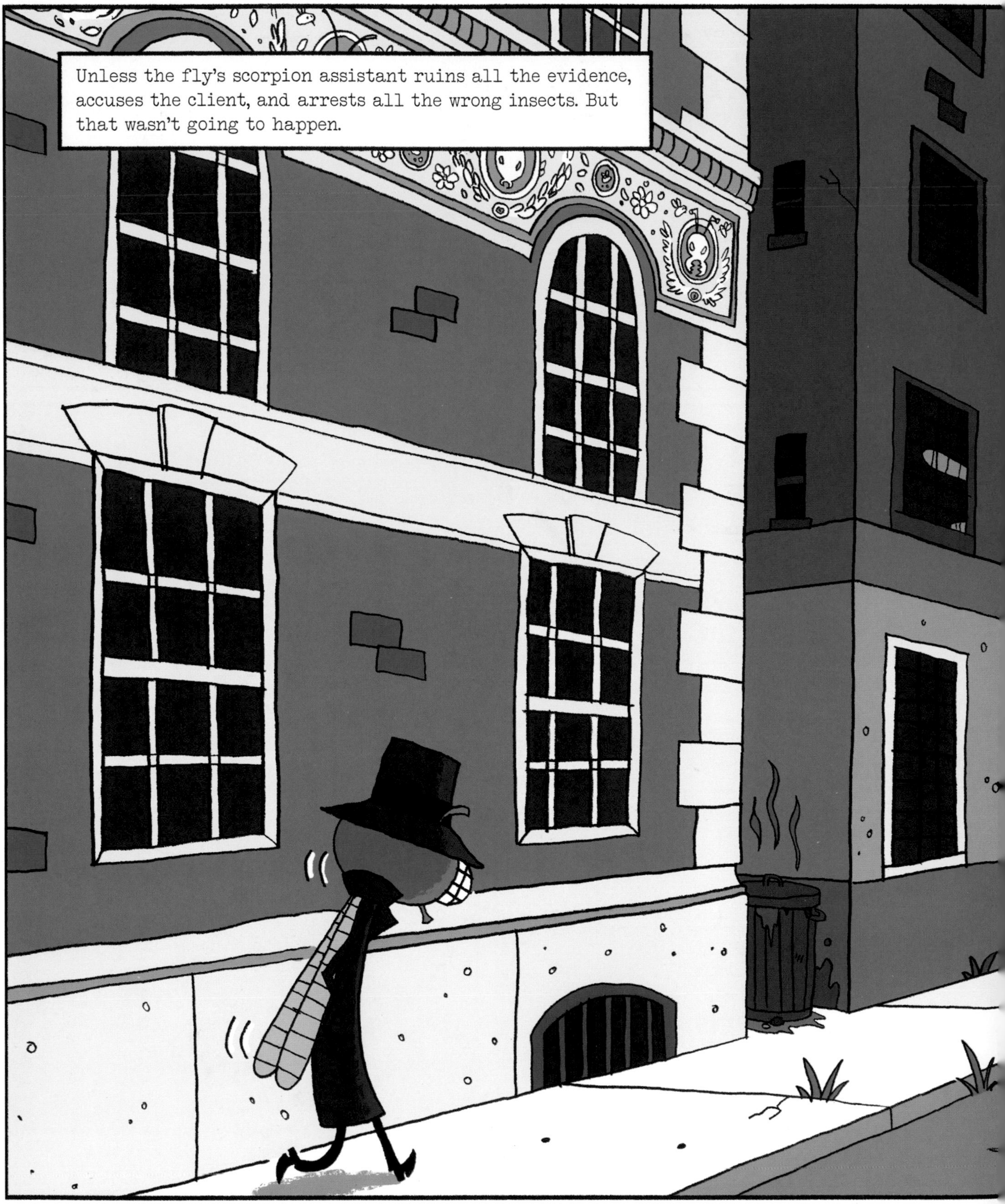
Unless the fly's scorpion assistant ruins all the evidence, accuses the client, and arrests all the wrong insects. But that wasn't going to happen.

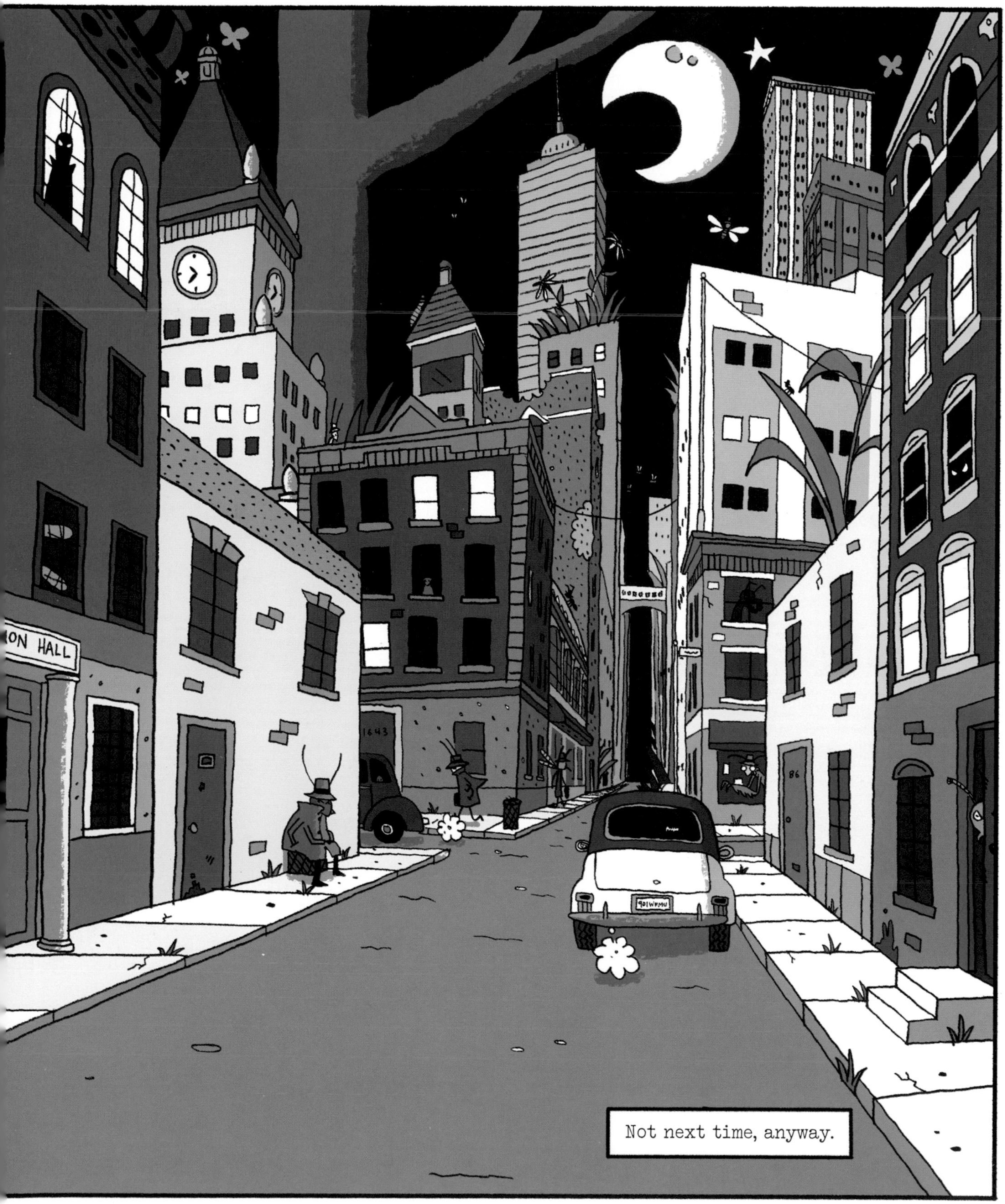
ON HALL
1643
86
901WFMU
Not next time, anyway.

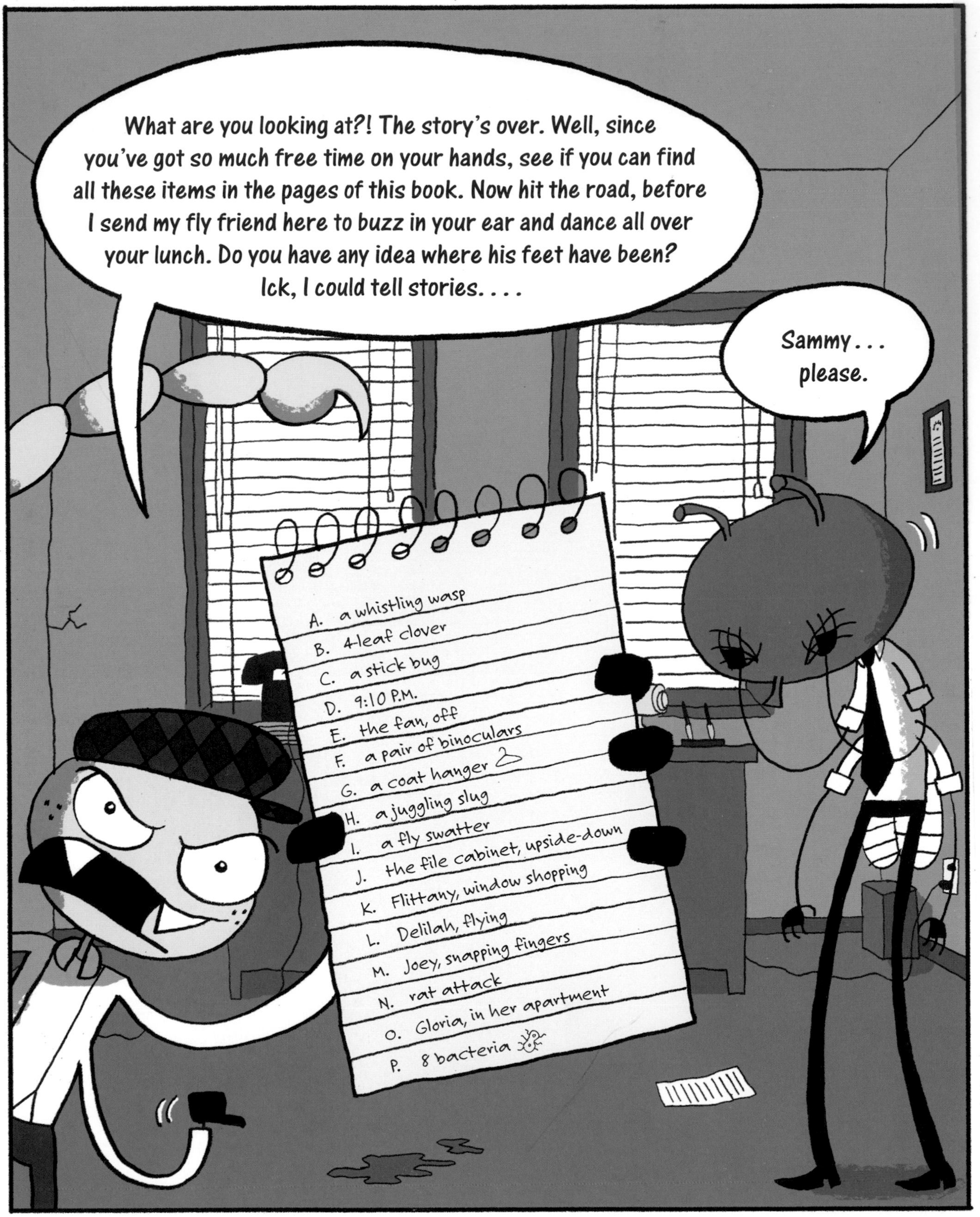
What are you looking at?! The story's over. Well, since you've got so much free time on your hands, see if you can find all these items in the pages of this book. Now hit the road, before I send my fly friend here to buzz in your ear and dance all over your lunch. Do you have any idea where his feet have been? Ick, I could tell stories. . . .
Sammy . . . please.
A. a whistling wasp
B. 4-leaf clover
C. a stick bug
D. 9:10 P.M.
E. the fan, off
F. a pair of binoculars
G. a coat hanger
H. a juggling slug
I. a fly swatter
J. the file cabinet, upside-down
K. Flittany, window shopping
L. Delilah, flying
M. Joey, snapping fingers
N. rat attack
O. Gloria, in her apartment
P. 8 bacteria

Answers are on the copyright page.